ALL I SEE IS MUD

ANDREW DUNKLEY

Thanks Mum and Dad

INTRODUCTION

The more I learn about the men and women of the First AIF, the more I admire them.

They went to war seeking adventure and faced horrors unimaginable.

Their innocence was quickly ground into the mud and our country lost over sixty one thousand people who may have, had the war never happened, contributed greatly to the development of our fledgling Nation.

Of course, had there not been a World War I, there probably would not have been a World War II, but tensions in Europe at the beginning of the 20th Century were high and war was inevitable.

The desire to build a great empire was strong in the minds of Germany's Prussian leaders and they drew their allies into a conflict that promised a new world and European domination. Germany was essentially trying to become the World's first Superpower.

Australia's ties to Great Britain were very strong then, to the point where most people in Australia considered themselves British. In 1914 a cascade of events transpired in Europe which led to the conflict and drew in the British who, under an alliance with Belgium, declared war on Germany when they invaded Belgium as part of their plan to sweep through and take Paris. When the British declared war on August 4th, 1914, the fate of tens of thousands of Australians was sealed.

Germany's plan was designed to achieve swift victory against France and Russia, and they won the minds of the Young Turks who ultimately sided with the Germans believing they would be the victors. In real terms the Turks or Ottoman Empire gambled on who they thought would win the war before deciding which way to go and they got it wrong. Had the Turks decided to fight with the Allies, things might have been very different indeed.

Ultimately the quick victory Germany that the Axis powers expected did not happen and the Great War ground to a halt in the muddy wastelands of France and Belgium, on the Russian Front and in the sands of the Middle East and of course on the Gallipoli Peninsula. While there were many skirmishes on land, in the air and at sea in almost every corner of the World, the main point of conflict was Europe. The war would see millions die over a span of four years, three months and fourteen days; not forgetting the many thousands that died of wounds, effects of gas and illness in the many years that followed the Armistice in 1918.

This book is dedicated to the men and women of the First AIF and to my grandfather, his brothers and my parents who have all given me the drive to find out more about the Great War and keep the memory of the First Australian Imperial Force alive.

This is a semi factual account based on letters, anecdotal evidence, war diaries, reference books and discussions I had with my grandfather, Stanley James Dunkley when he was alive.

Some of the characters are fictional for the purposes of story telling.

Andrew Dunkley

Chapter 1

<u>A Raw Recruit</u>

New Year's Day 1917, I scribbled down the last few words of a letter. My hand was shaking as I wrote, it had to be just right.

The bearer my son Stanley Dunkley being in his 18th year has my permission to enlist for active service. I then scrawled out the signature, *Ernest Dunkley.*

I'd been practicing for a few weeks to get it down pat. I folded the letter, put it in an envelope and stuffed it in my bag before seeking out my father. I knew he'd be angry and that he'd try and stop me, but I was prepared for that.

Dad was in his armchair, dozing after the nights' celebrations. I don't know how much he'd had to drink, the same as any other day probably. His half tucked in; crumpled shirt was stained with the remains of last nights' dinner and beer swill. He looked like he'd been there all night. I took a deep breath and then said,

"I'm joining up Dad."

It blurted out in a much harsher tone than I'd planned. Dad jumped as my words broke through his slumber and I watched as the message sank in. His jaw clenched and his face reddened as a scowl exaggerated an already deeply furrowed brow. He lurched to his feet and looked at me through bloodshot eyes,

"The Hell you are! I won't allow it. You're just a boy and boys don't fight in wars," he slurred.

Dad stared at me expecting the usual back pedal. I'd been listening to his bluster and feeling his belt for ten years now and always feared reprisal, but I'd finally had enough,

"You won't stop me; I've made up my mind."

I fully expected him to raise his hand. That wouldn't have been unusual. He stepped forward and shoved his face uncomfortably close to mine, his greying hair mopping beads of sweat from his forehead,

"I'll bloody well stop you if I so desire. You can't talk to me like that!" he bellowed as I caught a rancid puff of his breath.

We glared at each other, and I immediately felt a welling of nerves in my stomach and blood pumping through my arms and legs,

"I don't want to fight you Dad, I'm going and there's nothing you can do about it!"

I felt terribly uncomfortable. I'd never stood my ground like this before, and he seemed utterly surprised by my defiance.

Just then my younger brother and sister burst into the room and Dad was quick to use them against me,

"What about Ruth and Eric, they need you here. You know I can't look after them."

I immediately felt terribly guilty about leaving,

"Please don't do that dad, you'll just upset them. I'm not going to change my mind."

There was quite a pause as he pondered a new tactic,

"The army doesn't have time to play babysitter; did you think about that? *Men* are dying over there; you don't stand a chance."

There was a wry smile on his face now and I was about to say something smug when I noticed my siblings were weeping. It was a heart wrenching situation. I had to get out of this place and live my own life but leaving Ruth and Eric behind ate at my insides. I looked at Dad again and was about to speak but he cut me off,

"Your older brothers are already over there; surely this family has given enough to the war."

"That's beside the point Dad; no-one's keeping score. Can't you just accept that the decision is made, I'm going right now?"

With that I knelt and gave my brother and sister a big hug,

"Don't worry you two. I'll be home soon enough, with Harold and Allan."

I'm afraid I didn't sound very reassuring. I tried to stand but they wouldn't let me go,

"Please don't leave Stan," pleaded Ruth.

"It's alright," I said as I broke away from their embrace.

I looked at Dad again and thought I saw a tear glisten in his eye, but he wiped it away very quickly and his demeanor had softened a little,

"Don't be foolish son, there's no need for you to go. You'll get yourself killed," he said calmly this time.

"I'm sorry Dad, but I have to do this," I paused before I said what I really thought.

"Why Stan, what possible reason could you have?"

"Duty? Empire?" I was really spouting a lot of nonsense now, "It doesn't matter does it?"

The truth would have hurt him too much. I thought he was a terrible father, but I wasn't going to tell him that he was the very reason for my decision. It would have finished him off; I was certain of that.

"That's all good and well Stan, but there are plenty of men over there already, they don't need to watch over a sixteen year old boy!"

"We'll soon see, won't we?" I said as I made for the door.

Ernest grabbed my arm,

"Think about your mother, she would have been heartbroken," he said in desperation.

I looked at him square in the eye,

"I know," and with that the let go of me.

I looked at Ruth and Eric,

"Be brave and look after each other," I told them.

They were crying uncontrollably now. I stood and offered a hand to my father. He looked at it but then turned away so I walked to the door, strode through and gave it a good hard slam when I stepped outside. As I made for the gate, I could feel his eyes burning at the back of my neck. I turned into Smith Street and caught a glimpse of my father out of the corner of my eye. He was peering through the front window, but I fought off the desire to look at him. He started yelling through the glass and I caught a few words,

"You'll be back...........home....tonight."

I didn't catch exactly what he said but the message sank in, and I did wonder if the army might just turn me away at the gate.

I walked briskly up the street, still feeling his eyes upon me until I turned the corner and was quickly out of sight. I let out a sigh of relief and then began to cry. I thought I'd have felt relieved to be rid of that terrible part of my life but instead there was a deep sadness.

As I walked, doubts buzzed around in my head. I wept for a while longer but wiped away the last of my tears as I approached Harry Robson's house. He was my best mate, and we'd agreed to join up together. We'd known each other since starting school and he was waiting on the front step as I approached. When I got a bit closer it was clear that something was wrong,

"What's up Harry? Where's your bag?"

"Sorry Stan but I can't go with you. Mum and Dad came down hard on me when I told them."

"What? Didn't you stand up to them? Didn't you tell them I was going too?" I demanded but he didn't answer me except to say he was sorry.

I stood there, stunned for a moment. Where did this leave me? It wasn't part of the plan. I never even considered that he'd back out,

"Well, this is a right old mess then, isn't it?" I suggested.

"I suppose it is," he said and there was a brief pause, "What'll you do now Stan? Go home?"

The thought was already at the front of my mind, but I'd finally had the courage to stand up to my father and going back was not an option. If I'd inherited one thing from him it was pride but going on alone didn't appeal either. Then something snapped in my mind. My thoughts became very clear, and I knew what to do,

"Well, I think I'll just go on without you Harry."

"What?" Harry was visibly shocked, "No, you can't go now. Wait until Mum and Dad come around. I'm sure I can make them change their minds in a day or two."

"Maybe, but I don't want to go home. It was hard enough getting out of there just now; I can't go back. I'll look like a fool, and he'll never let me out again.

Sorry Harry I've got to go."

He looked at me and then smiled,

"I understand."

Harry was a regular visitor to our place, so I didn't need to explain anything about my father,

"I'll see you over there then?" Harry asked.

"I'll be counting on it old chum," I said and we shook hands, "Bye Harry."

"Goodbye Stan. Keep your head down, or whatever it is you have to do," he said with a laugh.

"I will. Make sure you write me. Tell me what's happening back home. And drop in on Dad if you can, make sure Ruth and Eric are OK," I called as I got into stride.

"Will do Stan....goodbye," and he waved as I disappeared up the street.

My plans were in tatters, but I was carrying on.

It was a long walk to Sydney Showground, and I didn't know what to expect now. Two of us wouldn't have attracted too much attention but a sixteen year old boy on his own might just invite some unwelcome enquiries. I was more worried than ever, but I'd read about a boy who got in aged 14. I was hoping the letter I wrote would be enough to convince them that I was a genuine recruit. As I walked my mind started swinging from one thought to another. I remembered my mother, Elizabeth. She died giving birth. The baby girl died also. Dad called her Elizabeth too. He took the loss very heavily. I was only 7 at the time and have only scattered memories of that terrible day but I know my older brothers were devastated. Dad took to drinking and our little corner store business suffered. We all tried chipping in to help but there wasn't much we could do with Dad in such a bad way. Somehow though the business survived but we always seemed to lack money. Dad took his frustrations out on Harold and Allan and then turned on me as I grew into my adolescent years. When he finally met someone new we all hoped it would be for the better but were wrong. She had her own son, also named Harold and she didn't want anything to do with us. Dad was smitten and we were a burden, so things just got worse. I hated leaving Ruth and Eric in that messed up place, but I couldn't stay a moment longer.

My brother, Allan was a good writer and sent us plenty of letters. I read as many as I could and was amazed by some of the stories he had to tell. My other brother Harold wrote occasionally but he wasn't much for letters. Most of the mail was heavily censored so they didn't go into a lot of detail when it came to military activities, but I was certainly swept along with patriotism. The truth is the war gave me the perfect excuse to get out, and I grabbed it with both hands. Once I'd settled on my decision I tried to keep up with the news of the war through the papers. They were always available at Sydney City Council where I'd worked as an Audit Clerk for the last two years after leaving school at 14. I'd given up the job to join the army and hoped to return there after the war.

Just then I spotted a figure across the road. It was clear he wasn't from Sydney. He wore a pair of dirty old trousers, well-worn boots, a long sleeved shirt rolled up to the elbows and a felt hat with the worst sweat stain I'd ever seen. He carried his swag over his shoulder and had the dark tan of a bloke who worked the land. I thought he must have been about forty years old. He'd already seen me and hurried across the road to catch up,

"Joining up young buck?" he asked.

He was a fit looking man and spoke with an odd country twang.

"Yes indeed, you too?" I enquired.

"Too right, I don't know why I waited so long."

He peered at me for a moment and I knew exactly what he was thinking,

"Geez mate, you're a bit young, aren't ya?" He suggested bluntly.

I felt the hair on the back of my neck bristle up and a shot a scowl in his direction. He picked up the message,

"Well, it doesn't matter I suppose, you know what you're doing by the looks of it."

I took a moment to calm myself and replied, "Yes I do."

He skipped slightly to adjust the weight of the swag on his back which appeared to be quite heavy, but it wasn't slowing him at all,

"The name's Tom, Tom Bower, from West Wyalong," he stated as he offered his hand.

"Stan Dunkley," I said and he gave me a crushing handshake.

We walked along chatting all the way. He told me about his wife and two boys and explained how he couldn't join up any sooner and had to wait until his children were old enough to run the farm. Like my father, his wife was furious with him, but he was determined to be a part of the Great War,

"So where do we go Stan?" he asked, "I don't know my way around Sydney. Never actually been here before."

"Really?" I asked with surprise.

"Nope. You ever been to West Wyalong?"

"Well no. I've never been over the mountains," I replied.

"Well, there it is then," Tom said and we both laughed.

I told him where we were headed,

"There's a camp at the showground, I expect that's our best option."

"OK then Stan, lead the way."

We walked for hours and really got to know each other. He was a nice bloke, and we really hit it off. He told me he was pretty good with a rifle and promised to teach me how to use one when we got our hands on them,

"I don't know what those army blokes are going to tell you, but if you stick with me, you'll be better than average," he assured me.

It was a hot day, and all the shops were closed. There was no public transport running, so I was feeling the effects of the long walk. My feet were hurting with blisters starting to bite and the perspiration was running down my face which I'm sure was bright pink. Tom, on the other hand, didn't appear to be suffering any ill effects. He gave me a quick glance and smiled but didn't make any comment. I'm sure he thought me a bit of a tender foot and he was right.

After a while we reached the gates of Sydney Showground. I could see rows of bell tents and a dry dustbowl where the grass used to grow, no doubt crushed under many hundreds of boots over the last few years. Guards stood at the gate with rifles slung over their shoulders. They were wearing khaki uniforms and slouch hats, but I got the impression it was only for show as they didn't take much notice as we ambled through the gate.

The first tent we came to was very large and had a sign above the entrance that said *Recruitment.* Tom lifted the flap and we both stepped through, the warm air was thick with the smell of canvas. There were a few desks and chairs dotted about and a main desk where an officer sat scribbling notes. He looked up as we approached,

"Good morning, what can I do for you today?" he asked politely.

I felt a pang in my belly and became incredibly nervous; I was scared on so many levels. Would they see through my ruse, what if they sent me home? All sorts of doubts were in my mind.

"We're here to join up," Tom announced,

"My name's Tom and this here is Stan."

"He's a fine looking boy, you must be proud of him," suggested the officer.

Tom let out an almighty laugh,

"He's not my son, but he sure is a good bloke."

The officer looked me up and down as I blushed,

"How old are you son?" he asked.

I'd anticipated the question and made the mistake of answering so fast I almost cut him off,

"Eighteen...sir!"

He still didn't seem to be convinced, and then Tom saved the day,

"Stan was telling me he often gets told how young he looks, must be hard for you sometimes eh Stan?" and I saw him wink.

"Indeed, I have a letter from my father if that helps," I suggested and rummaged around for the envelope.

The officer looked it over, pondered for a moment and finally said,

"Here are some forms. Please fill them out and bring them back to me when you're done. If there's something you don't know, leave it blank and we'll sort it out later," and he handed over a wad of papers and a quill to each of us.

We found a place to sit and began filling in the forms. The declaration required permission from the parents of anyone under the age of twenty one, so the letter was inspected and accepted without further question, much to my delight. Interestingly there was nowhere on the forms requiring me to state my date of birth. I wondered if that was an oversight or a very clever omission. We filled in as much as we could and were then shuffled off for a medical assessment. We were weighed, measured and had some basic medical tests done. Our bodies were checked for birth marks and scars, which were noted on drawings of human bodies on our papers,

"What's the point of that?" Tom enquired.

The doctor explained that these records would help to identify us if we were killed and our bodies were beyond recognition. The thought didn't sit well with either of us. Finally, the doctor jabbed me with a needle and I winced in pain,

"Sorry son, smallpox. You might feel unwell for a couple of days."

My papers were then stamped, *Fit for Active Service.*

Tom didn't have any trouble either and we returned to the recruitment officer,

"Right then, you're all set. Sign here," he ordered and pointed at a line on the application.

I picked up the quill and dipped it in the ink well. I hesitated for a moment then scribbled my signature on the form. Tom did likewise and the officer collected up the papers,

"Thank you, gentlemen, and welcome to the 18th Battalion," as he handed us our pay books, "Look after those, you're sunk without them."

"Thank you, sir!" we said in unison.

I felt a jolt of pride and a bit of relief knowing the hard part was over.

"Now if you'll report to the quartermaster, he'll look after you from here. Out the door and turn Right."

"Yes sir," I barked and we left without another word.

Tom and I made our way to the quartermaster's tent and were met with a totally different reception; the little man was almost hostile. I wasn't sure if he had a chip on his shoulder because he was the shortest man in uniform or if he felt that everything in his tent was a personal possession. He looked over our paperwork and groped though the piles of uniforms, preparing a kit for each of us. A few minutes later we both had new uniforms, kit bags, packs and all the paraphernalia of a soldier. The last thing we got was a felt hat each. The AIF uniform was indeed impressive, and the slouch hat really finished it off. I'd seen many soldiers in the city in the last few

years and was always struck by how manly they looked.

"Sign here," demanded the Quartermaster in a gruff and disinterested tone and we took possession of our kits. He then he directed us to a bell tent where we'd stay until it was time to ship out. He pointed out the mess and a few other essentials, like the latrines and sent us on our way.

"Nice bloke," Tom said sarcastically as we left the tent.

I didn't have to reply and just nodded in agreement. We wandered along the rows of tents until we saw our tent number. I threw the flap open and startled the five occupants. They all stared as I entered the tent with Tom close behind,

"Well look here fellas, some new boys," said one of the group.

"Put a sock in it Frank. You don't need to act like a thug every time someone arrives," said another.

There was an awkward silence until Tom piped up. He seemed to be good at breaking the ice,

"G'day. Tom Bower's the name, from West Wyalong. This here's Stan Dunkley. He's from Sydney."

"Nice to meet you blokes, I'm Mick Hogg, this is Frank Curry and these others are Les Giles, Bert Thorn and Dick Jones," and they all greeted us in unison.

"You can stash your gear wherever you can find a space," suggested Mick.

"Thanks Mate," replied Tom.

We both found a place to bed down and sat to learn more about camp life. Mick did most of the talking and explained how things worked,

"And the early starts don't go down well with too many of us. Up at five and on parade before calisthenics, marching, drill and work around the camp. But the discipline isn't too bad really."

I noticed that Frank was eyeing me closely,

"Stan, isn't it?" he enquired.

"That's right."

"How old are you?" he asked pointedly.

I felt my face redden again and knew my ruse wouldn't hold up here. Just then Bert Thorn spoke. He'd been incredibly quiet up until now,

"Leave him be Frank, no business of ours."

"Look at him. He's gotta be fifteen at best," Frank suggested.

I didn't know what to say and felt it best to ignore him.

"You're only just out of nappies yourself aren't you, Frank?" laughed Dick.

"That's not the point. He's underage and we'll get stuck with looking after him. He might even get us all killed," Frank said accusingly, looking me square in the eye.

There was an awkward silence again and I had no answer.

 "Leave the kid alone Frank," came a chorus from the rest of the group.

 "Don't you worry about old Frank here Stan, he mature beyond his years," Mick suggested and everyone laughed, but I didn't see the joke.

I learned more about the men as we talked. Frank was twenty one and worked on the docks. That certainly explained the tough exterior. Waterside workers had a reputation for being rough and Frank was, at the very least, putting up a good front. Mick Hogg was a jovial chap, very friendly and didn't mind a chat. He was very likeable and seemed to get along with everyone. I guessed he was around thirty. Bert Thorn was the quiet one. He didn't say much at all, but when he did it was usually direct and no-one ever argued; I liked him. Then there was Dick Jones. He liked people to call him Dickie, and he was a good fellow, although I detected that he was very pessimistic. He didn't seem to be too confident about very much. Les Giles seemed pretty sure of himself but didn't give much away either.

Tom and I then followed the group to the mess hall where we had our first army meal. There must have been about one hundred men at the camp and there was an excited buzz in the room. They were all expecting that we'd be shipping our in the next few weeks. I took my first mouthful of army food and almost threw up. I thought I could eat anything, but this was the worst mush I'd ever tasted.

"You OK Stan?" asked Mick as the others smirked.

"I don't really know, what on Earth is this?" I asked.

"Well, we're not really sure, but I suspect that the cook is scraping the bottom of the pot every night," suggested Mick.

"That explains the metallic taste then," I replied.

We laughed and somehow managed to finish our meals. I met a great many new recruits and saw quite a few fellows who, like me, were clearly younger than they claimed. I felt much better about my situation after that. When dinner was over, we headed back to our tent and after another long discussion the order came for lights out. I fell asleep almost immediately.

Chapter 2

<u>Training and travel</u>

The next morning, I woke to the strains of a bugle. There was much activity and I could hear men running outside. Mick and the others were already getting dressed into their uniforms and filing out of the tent. I then noticed that I ached all over after sleeping on a soil floor all night with nothing more than a blanket to lie on and my pack as a pillow. Frank turned back towards me as he opened the flap of the bell tent,

"Better get a move on, you don't want to be late for parade," and he left.

Tom already had his pants and boots on and left while putting on his shirt. I rummaged through my kit and found my uniform. I rushed to dress but the faster I worked the more difficult it seemed to become. I was in an awful state as I burst out of the tent and ran towards the parade ground. As I did, I looked for Tom and the others. Most of the men were already assembled in lines facing a flagpole. Just then I spotted Tom who urged me on with a wide smile. Suddenly, his smile vanished and a look of horror took over. Next thing I knew I was sprawled on the dusty ground and could hear the roars of laughter coming from the ranks. Then a voice broke through the commotion,

"Are you OK son?"

I looked around and saw another man propped up on one knee. His uniform was very smart indeed or at least used to be. Now it was covered in red dust and dry grass. I wasn't sure of his rank.

"I'm so very sorry, I didn't see you," I explained.

I was expecting a tirade, after all this was the army but he looked at me and said,

"That's completely alright, I didn't see you either."

He stood and brushed himself off then offered me his hand. I reached out and he drew me up on my feet. I brushed off the dirt and grass and look at his face. He had a gentle way about him, nothing like I expected of an army commander. A thick moustache covered his top lip, and his hat only slightly hid a receding hair line. He was around forty-five or fifty and he carried a riding crop,

"Are you OK young man?" he inquired.

"Yes sir, I'm very sorry sir."

The one hundred recruits had suddenly gone very quiet. I think they were as shocked as I was that there was no shouting or hostility. I must say I was very relieved.

"You're new. What's your name?"

"Stan Dunkley sir, arrived yesterday," I explained.

"Well Private I'm very pleased to have you here. Please join the other ranks," and he saluted.

"Yes sir!" I replied but my attempt to salute felt rather clumsy.

Being called by my rank had caught me a little off guard. I hastened to the line and took my place next to Tom, he was smiling broadly,

"I think he likes you," he said and a few men within earshot chuckled. I didn't bother to reply but couldn't help but smile. We stood on the parade ground, eager for some news.

"TEN SHUN," came an order from one of the ranking officers at the front.

Everyone stiffened to a ramrod straight stance. Quite a few of the new chaps were slow to respond. Then the officer I had just collided with began to speak,

"Stand easy men," and everyone relaxed, "My name is Colonel James Braidwood, for those of you who joined us most recently. I am commanding officer here," he announced.

 I suddenly felt like a real idiot as Tom dug me in the ribs and the others stifled their laughter. The commander continued,

"I trust you didn't overdo it for New Year, although I must say there were signs of excessive celebration on the parade ground this morning. I do hope you feel better now."

Several men murmured and laughed somewhere in the line. Just then the Commander took some papers from his batman and cleared his throat,

"The war continues in France, Belgium and the Middle East and you will soon be called upon to do your part for the Empire. I've received orders asking that you men be send forthwith to England where you will be trained for duty on the Western Front!"

A mighty cheer rang out all around at this news. I must say I got caught up in the moment and felt a jolt of excitement. Tom's face was beaming a huge smile and even Frank seemed to have softened just a little. When we'd settled down again the commander told us more,

"You will be the 19th reinforcements of the 18th Battalion. I don't need to tell some of you that things have been difficult for our lot on the front line in the last year. The 18th Battalion spent a good part of August in a major battle for the town of Pozieres, twice having to take the ground from the enemy. They were lucky to have had something of a spell in Belgium on a quiet section of the front until October when they were sent back to the Somme. And now, it seems the Germans are on the run."

We all cheered again as the commander continued to talk of the exploits of our battalion. If he was trying to build pride and confidence in the new recruits, it was working. My heart swelled as I listened to him talk of our successes.

"Men, we are on the verge of a great victory, and you will play your part. Despite the bleak European winter and the difficulties of trench life, we have made much progress and expect to continue pushing on in the coming months. When you arrive you may well be part of the final battles which will settle this war once and for all."

Another cheer quickly evaporated when the Colonel chose not to pause,

"We will bring the new recruits up to task quickly before you ship out. Thank you, men."

With that he saluted as another officer ordered us to attention and we returned the salute. The commander marched off and didn't look back.

"What now?" Tom enquired.

"Don't ask," replied Dickie.

Just then we were ordered into four groups and told to start jogging. We ran laps around the perimeter of the camp before performing endless calisthenics. After that came work detail, cleaning up the camp and repairing buildings and fences.

In the coming days we performed many drills and exercises and learned how to disassemble and assemble the Lee Enfield .303 rifle, the standard weapon of a British soldier. Most of the men quite liked the rifle as it was very reliable, but we were warned not to let dirt get into the firing mechanism or the gun could jam. Practicing on the range was intimidating at first. Tom's experience with guns was obvious and, as he promised, he trained me on its use when the instructors weren't looking. I became quite adept with the weapon in a very short time and overcame my fear very quickly. We were told how a crack unit could fire at such a rate that the enemy would think that they were under machine gun fire. I had to agree as the weapon was easy to load and fire repeatedly; I could fire off ten bullets in just over a minute. I still wondered if I would be able to point the thing at another human being though. Shooting targets wasn't quite so threatening. Most of the country boys were handy shots but I did manage to keep up with many of them. Tom was very pleased with how I adapted to using the rifle and was proud of himself for being such a good instructor. We familiarised ourselves with a great many weapons while in camp; mills bombs, mortars and the most dreaded weapon of all, the bayonet affectionately known as a tin opener. We did practice drill with these blades attached to the end of the rifles, running headlong at a row of straw men hanging on wooden beams. We'd thrust the bayonets deep into their hollow stomachs screaming at the top of our voices, withdraw and stuck them again before charging on. I really hoped never to have to do anything like it.

Of course, camp life wasn't all hard work. We got to spend time off in the city. Army wages weren't much but our food and clothing were taken care of as were our health needs and general amenities. The money we were paid was more than enough for a good night out. It seemed that wearing a uniform got me into places that wouldn't have welcomed me otherwise and I took great advantage of those opportunities. Drinking was new to me, as was smoking but I didn't want to look like a toff, so I indulged in these vices with glee and paid quite a price a few times too. Trying to do calisthenics after a night in the city wasn't fun at all but you couldn't fall behind or there would be repercussions. Marching was almost comical. Drill sergeants would yell and scream instructions, but no matter how hard they tried there was always someone out of step. I heard one bloke ask how marching made us better soldiers. He spent the rest of the day cleaning toilets. We also sat through many lectures about tactics, discipline, hygiene and safety. There was always something new to learn. When it came time to find out about the weapons used by the Germans, we were keen observers. The Mauser rifle and the infamous Maxim machine gun, which they used to great effect early in the war, sent shivers down my spine. We were tested in the use of the Enfield regularly; disassembling, cleaning and reassembling the rifle before firing the next shot. It was all designed to make the process automatic so we could do it under fire. My youth was also an advantage on the obstacle course, and I soon became quite fit and athletic, without so much as an ounce of extra fat to speak of. I was developing into a model soldier or at least I thought so.

On February 7th, 1917, we were ordered to embark the HMAT Wiltshire. There were one hundred and fifty four of us, mostly reinforcements but many heading back after time at home recovering from wounds. It was easy to pick them from the rest; they were quiet and intense and kept to themselves. We were quickly sorted into alphabetical order and allocated our service numbers. Mine was 6536. We marched to Woolloomooloo to board our ship, a huge steamer weighing in at seven thousand eight hundred tons. She'd been plying the Indian Ocean for the last two years, carrying Australian soldiers to England. Wiltshire was an ugly ship and nothing like the great ocean going cruise liners I'd seen in Sydney Harbour in the past. She was a heavy haulage vessel that had been converted to carry troops. The superstructure was jammed up towards the ship's stern with a single funnel belching black smoke as she built up steam. While we clambered up the gangplank I couldn't help but notice three T shaped masts that looked ominously like crucifixes. I shivered.

Once on board the Wiltshire we were placed under the command of Captain Andrew Thomas. He was a veteran of the war and was returning to France after being wounded a year before. He'd recuperated in Australia and rejoined once he had enough strength. His experience made him a perfect candidate to look after our bunch. We were all very excited to be on our way at last. Family, friends and well-wishers crowded the docks while press photographers documented the whole event. Soldiers crowded every vantage point on the ship waving and shouting to loved ones.

I stood there on the deck with my friends, Tom Bower, Mick Hogg, Frank Curry, Bert Thorn, Dickie Jones and Les Giles. I'd grown quite close to Tom despite the twenty six year age difference, and we'd agreed to watch out for each other no matter what. We all stared down at the well-wishers as the ship slid away from the dock. I felt the bump of the tugs as they lurched at the heavy ropes and started guiding our ship towards Sydney Heads. We looked down at a sobbing mass. Men, women and children on the dock cried, waved and screamed to their sons, brothers, nephews and uncles. For me it was an isolating moment. Tom and Mick were also feeling a little left out and we watched while Frank waved madly to his sister Jo, tears in his eyes, screaming out a promise to be home soon. We all hoped he was right.

Before long the crowd disappeared, and the Wiltshire was passing through the heads under its own steam. We moved off to find our berths and discovered that the accommodations were very basic indeed. Men were crammed into small ward rooms with bunks stacked against the walls. There was barely room to move about when everyone stepped inside. We stashed our gear and headed back on deck.

We then moved into open water and turned south, following the New South Wales coast. I heard from the sailors that we should keep an eye out for enemy shipping. One in particular had them worried, a ship they called the Wolf. It was a converted German merchant ship, designed to look like a civilian vessel. When she came across her prey she would suddenly switch into a fighting vessel with guns emerging from hidden compartments. Accounts of her activities had been reported in the papers, and her reputation had panicked a great many, including us. The Germans operated like pirates, pillaging ships and taking the crews prisoner. We didn't like to think what they might do if they took on a troop ship. Most likely start shooting and leave us for dead. At first things were fine and I felt well, but the waters became quite choppy as we turned into Bass Strait. Tom and I were seasick,

"Geez Stan, I don't think I can recall feeling so lousy," Tom suggested.

"It's terrible," I replied as my lunch spattered onto the waves below.

First stop was Melbourne where we took on more recruits, then on to Albany and Fremantle. Thankfully there was no sign of the Wolf. When we started to cross the Indian Ocean, the ship was crammed with one thousand seven hundred and seventeen men. We settled into life on board the ship and eventually got over our sea sickness, although it seemed to make a sudden return whenever the swells got bigger.

Days at seas were boring and uncomfortable. We did our best to keep ourselves entertained by

playing cards, smoking, singing and sleeping. Boxing matches were held on deck and some men even managed to manufacture basic musical instruments and do some shows. We were ordered to wear our boots for several hours a day to get used to them. I'm afraid my feet didn't fare too well as I suffered many blisters. We were regularly lectured on ship safety and what to do if the hull was struck by a torpedo and we took turns on submarine watch.

After a few weeks we arrived at the South African port of Durban where we spend a few days ashore. We visited bars and it was clear that the local people knew Australians very well after welcoming so many in the past couple of years. Everyone had something to sell, from small boys to old men and women. Fruit, eggs and souvenirs were plentiful, and one had to watch his pennies as the pick pockets were quick and crafty. While Military Police tried to keep the men in line, there was always trouble and many a recruit found himself in lockup or banned from shore leave. Thankfully we avoided such problems and took in the sights, sounds and some of the very bad smells of this exotic place. The people of this land were strange indeed. I was intrigued by the black men. I'd never seen such types before and watched them work on the docks. They regularly called for us to toss coins into the water, and they'd dive in after them, some even fighting over a sixpence or a shilling. I suppose it was an awful lot to them. Sometimes they'd even get paid to fight and were urged on by Australians on the ship, the winner being showered in pennies.

From Durban the Wiltshire travelled to Cape Town and finally started heading north, up the coast of West Africa to England. As we approached British waters we were again warned about German subs. They were doing their best to cripple merchant shipping across the English Channel and in the North Sea, but from what we'd been told; most of the German Navy was bottled up in a blockade after the Battle of Jutland a year ago. I'd read about the battle in the newspaper and found it hard to comprehend that as many as ten thousand men were lost along with scores of ships from both sides.

Excitement grew amongst the men as we spotted the English coastline. Our were heightened more when we were joined by British destroyers which danced about like little nymphs trying to reduce the chance of a torpedo attack. Our men called out to the English sailors, but they were too well disciplined to respond. We were very relieved to finally dock in Plymouth Harbour; our journey uneventful when all was said and done.

On April 11th, 1917, two months after departing Sydney we stepped onto English soil. We were very keen to hear news of the war. Our time at sea had closed us off so we were unaware of any recent developments. A group of British soldiers met Captain Thomas, and he talked with their leader. The pair had quite a long conversation and a few of the other Tommies took the opportunity to fill us in,

"The Hun made a run for it; gave up just about all the ground they gained in the last two years!" said one fellow.

"Geez, there won't be much left for us," Les Giles suggested.

"That's fine with me," said Frank who wasn't the least bit thrilled with the cool spring air of England.

The soldier went on the explain that the commander of the British Forces in France and Belgium, Field Marshall Douglas Haig had spent winter driving the German's all the way back to their last line of defense, known as the Hindenburg Line. Bits and pieces of information filtered through about other events on the Front. We learned of the successful Canadian attack on Vimy Ridge where four Victoria Crosses had been won. Then we heard of the failed attempt by the French to end the war in one fell swoop at the River Aisne. They sent one million men in against the Germans and lost one hundred and seventy eight thousand of them in the worst defeat of the war to date. As a result, the Chief of the French Army, Robert Nivelle was dismissed. The news was shocking to us, so many men extinguished so quickly and easily. Then someone said that the Germans had signed an armistice with Russian, freeing up hundreds of thousands of troops for the Western Front. Our hearts sank at this news. There was also talk that the United States had finally agreed to send troops to France, as many as one million. It was hard to tell fact from fiction. How could so much have happened in such a short time? We didn't know what to think.

Finally, Captain Thomas broke off his conversation and called us to attention. We were to march to the Plymouth Railway Station and then travel to Salisbury Plain where the British Army training facilities were located, approximately one hundred and thirty miles to the north-east. Three trains stood at the station getting their steam up, ready for the journey. We clambered on board and found ourselves some seats. Our carriage was old and worn out, the linoleum floors etched with skids, scrapes and nicks from hundreds of boots. Before long all the recruits were on board and the trains began to move away. We looked out over the English countryside, wide eyed and in awe. We travelled through pristine forest and caught glimpses of the coast from time to time. It was a refreshing change for most of us after so long at sea. We passed through the town of Exeter and noticed a sudden change in the landscape. The forest was replaced by grassland and hills. The further we went the less impressive it became. I started to think of England a dreary, desolate place with a forest around the edge. It didn't seem beyond the realms of possibility. Many of us soon grew bored with the dreary view and went to sleep. After many hours trundling along the English countryside our train approached Salisbury. A few of the educated amongst us realised we were in the vicinity of the famous Stonehenge and scanned the horizon for a glimpse, but it was probably several miles away and out of sight.

At last, we stopped and tumbled off the train to be met by the camp commander, Colonel Robert Dunning. He was typically British, with that stiff upper lip and strong, posh accent. He made us stand there for an eternity as he told us about the history of the region and the rules and regulations of the facility,

"I believe most of you have already been through basic training back home. I imagine that many of you are feeling a little weak in the knees. We'll knock that out of you in a jiff."

 The men groaned at the thought.

"Some of you will be here longer than others, depending on the kind of training your battalions require. Most of you will be joining the infantry but there is a need for signallers, trench mortar, Lewis gunners and snipers. You will be trained in the use of all weapons, dressing wounds and trench warfare."

He seemed to speak for hours and after a while most of us struggled to keep our minds from wandering. We learned that he was a Gallipoli veteran, and I noticed a distinct limp which would no doubt have encumbered him at the front, so I imagined that a training post was his only way of contributing. He was in command of a facility that covered over three hundred square miles, and he clearly took the role very seriously. He eventually finished talking, much to our relief,

"So, welcome and I hope your stay here is very rewarding. Dismissed!"

With that we were left to our commanders who were busily trying to learn more about our billets. This gave us a chance to have a good look around and Frank was the first to say something,

"I've never seen a more pitiful place in my life. How bloody sad is this?"

It wasn't a pretty sight, a vast expanse of nothing but grass, dirt and white rock which we were told was chalk. Soldiers had been coming here since the late 1800s, and it was not wonder. There was absolutely nothing else you could do in a place like this!

After a long wait we were finally allocated our billets. We weren't to stay at the camp itself. The conditions there were quite unsavory and the accommodations had been abandoned some time back. Instead, we travelled a short distance to one of the nearby villages. Men were spread out far and wide, there were almost two thousand of us from all parts of the world, Australia, New Zealand, England, Scotland, Africa and a raft of other places.

It didn't take long for us to settle into our new accommodation and learn the routine. By day we trained and by night we drank and enjoyed ourselves as best we could. There was very little in the way of entertainment in the village and I would go so far as to say it was one of the most uninteresting places I've ever been but, as always, we made the best of it.

Over the following weeks we spent a great deal of time learning about tactics and trench warfare. Going 'over the top' was drummed into us constantly. Most of us had never seen combat before and only had ideas from reading newspapers or letters from our relatives. The training only taught us the physical processes involved in achieving any task. Doing the same thing shrouded in fear might prove a very different concept indeed.

We continued to work on our musketry at the range, and I quickly improved and became quite a crack shot. Again, Tom was instrumental in adding to my understanding of using the rifle effectively. We were told that the use of Mills Grenades would be something we all needed to know. It seems a harsh lesson had been learned by the AIF during their first sojourn on the Western Front at a place called Fromelles. The attack went badly with all the Mills bombers killed leaving the infantry without anyone to support them in the enemy lines. The battle quickly cascaded into calamity. If everyone had known how to use bombs, perhaps the story would have been different. It was decided from then on that all front line personnel would be trained in bombing techniques. Unfortunately, we regularly attacked the straw men with bayonets. I don't really know why I found it so unsavory, but it really didn't sit well with me. I suppose the thought of stabbing someone was much harder to accept than shooting them from a much greater distance. There was also specialist training in any number of roles from signalling to machine gun operations.

We received news that the 2nd Division, which included our own unit, the 18th Battalion had just come out of a major battle at Bullecourt. Australian and British Divisions joined up to take part in the attack but were cut up badly. A few weeks later they tried again. This time they took the town but again the losses were horrific. We were very pleased to have been in England on hearing such news.

It came time for us to do our marksmanship test. The best shooters would be selected for further training on the Lewis Gun or as snipers. I suggested to Tom that he would be a shoe in,

"No bloody way mate. I'm not joining the suicide squad," he announced.

"But Tom, you're a perfect shot, you'll be a great sniper," I suggested.

"Maybe, but I don't think my scores are going to impress these blokes today."

And he was right. He shot poorly and didn't make the list. My turn came and I lay as still as I could and squeezed off my allocation of bullets. The targets seemed so much smaller and nervous tension made it difficult to keep the barrel steady. I tried my best, but the pressure got to me and many of my shots strayed. Mick, Frank and Les did marginally better, but Bert and Dickie were most impressive. They scored quite highly and were offered further training on the Lewis Gun. I must say I felt a little disappointed that I'd done so poorly but I realised there was more to shooting than just blazing away and again wondered how the pressure of battle might impact on me. Bert and Dickie were justifiably proud of themselves, but Tom didn't join in their celebrations,

"You blokes are as mad as cut snakes. You're just making yourselves targets for German snipers," he suggested.

"Well, that's where you blokes can help," suggested Dickie, "They tell us we need a crew of at least five for the gun, so why not you blokes?" he asked.

"Not me mate," retorted Tom.

Frank too dismissed the idea flat out but the rest of us thought it over and agreed. It would mean we'd stay together and there was more pay for Lewis gun crews. The arrangements were quickly signed off and we were set.

Before long we were on the range gaining instruction on the Lewis Gun. Our instructor was Sergeant Ronald Spears,

"This ere is a Lewis Gun and you better get to know it very well," he said as he squinted at us intently. I found his thick cockney accent quite amusing.

"This lil beauty'll shove six hundred rounds into the Germans before he can draw bref. Anyone used one before? No? Right then, we best get darn to basics then!"

With than he knelt next to the machine gun and started pointing out its functions and features and I must say it had quite a distinctive look. From the stock it resembled a typical rifle but that's where the similarity finished. Circular ammunition panniers sat on top of the guns' breech and dropped bullets into the firing chamber. Panniers held forty eight bullets and if you fired continuously, it only took five seconds to empty. The barrel was unlike any other gun I'd seen so far. It reminded me of a stove pipe. The sergeant explained that the Lewis gun was air cooled and the barrel's chamber was designed to keep the barrel from overheating. All up the unit weighed in at about thirteen kilos. In the days that followed our crew learned how to pull the Lewis gun apart, clean it, put it back together, how to load and reload the breech and refill the panniers with bullets. The gun had been modified to take .303 bullets, to avoid any confusion with the Enfield rifles which was a problem the English still faced. They had to carry two types of rounds depending on which gun they were using. Bert was made the number 1 of the crew and Dickie was his second. They discarded their rifles which were replaced with Webley revolvers. The rest of us would keep our Enfield rifles and provide support for Bert and Dickie. That simply meant, carrying ammo and tools. We'd also need to learn how to use the gun should something happen to the number 1 or number 2. As with the rifle, maintenance procedures were drummed into us every day.

"The weapon is only as reliable as you make it. Keep her clean and oiled and she'll look after you. A dirty gun will get you killed!" explained Sergeant Spears.

We worked hard, honing our skills and soon became quite a team. Bert was an excellent gunner. He never got flustered. He had a keen eye and seemed very natural behind the barrel. Dickie was quick at changing panniers and the rest of us didn't do too badly either. One of the most critical jobs for us was to keep watch for the enemy. Lewis guns were always targetted and we were expected to look out for any trouble that Bert and Dickie otherwise might miss while they were focussing on their target lines. The Lewis gun had some great advantages over the German Maxim machine gun. Theirs was water cooled and tended to overheat if used to excess. Ours was also lighter and could be fired from the hip in an advance if the need arose. The only problems were a lack of bullets in the magazine and lack of range. The Maxim could fire nearly six hundred bullets without having to reload and had a range of two thousand yards: triple that of the Lewis Gun. I guessed that the pluses and minuses of both guns balanced things out tactically on the Western Front. Sergeant Spears was an excellent trainer, and we grew in confidence and skill.

The time soon came for some of the recruits to head to France and join their battalions. Several hundred men were about to ship out, and they included Tom and Frank. We decided on a fitting farewell that night. Tom, Frank, Mick, Bert, Dickie, Les and I visited one of the town's small pubs. It was something we'd done regularly since arriving several weeks ago. Australians had a reputation for being rowdy and drinking too much and occasionally getting into trouble, so there were plenty of Military police about to keep an eye on us. It was hard to tell who hated us more, the MP's or the Tommies. They didn't take kindly to the way we made ourselves at home. Naturally we got horribly drunk and that attracted some unwanted attention,

"Ay, keep it down for Christ's sake won't you," someone shouted from across the room in a thick English accent.

We immediately swung around to see who we might have offended but Frank Curry had other ideas. He had a fiery temper and didn't mind a bit of a stoush now and again. Growing up on the waterfront made him very streetwise and he'd seen his fair share of biff back home. There was no love lost between the Australian and English soldiers either. We'd heard many stories about Australians winning ground from the enemy, handing it over to the English only to have it lost again a few days later. It was probably an unfair assumption on our part, but Frank didn't really care.

"Who's askin?" Frank yelled, the beer amplifying his demand!

The room fell silent as the two groups stared each other down. I must admit I felt quite intimidated. They were big fellows, all of them and any one of them could have flicked me away like an insect.

"We're not asking!" replied a bullish looking young Pom. He had red hair to match his angry red face, and I watched him clench a fist. The rest followed suit.

"Well, I'm afraid we cannot comply," said Frank who was attempting his best English accent.

It was likely these men were all conscripts. They probably hated the idea of fighting in France and were about to be sent to the trenches like our boys. The fact that we were all volunteers fuelled their anger. Just then another in their group mumbled to his mates,

"God help us is they think these fellows can help win the war!"

It took a few more seconds for the words to sink into Frank's beer soaked brain, but when the realisation took hold, he jumped. Before anyone could move the Englishman was flat on his back courtesy of a Frank Curry haymaker. He started laying into the brute, flailing wildly and landing several blows before his mates came to the rescue. As they moved, so did Tom, then Mick. I knew it would be a mismatch, but I quickly followed, hoping the whole thing would blow over. That hope was soon dashed when Mick hammered the first Pom he came to. Tom got stuck into the next bloke leaving one fellow for me. I looked him up and down and realised I was hopelessly outgunned. He was a huge fellow with a pair of mallets for fists and the girth of a barrel. I knew I was done but before I could move several other Australian rushed into the fray, which attracted more Tommies and before I could blink everyone in the pub was in on the fight. Punches flew and men crashed to the floor. Furniture broke as bodies were flung all about. I was standing my ground trying to avoid being hit, shoving anyone who bounced my way back into the brawl. The fight attracted even more men from outside and soon there must have been twenty or thirty bouts going on. I decided it might be best to slip away. I'd never fought once in my life, not even in the schoolyard and didn't like my chances here, but before I could take a step a fist crashed into my stomach. Winded, I crumpled to the floor. I struggled for breath amongst a herd of stampeding boots and looked up just in time to see the heel of a boot bearing down. I turned my head just as it crashed into my temple and then everything went black.

When I woke up, I was propped in a chair. I felt groggy and there were still stars in my eyes. I could hear a piano playing and the strains of some dreadful singing. I shook my head to try and clear my vision and soon realised that the fight was well and truly over. In fact, everyone was having a great time. Tom looked around and saw that I was awake and made his way over,

"You OK sport, you took a heavy blow I, see?"

"I've got a headache," I replied.

"That's no surprise and you'll have quite a black eye too I expect," said Tom.

"What happened?"

"Well, I'm not sure. Someone yelled out that it was his shout and the fighting just stopped. We've been having a sing-along for the last half hour," Tom explained.

"Didn't the MPs break it up?"

Tom let out an almighty laugh,

"That's got to be the funniest thing you've said. They'd be the last bastards to try and break up a fight. They're bloody cowards," and he laughed all the way back to the crowd and shared the joke with Mick and Frank.

Next day we were back at camp, a little worse for the experience but no long term harm done. Tom and Frank jumped onto a waiting lorry with the rest of the recruits who were head out.

"See you over there Tom," I suggested.

"Hey, what about me?" Frank demanded.

"You too Frank," said Mick.

"We'll save a spot for the rest of you," Tom promised and with that the convoy of lorries jerked away and soon they were gone.

We went straight back to training and spent the next few weeks honing our skills. Then it was Bert, Dickie and Mick's turn to leave. I didn't quite understand why I wasn't going with them, but I couldn't do much about it. That just left me and Les Giles. With my Lewis Gun crew gone I was re-tasked and spent quite some time being trained as a medic. I learned how to stop bleeding, administer a pain killer called morphia, set broken limbs and how to use a field dressing. I was astonished by the amount of paperwork that a medic was expected to do even while under fire. I had to learn to assess a wound, write the details on a tally note and colour code the cases based on severity, a red tag meaning critical care was needed. There was so much to remember, and the training was intense and I hoped never to have to use these new skills.

One night we were woken by an incredible roar. None of us had a clue was had happened but later learned that a major offensive had begun at a place called Messines in Belgium. The roar we heard was a series of huge bombs that had been placed under the Germans by Australian miners who'd been recruited for the task. The tunnellers took two years to do the job and then in one night watched as their nineteen mines obliterated the enemy with a million pounds of explosive. I heard that as many as ten thousand Germans died in those few horrific seconds.

As we continued to be trained news soon arrived that we were involved in yet more offensives at Menin Road, Polygon Wood, Broodseinde and Passchendaele. Reports suggested that the Australians were again decimated and the Canadians were sent in to finish the job. For us there was only more marching, musketry, pack drill and trench tactics. I was starting to think I'd never be called upon to join the battalion but then on October 5th, 1917, my 17th birthday, orders were issued and this time we weren't left out.

A few days later, thirty five of us were taken to Southampton and boarded a chip called Invicta. This ship had the unenviable task of crisscrossing the English Channel, carrying troops to and from France and had been at it for the last three years. We were accompanied by destroyers and followed a zigzag path to try and avoid torpedo attack. Some ships were emblazoned with words like *relief* to try and fool German submariners. I wasn't convinced that the enemy was that dumb. After a journey of many hours, we reached the French coast and soon disembarked.

Chapter 3

<u>France and Belgium</u>

Le Havre was a very busy port in the northwest of France on the famous Seine River. It was cold when we arrived, about sixty degrees but we'd managed to adjust to the conditions after six months in England. Our woollen uniforms were still in good condition, so keeping warm wasn't a problem for now.

Havre was known as the Harbour of Grace, established in 1517. It was astonishing to think that something could have been around two hundred and fifty years before Australia was even discovered. This was the main port of entry into France and housed two Allied General Hospitals and a convalescence unit. Thousands of soldiers were said to have been here at any given time. During my training as a medic I was told about the way the network of medical facilities worked and how the wounded were evacuated from the front line. Stretcher bearers would carry them to facilities behind the fighting. Carrying a stretcher was one of the most dangerous jobs you could have, unarmed and unprotected while the fighting raged all around. The wounded would be taken to casualty clearing stations and triaged. The severity of a wound determined what happened next. They could be treated on site and return to duty if the wound was minor or sent all the way back to the French coast or even England in severe cases. Sadly, we weren't spared any details when it came to the survival rate of those with bad wounds. They may well survive the damage only to die from infection days or even weeks later.

As we walked down the gangplank we came across scores of men, all bandaged ready to be shipped over to England, no doubt from the most recent campaign at Passchendaele. The look of them was most disturbing. Ashen faces, missing limbs, blood stained uniforms and the smell of iodine. Most seemed utterly miserable and yet, amongst them a few were in high spirits,

"Where you blokes from?" enquired one fellow.

"Sydney," I told him.

It was only at that moment I noticed that his right hand was gone and a bloody bandage covered his stump. I couldn't help but stare,

"It's just a scratch mate," he suggested and he chatted to everyone as we marched by.

I looked down at the poor devils as we moved along; some already appeared to be on the verge of death; their war torn bodies soaked in blood and mud. They were truly exhausted and I began to wonder about Tom, Frank, Mick, Bert and Dickie who had been on the front a few months now. I was pleased not to have recognised anyone.

Acting Corporal Arthur Freeman was in charge and barked at us to step it up. As we marched, words of encouragement came from those who could muster the strength to talk. We moved away from the dock and into the town. I was again astonished by the sights before me. Old buildings and cobblestone streets; an amazing rail network and a mass of people moving in all directions, both military and civilians. Horses, carts, lorries, trains and limbers of all sizes moved here and there. It was hard to imagine how they all knew where they were going. As for us, we made our way to the Australian Base Reception Camp a rally point for soldiers moving in and out of France.

We soon settled into a row of bell tents inside the camp which was every bit as busy as the streets of Le Havre. Dispatches were sent to advise headquarters of our arrival so for now all we could do was wait for our orders to arrive. We spent our time gathering supplies and cleaning our weapons. It gave us a chance to catch up on news from the front.

We soon met other Australians who were coming into camp. They told us there was a lot of talk about a German offensive before winter set in. It wasn't the kind of news we welcomed and between the thoughts of an attack, the cold and the noise, I didn't sleep well that night.

We soon received orders to move out and were told we'd be heading for the Ypres Salient in Belgium, just north of the French border. Ypres was one of the most dangerous sectors along the entire front. The Allies considered this a critical area which had to be defended. Any breach in the line could see the Germans take the Channel Ports, cutting supplies to Allied soldiers. That would effectively end the war and hand Germany the victory.

The Ypres sector had already seen three major battles, and no-one was sure how many had died in the region over the last three years, but it was probably in the hundreds of thousands. We were to travel to the region and join up with the 18th Battalion as soon as we were able.

We didn't waste any more time and began marching two by two. As we moved out, we saw soldiers filing into the camp, many were battered and dirty, like those we'd seen at the docks. Some were headed for hospital;

others were on leave. They eyed us with cold, blank stares and few words passed between us. Others were more receptive but most just ignored us. As new recruits we hadn't seen any action and didn't have much in the way of status as far as these men were concerned. Our shiny boots and spick uniforms were once again like warning beacons to these men. It was clear one had to earn his place in this fight, so for now we were considered a burden.

We arrived at the railway station and found a train waiting to take us east. We were ordered on board and pushed in like cattle. We crammed into the filthiest box cars I'd ever seen. The air stank of a vast array of uninviting odours from blood to manure. The floor was covered in slime, and we had no choice but to sit in the refuse of previous journeys. Once on board the carriage door was slammed shut. There were no windows and little in the way of fresh air. Some lucky fellows were close to vents or knotholes and were able to look outside. I took out my bayonet and started drilling out a little hole to look through. By the time I was done we were travelling in the French countryside. It was simply beautiful with rolling fields, tall green woodlands and wide open farmland, nothing like the dismal, chalky training grounds of Salisbury Plains.

Despite the conditions on board the train we managed to relax, every man finding a small piece of floor to squat on. Some of us played cards, others chatted and some even managed to sleep. I certainly envied them. The train moved along at a terribly slow pace, and someone explained that we couldn't go any faster just in case the lines had been sabotaged. French soldiers sat on the rooves of our cars keeping watch for enemy aircraft. It seemed we were a significant target, and no German pilot would ignore the opportunity to strafe us if he could.

Several hours went by without incident. I must have dozed off at some stage and was woken by a series of jolts as the train jerked to a crawl, then a stop.

"Where are we?" someone enquired.

"Amiens!" was the reply.

We'd only travelled about a hundred miles or so. It didn't seem possible to travel such a short distance in such a long period of time. We were only about halfway to our destination.

I peered through my knot hole and caught sight of yet another hub of activity. More rolling stock, horses, limbers, motor lorries, staff cars and equipment crowded the road. It was impossible to guess how many soldiers were here, but a great many were marching in and out of the city.

Amiens was a major rail hub, the major rail hub of the Allies and it was clear that it had been under siege for some time. Some buildings were shattered and shell holes could be seen here and there. The front line was about thirty miles from us now and for the first time I could hear the din of battle in the distance. It was a low but unmistakable rumble, like a thunderstorm beyond the horizon and my stomach knotted up as the realisation hit home. It appeared I wasn't the only one to notice, everyone muttered to each other as the sounds crept into our carriage.

Suddenly the carriage door ripped open, and the light blinded us momentarily, it was an officer that none of us recognised.

"Right, you lot, rise and shine. Grab your kits and get yourselves organised," he demanded as he strode to the next carriage.

We slowly rolled out onto the rail siding and stood waiting for our next order. As my eyes adjusted to the brightness I got a much better look at Amiens. It had been pulverised in places. While some building were untouched, many were just rubble. The rumbling of guns in the distance seemed much louder now and we could see a steady stream of wounded tricking into the city from the east. The civilians had been evacuated some time back and so the area was now purely a military zone. The last of the men were now off the carriages and standing in their respective groups. We were ordered into the city and began to march. Just as we set off a whistling sound could be heard in the sky. It grew louder and someone shouted,

"TAKE COVER!"

Almost instinctively we all dived for the ground. As we did a huge explosion shattered another piece of Amiens. I looked up to see a plume of smoke and dust erupting from the middle of the city.

"What the Hell was that?" cried Les.

"That was a Krupp," replied the officer who just herded us off the train.

"A what?" someone blurted.

"A long range Krupp field gun. The Germans have them well behind their own line, but they have a range of 80 miles or more so they're firing on us all the time. They've even been able to fire on

Paris," he explained.

I was stunned at the thought as the officer offered more details.

"The Germans really want to take Amiens. It would give them all the rail access they need to win the war, that's why they're paying so much attention to us. They're raiding Amiens at night with Gotha bombers and shelling us by day, so you best find a nice secure place to sleep!"

We'd only been away from England three days or so and already seen much to unsettle us. It was getting late and after the officer led us to what he described as a quiet place on the edge of the city, he bid us goodnight and said he'd return in the morning to see us on our way. Corporal Freeman resumed command and barked at us to get settled. Night descended quickly and we were ordered not to light any fires in case of enemy aircraft attack, so we ate cold bully beef and dry rations. We couldn't even have a cup of tea.

I looked out into the void and saw what appeared to be lightning in the distance,

"See that?" I exclaimed to anyone who was within earshot.

"Yeah, artillery. It looks pretty, doesn't it?" someone replied.

We tried to make light of the situation but most of us just sat nervously hoping to get some sleep. That was soon made impossible as another shell from the Krupp canon screamed in and exploded about a mile away from us. I saw the flash of the explosion and heard the boom a few moments later. As the sound faded another noise filled the air. It was the drone of many engines, and it soon became clear that an air raid was upon us. Search lights came on, their fingers raking the darkness for the enemy. Almost immediately anti-aircraft fire lit the sky. I couldn't tell if the gunners could see the planes or were just firing blind. I certainly couldn't see any of the bombers, but their drone was unmistakable.

Within a few minutes bombs were crashing down on the railway lines. Even though we were well away from the action we stayed low as the strobing light of explosions flashed against the shattered buildings of Amiens. Men around us were firing into the air and I wondered how it was that no-one was hitting the planes with so many guns aimed skywards. I joined in, trying to aim at the sound of the planes but they were too far off. I emptied a magazine and loaded a new clip just as a searchlight caught the wing of a German plane. The beam steadied and held the plane which was weaving to get out of the light. All guns trained on the target, and I took a few more pot shots as did the rest of the recruits. There seemed little hope for the poor fellows but they somehow managed to ditch their bombs and turn away from the city. I had no doubt that the plane was hit but most of the bullets must have simply cut through the fabric and done little damage. Their luck was in and the plane soon disappeared.

The raid was over a few minutes later and the other planes turned for home after dropping their payloads. If our men had hit any of them little damage was done and they got away having executed what appeared to be a successful attack. Fires were everywhere and we could see men running here and there trying to douse the flames. It took over an hour to quell the fires and the rest of the night passed without further incident. The sounds of distant thunder eventually lulled me off to sleep.

Next morning we rose early feeling very tired; none of us had slept very well. We stared at the damage from last night's raid. Train carriages were shattered and lay smoldering on twisted tracks and several buildings appeared to have been further damaged judging by the bricks that littered the roads. Crews were already at work cleaning up the refuse and repairing the rail lines. Things seemed to be dealt with very quickly around here, an indication of how important this rail hub was to the cause.

We were ordered to help with the cleanup and spent the morning clearing the roads of debris. Rail crews worked frantically on the tracks while others cleared the shattered carriages from the lines. Thankfully none of the steam engines were damaged but it was clear our departure would be delayed.

Once we'd cleared our section of street it was near mid-morning. Corporal Freeman was advised that we'd have to wait another day before we moved as more urgent transport issues had to be dealt with. We had the rest of the day off and used the time we had to find the mess and have a hot breakfast, although it turned out to be lunch given the hour. It was the first decent food we'd had for a good few days and it was very welcome indeed.

We were warned to stay close to camp and not venture into the city. Several areas were declared unsafe with a very real risk of buildings collapsing due to pervious bombing raid. Some fellows ignored the advice and went souvenir hunting, most returning empty handed. The town had been well and truly cleared out long before we arrived. That afternoon we caught up on some sleep but woke before nightfall. We'd learned our lesson from the day before and cooked up a meal before dark which left us quite satisfied. The night passed without incident.

October 13th, 1917, we rose early and ate a hot breakfast. The weather was clear, but the air was cold. We again crowded onto windowless boxcars and were soon creeping along the rail sidings of Amiens. Engineers had done a grand job of repairing the lines and removing damaged rolling stock, but we still had to detour from one line to another to bypass the unrepaired tracks.

The bombing raids were concentrated on the city's rail infrastructure itself, so once we cleared the outskirts the line was untouched. We headed north now, towards Ypres and once again we crawled along at a painfully slow rate, the driver wary of track damage and sabotage.

We learned that enemy aircraft had been very active in this sector of late so things were tense. The train would again prove a very easy target for a patrolling German fighter with the slowness of our progress adding to the frustration. French lookouts were perched on each carriage manning their guns but somehow it wasn't reassuring. A betting man would put his money on the pilot and get very short odds. We'd been underway for about an hour when should rang out,

"Is it one of ours?" I heard someone yell.

We crowded around whatever openings were available to see what was going on. A moment later the train began to shudder, and we were thrown off our feet as it braked heavily. I could hear the French gunners yelling at each other above us, but no shots were fired. Then the drone of an engine caught my ear. Men began to panic and as soon as the train stopped someone ripped the door open and people started piling out. I got caught in the scrum and was propelled towards the door. It happened so fast I was unable to grab my rifle which lay on the floor where I'd been sitting. A few seconds later I hit the ground, landing awkwardly, the wind knocked out of me. I could hear the aircraft's engine clearly now and tried to catch a glimpse of the plane, but I was struggling to catch my breath. Men fumbled with their rifles and some even peeled off a few shots,

"Is it German," came another voice.

More shots split my ears as men shouted at each other. The French gunners still hadn't opened fire but were ready to do so. They seemed to have a better idea of what was going on. Then the plane passed low over the train. I could see red, white and blue circle markings under its wing and it was even low enough for me to catch a glimpse of the oil stains around the exhaust pipes,

"Don't shoot, it's one of ours!" came the order.

Even so, someone let fly with one more shot and a few unsavoury remarks were quickly directed towards him. We presumed it was an Allied reconnaissance aircraft returning from a mission. The pilot probably didn't have a clue about the mayhem he'd causes flying so low over us. If he'd seen the soldiers spread out all over the grass, he might have thought we'd stopped for water, or the engine had broken down. I'm not sure why he didn't notice the bullets whizzing past his plane, but then the panic I witnessed may have meant they missed by a significant margin. The plane flew on without deviating from its course.

Officers screamed at us to get back on the train and yelled at the shooters calling them all sort of insulting names. All up it had been an embarrassing misunderstanding but in the end no harm was done. I doubt that anyone even bothered to write a report about the incident. We were soon on the move again bumping along at the usual snail's pace, everyone still on edge after out little scare.

The landscape seemed more baron and unimpressive through the slit I'd found near my piece of wall. We were moving parallel to the Western Front and the only people we saw were occasional groups of soldiers and transport equipment on the roads that we crossed or travelled along.

After several more hours in our cramped compartment we arrived at a place called Hazebrouck, about a hundred and twenty miles north of Amiens. We were close to the French, Belgium border now and we eagerly leapt off the train and had a look around.

"Crikey, look at this place," cried Les Giles.

I'd already noticed what he was referring to.

"Look there," someone else remarked, pointing at a shattered cathedral.

Hazebrouck was another important hub in the Allied rail network and, being so much closer to the front line had been savaged by enemy artillery. The town was shattered beyond recognition.

"God almighty," came another remark.

We'd never seen such damage. Amiens looked cosmopolitan compared to this place. The rumble of war sounded closer than ever as we assembled. We were to complete our journey on foot. Everyone grumbled at this news but there was no time to waste as we only had half a day to make the fifteen miles to Ypres with full packs. We left Hazebrouck behind and started marching northeast. The ground around us was desolate with the occasional piece of broken down equipment or an abandoned village. The absolute lack of human activity was testament to how dangerous this region was. We marched along for hours and crossed the Belgian border reaching Ypres late in the afternoon. Road traffic was more prolific here as it was the only route to the front line. Few words passed between us and the soldiers on the opposite side of the road. They looked tired and dirty and barely paid any attention to us. It was hard to tell where they were from, but none were Australian.

Passing through Ypres we were again met with wholesale destruction. This town too had been razed to dust. Almost every brick has been shattered loose, and they lay in huge piles next to the streets we walked along.

We forged on, toward the famous Menin Gate, a favourite target of the German artillery. Of course there was no gate, just a gap in the ancient battlements and a bridge. The fortress of Ypres was a star shaped wall, surrounded by a moat. These defenses harked back to a time when people fought with swords and arrows and clearly provided no protection from modern warfare. As we moved along, sentries directed us to the town's exit point, Menin Gate. The Germans had it well targetted and shelled it constantly. We turned down another street and walked through more rubble, finally reaching the eastern edge of Ypres where we were ordered to stop. We took refuge next to the earthen embankments of the old battlements waiting for our guides to arrive.

The entire town resembled a wasteland. Almost every tree and every blade of grass was gone. As far as the eye could see there was rubble or gaping holes from German shells, most filled with rancid water. I caught the whiff of something foul in the air.

"What's that smell?" asked Les.

"I don't think I want to know," was my reply but I'd smelled it before when I had to retrieve a dead cat from under our house one time. The air was filled with the stench of death. We could hear the whistle of shellfire and the boom of explosions a short distance away now.

Presently a voice barked out at us,

"Are you blokes looking for the 18th battalion?" asked a tall, stringy looking fellow, flanked by two others.

"You know we are, "replied Corporal Freeman.

"That's good because we're here to take you in," explained the soldier.

He looked us over but didn't say anything. He seemed tired and his uniform was old and torn. The other two weren't much better off. He quickly turned his attention back to the Corporal,

"We have to wait until dark, so I suggest you get some rest before we start moving,"

"We're not waiting till morning then?" asked someone.

"Mate, you're near the front line now...no-one walks around in daylight, especially fresh meat like you lot. We travel at night!" he was quite abrupt.

He addressed Corporal Freeman again,

"You'll maintain control of the ranks until we reach Steenvoorde. You'll then hand over the recruits to the battalion. We've got about an hour before tackling Hellfire Corner."

Hellfire Corner, the name sent shivers up my spine. There must be a good reason why it was called that. Les was thinking the same thing,

"What's Hellfire Corner?" he asked. The fellow looked at Les as his two comrades chuckled. He then noticed that we were all peering at him hoping for an answer,

"It's just the most dangerous place on the entire Western Front lads. There's no other way to get to the trenches from here and the Germans know it. They have artillery aimed at the place all the time and they're relentless. It's not the kind of place you want to sit around for too long," he said.

The information quickly sank in, and I would have been surprised if none of us felt apprehensive. Almost on cue more loud explosions could be heard in the distance. We sat nervously waiting for darkness but none of us was in a hurry.

As we sat in our little group more Aussies sat themselves down nearby. I watched as they settled into a shell hole across the road. They took a billy out and got a small fire going and began to make some tea. We didn't even dare light a cigarette, so it was clear that these fellows were veterans as they didn't appear at all phased by the threat of enemy fire.

I suddenly realised how hungry I was and rummaged around for some dry rations. I looked up at the men again and caught the eye of one. He looked at me for a moment and then smiled,

"Would you like some tea young fella?" He asked.

At first, I wasn't sure who he was talking to, so I pointed at myself like a school kid called to the front of the class.

"Yes you, come on over!"

With that I jumped up and wandered over the road.

'Take a seat," he suggested, "I'm Sid, Sid Kohn and these are my mates Nev and Henry."

They greeted me and we shook hands,

"Stan Dunkley from Sydney," I explained.

"Nice to meet you, Stan. I'm guessing you blokes have just arrived," Sid enquired.

"Yes, how did you know?"

The three men laughed,

"Well, those shiny boots and clean uniforms aren't really hiding much," he said.

"I don't suppose they are," I replied as I looked at my spotless tunic and puttees.

"Here you go Stan," Sid took my mug and filled it up. He was a nuggetty little fellow, with kind eyes and a cheeky grin. His hair was short and blonde, and I felt comfortable being in his company.

"Who are you blokes with?" I asked.

"22nd Battalion. Most of us are from Victoria. The three of us are from Melbourne. I see you're with the 18th then?

I took a sip of tea and was surprised by how very good it was,

"That's right, you know anything about them?"

"Yeah. We cross paths from time to time. I heard they just came out of Passchendaele. Nasty business that," he said but he didn't elaborate.

"How long have you been over here," I asked Sid.

"Well," he paused, "if you include Gallipoli, I reckon it would be two and a half years."

I almost choked on my next swallow. I hadn't noticed their ANZAC shoulder patches. Only soldiers who'd fought on the Peninsular wore them. I felt like a fool,

"Hell's teeth!" I blurted out.

"No mate, this is Hell," suggested Henry and the trio laughed again.

I realised I was with some real fighting men. They'd have been involved in some major battles that was certain. To us they were to be respected; people of high standing even to raw recruits like me.

"Tell him about those medals you didn't get Sid!" urged Nev.

"Nah, Stan doesn't want to be bothered with all that," Sid exclaimed.

"Go on...or I'll tell him," Nev turned to me and started telling the story, "Sid was sniping and...OUCH!"

Sid clipped Nev's ear,

"Shut it Nev! I'll tell him, you'll just mess it up!"

I was very keen to hear the story and Sid didn't disappoint,

"We were in this trench, keeping to ourselves. You could hear shells whistling overhead and Turk rifle fire in the distance. Someone was having a good old scrap that was certain. Suddenly, the ground around us lifted like I don't know what. I still haven't heard the explosion, but a shell had burst right by our section. A bunch of us were completely buried under dirt and sand and rocks," Sid explained and paused to sip on his tea.

"I was knocked out cold and only survived because a few blokes close by managed to dig me out. It's a miracle that none of us were killed! Anyway, I woke up and someone said I should go see the doc,"

Sid paused again.

"Tell him what happened next Sid," urged Nev.

"Righto, steady on, will ya? Anyway, I went to see the doc and he looked me over. He couldn't find anything wrong, not even a bruise so he sent me back to my unit declared fit."

"Tell him the rest Sid," shrieked Henry while both he and Nev started to laugh.

"There was this other night when I decided to try my luck at sniping," Sid went on.

"Sniping, eh?" I inquired.

"Yeah, taking a few pot shots at the Turk muzzle flashes. Sometimes you get lucky you know?"

I nodded while Nev and Henry continued to chuckle uncontrollably. I still didn't see the joke.

"I saw a muzzle flash in the distance right and fired a few shots in that direction. Suddenly, I'm knocked flat on my back, the wind knocked out of me. It took a few moments to figure out what happened. It seems some Turk was snipin' too and saw my muzzle flashes. So, he fires back at me. His bullet hit the barrel of my rifle and travelled along till it hit the stock and knocked me over just like that!" Sid revealed.

"What happened after that?" I asked.

"Well, I'm off to the Doc again, aren't I? I'd been shot after all. So, he looks me up and down, makes a note about the bruise on my shoulder and then sends me back to the unit declared fit!"

Nev and Henry were rolling on the ground laughing hysterically,

"No stripes for you Sid!"

"What do they mean? I asked.

"Well, nothing broke my skin either time, so I wasn't considered wounded. That means I don't get wound stripes for my uniform!"

I suddenly understood what was so funny and began to laugh too. It seemed so strange to be laughing over someone nearly being killed but it was totally natural to these men. Sid had cheated death twice and had nothing to show for it.

As we sat the trio opened up to me and told a great many stories about the battles they'd been involved in and what they did behind the lines. I liked them very much and felt privileged to have been allowed into their confidence, although I didn't really know why. I learned a great deal about what had been happening over the last two years on the Western front and what conditions were like. It was interesting to hear a perspective that never seemed to make the papers. It was clear that the AIF men didn't think much of the British brass or the English Tommies, but I was already aware of that.

The time sped by and we were soon called upon to start moving again. We'd be heading through the Menin Gate and rounding Hellfire Corner in pitch black darkness, and I was feeling rather nervous. Sid must have noticed the concern on my face,

"Where are you headed Stan?"

"I heard the guide say Steenvoorde I think."

"That's behind the line. Sounds like your blokes are resting, so you won't be in the trenches straight away. That's a good thing," said Sid.

"Anything else I should know?" I asked hoping for some sage advice.

Henry jumped in before Sid could reply,

"Yeah, shoot straighter than they do!" and he and Nev cackled some more.

"Never mind them," Sid remarked, "Listen, they might have shown you how to shoot a gun and stab a straw man, but you've got to rely on your wits. It gets confusing out there and you can easily lose your way. They can't prepare you for the smoke, the noise, the panic or the fear. Just keep your head, understand?"

I gulped down my last swallow of tea and nodded. I wouldn't forget the message and how sincere it was. I jumped up and brushed myself off and we all shook hands,

"Thanks for the tea and...everything else. It's been a pleasure," I remarked.

Sid gave me a wink while Henry and Neville said their goodbyes. I walked back across the road to re-join my unit, looking back only once. Neville and Henry were looking at me strangely, which made me feel a bit queer. I didn't quite know what they were thinking. Sid seemed to be unimpressed with whatever it was they were talking about. I decided to let it go. As I got back to my own men I was met by Les Giles,

"Where the Hell have you been mate?" he blurted.

"Off for a spot of tea old chum," was my reply.

The look on his face was priceless,

"Sometimes Stan, I don't know what to make of you!" and he grinned.

Chapter 4

<u>The Front</u>

Darkness had finally shrouded Ypres and we gathered our rations, billies and tin cups, stashing them in our packs.

"Listen up," ordered Corporal Freeman, make sure your kits are secure and don't leave anything metal hanging out to clank as you walk! Let's move."

We stood up, picked up our weapons and started to march. The sounds of exploding shells and the boom of guns seemed to have amplified and they never seemed to stop now. Sid had told me that the Germans were well known for firing random shots behind the Allied lines just to see if they would hit anything. If they saw smoke they'd concentrate on the target with a severe barrage hoping to inflict as much damage as they could. Another tactic was that of focussing on bottlenecks in the Allied transport lines and we were coming up on one of those right now.

As we passed through the Menin Gate, which was simply two earthen resembling a cutting, the road became very thick with lorries, cars, horses, carriages and men moving to and fro. There was a constant stream of traffic now, heading in and out of Ypres. There was little wonder why the Germans paid so much attention to this place. We were now on the Menin Road, walking slowly towards, who knows what? To our left a series of dark ridges showed us the German positions. They certainly had good ground.

As we approached Hellfire Corner the ground was very much open to enemy view, and I noticed a series of pathetic canvas screens. They were supposed to keep us hidden as we passed through. I must say I didn't have much confidence in this defensive system, but I was pleased that no shells were falling in the area for the moment. A unit of Pioneers was busily repairing sections of road that had been blown away by recent bombardments and then there was that smell again. It lingered in the air like wood smoke and seemed much more intense in the cool night air. Decomposing men and animals mixed with the stench of mud all combined to create to most foul of odours. There was no escaping it and I winced with every breath. It was very dark, but we were able to see the verges of the road in the moonlight. Distant flares also gave us an occasional flicker of light. I peered towards the front line, still quite a distance away. The lightning danced about as far as the eye could see. Just then I caught a glimpse of something in the mud only yards from the road.

"What's that?" I whispered.

Les Giles moved over and took a look,

"That's a dead man!"

I was mortified. I could see him now lying in the mud, crumpled and disfigured. I couldn't tell if he was friend or foe, but he was most certainly dead. His face was buried in the mud, but I could see the nape of his neck, white against a dark uniform. He was curled up with one arm folded under his body, the other falling across his back. My spine tingled and I suddenly felt ill. I stopped and unloaded my dinner onto the road. No-one said a word. I think most of us felt equally horrified by what we'd seen. I spat out the last of my meal and stood, sprinting back to my position in the formation. I'd never seen a dead man before and even though I was expecting to come across something sooner or later, it caught me completely off guard. Conversation amongst the recruits had been totally extinguished and our pace seemed to have quickened somewhat.

We marched for the next several hours, well into the night, resting only occasionally and briefly. Our guides kept us moving, keen to get us to Steenvoorde before dawn. We'd learned that the 18th battalion was resting behind the line after coming off the line after the battle of Passchendaele. The battle was a victory but terribly costly. I wondered if my mates came through unscathed.

The crunching of our boots on the gravel warned sentries of our approach. They challenged us with a demand for the password, to which one of our guides replied,

"Shut up Dobson, you know who it is!"

There was a little chuckle from one of the sentries,

"Yeah, righto Jacko, the old man's over there," and Dobson pointed somewhere into the twilight.

We followed the guides into the town of Steenvoorde and after a few minutes we were ordered to stop. Corporal Freeman chatted briefly to the guide and then told us we could rest. Most of us dumped everything immediately. Packs, rifles and bodies crashed to the ground. We were exhausted.

As we waited for whatever was to come next, I looked around at the town. The morning light was beginning to eek away at the grey, adding colour to the buildings and countryside. Steenvoorde was one of many small villages in this sector of Belgium. The people still lived here and helped the Allies by providing food and shelter. Like most of the villages we'd passed through it showed signs of shell damage, but it was in better condition than many. Little farmhouses were dotted along the cobblestone road with most attached to stables or pens. Chickens ran here and there as did a few local dogs.

Our marching must have disturbed some of the soldiers. I could see some of them as they appeared from the strangest places. Some came out of barns, other from little iron shanties. Even more rose from a few little houses; all were converging on us. Before long we were surrounded by dozens of men who eyed us suspiciously. They muttered amongst themselves, but I couldn't hear what was being said. I looked at their faces, hoping to see my old mates but was soon interrupted,

"TEN-SHUN!"

We all jumped to our feet and formed two straight lines. The soldiers around us just laughed. It was then I noticed a group of men approaching, one of them in a very smart uniform. As the other soldiers noticed him, they too stood to attention. Salutes followed, papers were handed over and after a brief exchange of words the officer turned his attention to us,

"Good morning gentlemen. Welcome to the 18th Battalion. I am your commanding officer Lieutenant Colonel George Murphy. Stand easy men, I know you've been on the go all night."

He seemed quite a delightful man on first impression. He was tall and thin, had very short grey hair and I was guessing he was around fifty years old. His face was pale and he showed all the signs of a man with much on his mind,

"The Western Front is that way," and he pointed behind us, "and we'll be back there soon enough. In the meantime, we'll get you sorted into your companies, and they'll find you jobs that suit your various talents."

We stood silently as he spoke and I looked across at the soldiers who had assembled. Most looked quite disheveled; many were smoking now and talking quietly to each other. Some pointed as us shaking their heads or rolling their eyes. The commander continued,

"You won't have too much time to get settled, so you'll need to learn as you go. Your CO's will take care of that. Thank you, men!" With that he saluted, turned and walked off.

A bugle call then rang out and more men started popping up from all over the town, some emerging from shell holes where they'd no doubt been sleeping.

Before long, it seemed that the whole battalion was assembled before us. The thirty five of us were about to be broken up and handed over to any of four companies. Within them were smaller platoons, each with its own command chain and pecking order. I don't quite know why I felt scared by the prospect of change, but it was quite intimidating to say the least.

Company commanders peered at our paperwork and sorted out their needs. They then approached us and the first spoke,

"The following men will report to A Company," and he called out the names. Around ten or so recruits were hustled into their new unit, "These men report to B Company!"

Mine was the first to be called out and I immediately gathered my pack and stepped out of line, walking towards the men of B Company. More names were called and soon Les Giles was beside me. In a few moments we were lined up with our new company. It didn't take long to sort the recruits into their respective companies. The rest of the parade went quickly but I didn't really hear much of what was said. Several pairs of eyes on me and I felt quite intimidated and insecure.

As soon as the parade was over, I stood for a moment, unsure of what to do next. Suddenly a voice bellowed behind me,

"Well, they really did scrape the bottom of the barrel this time!"

I'm might have been scared but I wasn't going to stand there and take that. I turned to give the individual a mouthful back and was greeted with three beaming smiles, Tom, Mick and Frank. I immediately broke into a smile myself,

"Gee it's good to see you blokes!" and with that we all shook hands. Even Frank seemed pleased to see me.

The sun now broke over the horizon and its warmth added to the joy of rejoining all my mates. It was such a relief to be with my old mates and my fears dissipated immediately.

"So, they finally let you out huh?" suggested Tom.

"Yes indeed, I was getting into too many pub fights!"

"Well, you missed quite a party," explained Tom and the rest agreed.

Quite a few men were sporting bandages, others carried scars. They'd seen a lot of action recently and many were still recovering.

"Passchendaele must have been bad," I remarked.

"Yeah, well, we'll tell you all about it later. Are you hungry?"

"My word yes!" I told Tom.

"Well let's get some chow!"

Have you seen anything of Bert and Dickie? I asked but before Tom could answer,

"If he tells you no, he's a lying pig!" It was Bert and Dickie.

More handshakes followed and words of greeting. The whole group was back together. I couldn't have been more thrilled to find they were all OK. The reinforcements were welcomed cautiously by some and with warmth by others. I considered myself very lucky to be back with my mates. Will Spencer was with the 18th. He was a few years ahead of me at school, but everyone knew him and liked him,

"G'day Stan. What brings you to these parts," he asked with his customary smirk.

"Well, someone has to keep you in line Will?" I replied.

"Well, they should have sent your sister," and we both laughed!

"So, where's that mate of yours, Joe Crawley?"

Will's face changed and he looked down, struggling to find the words,

"He's gone mate; last week, a stray shell. Didn't know what hit him."

I was utterly shocked. Crawley and Will were as thick as thieves' right through school. They played rugby together and always made the representative side. It was no surprise to anyone when they joined up together. I could tell I'd hit a nerve,

"I'm sorry Will. I didn't know."

He didn't say anything for a moment but nodded an acknowledgement. We spoke a while longer, catching up on news from home before Will moved on. I turned back to my mates and looked them up and down,

"You blokes look like hell! What's been going on?"

"Well, I don't know where to start, it's been ugly," said Dickie. "We barely got our feet on the ground

and we were in the thick of it. Lost a lot of blokes at Passchendaele. Good thing you missed that one Stan!"

"Too right," said Tom. "We lost a great many good fellows out there. Bill Heap and Fred Hill. One minute they're right next to you, the next they're gone."

There was a long pause before Bert broke in,

"So that's why you're here Stan, making up for the losses!"

"Yes, I suppose so," I replied. I was still trying to process the news of more men that I knew being lost.

I soon caught up with quite a few men from training and even though several had been killed, everyone seemed to be in good spirits. We got some food and sat quietly to eat, catching up on all the news. They told me about the recent battle and how they fought in the mud and rain, barely able to move forward and under constant harassment from German artillery and machine guns. The guns we heard on the way to Steenvoorde were still firing on the enemy trenches. Passchendaele was yet to be taken.

After we ate, the men disbursed. Frank and Mick disappeared and Tom introduced me to his platoon commander, Sergeant William Wilton. He was a lean looking fellow in his thirties with bright red hair and a fair complexion and still had a freckles face despite his age. Not surprisingly everyone called him Blue,

"This is Stan Dunkley Blue. He's the one I was telling you about."

"Oh yeah, looks a bit scrawny. Is he up to the task?" Blue asked.

"I reckon so. He's quick on his feet and a mighty good shot. Taught him myself," explained Tom.

I wasn't entirely sure what was happening but decided it best to just stay quiet.

"Well then, we ought to make sure he's in our platoon then. How do you feel about that Stan?" asked Blue.

"Fine with me sir!"

"Sir? I'm no sir. Just call me Blue," and he gave me a wink.

Tom continued, "I was thinking he might make a good addition to the Lewis gun crew with Thorn and Jones here. Blue pondered for a moment, slurped down the last of his tea and looked at me again,

"You know anything about the Lewis Gun Stan?"

"Yes sir...Blue. I had extensive training on the gun in England."

"Are you two on board then?" he asked Bert and Dickie,

"Yup" said Bert, "Definitely Blue, without question!" replied Dickie.

"Then it's done," he replied with a chuckle.

"Thanks Blue," replied Tom. "I knew you'd come through."

We walked off to find me somewhere to call home.

"What just happened?" I asked.

"Tom just made sure you stayed with us!" explained Dickie.

"You didn't have to do that Tom." I suggested.

"Yes, I did, we look out for each other remember? I was just sticking to our agreement." He replied.

"Thanks Tom. I appreciate it."

"You're welcome, Stan."

We walked a little way before coming across a small barn,

"Here we are then, saved you a place!" said Tom.

It wasn't what I expected but at least it had a roof and the ground was covered in dry straw. It would do just fine.

As I got settled and stashed my gear, I noticed an officer standing outside. I jumped to attention and saluted,

"So young fella, where are you from? Asked the officer.

"Sydney sir!"

"Relax private, no need for formalities here," he replied.

I could smell a rat but was in no position to ready myself for what might be happening. Tom and the other were conveniently absent suddenly.

"And your name?"

"Stan Dunkley sir!"

"Tell me Stan, what brings you to these parts," asked the officer.

"Well sir, to be honest, I'm starting to ask myself that very question," I replied.

There was laughter from what seemed like a large crowd of onlookers.

"Good answer! My name is Joe Maxwell, welcome to the battalion Stan."

Perhaps I was wrong. Maybe he was just trying to be nice?

"Hey fellas, this is Stan from Sydney. Let's make him feel at home," cried Joe.

Before I could blink an avalanche of, I don't know what fell upon me from every direction. In a few short seconds I was smothered in the foulest smelling pile of dirty underwear and socks, all unwashed.

"That's about a month's worth of laundry Stan. Your first job is to get is washed!" Joe explained.

Welcome to the battalion indeed.

I wasn't the only one to receive an initiation. Les Giles ended up in a pile of manure and a few others were given a similar hazing. In the end no harm was done. I even managed to laugh about it, much later.

I was directed to the laundry house and got down to work. I found out that the men usually swapped their dirty clothing for fresh gear and that this lot would be handed over to the next unit to rest in Steenvoorde.

After quite a few hours I finished the job and headed back to the stable where I found Tom and the others dozing.

"How'd you go Stan?" asked Tom.

"Oh, alright I suppose. I got off easy I think."

"I tend to agree," replied Tom as he cast at glance at Les.

"Have you seen many Germans?" I asked.

"Bloody oath we have," blurted Frank, "The bastards are everywhere. They're tough too; real good soldiers and they've got this whole area tied up good and tight."

"And their artillery is accurate. They hit you day and night and they know what they're shooting at," said Mick.

I caught Tom looking at my face hard and I realised I must have been showing my fear,

"Don't worry Stan. You'll be an old hand at this before you know it. Just listen and learn. You'll figure it out. Won't he fellas?" suggested Tom.

The others nodded in agreement, except for Frank. He obviously still had reservations and leered at me like a schoolyard bully.

It was now October 14th, 1917, and I didn't have a clue what would happen to us next.

Chapter 5

<u>The Trenches</u>

We spent the next two weeks training behind the line at Steenvoorde. It gave me time to settle into a routine and learn the ways of my battalion, not that much different from camp life back at Sydney Showground in many ways, except for that incessant rumble in the distance. I noticed that the other Lewis gunners were operating with bigger crews and was a little confused as to why our team was so small,

"Why just the three of us then Bert?" I asked.

"Passchendaele," he replied with his customary economy.

"We lost half our crew in that fight but we're getting two new blokes today," explained Dick.

I decided to push my luck, "What happened?" There was a long pause as both men collected their thoughts, "It was a bloody mess," said Bert, "Mud, just mud everywhere,"

Dick was more forthcoming,

"It's hard to explain Stan. We just couldn't move you know? Mud, yeah there was mud all around. The trenches were full of water and so were the shell holes. There was no dry cover and no way to move fast. We were sitting ducks, all of us but they made us go anyway. It was never going to succeed."

"And then there were the machine guns and artillery," added Bert. "It's a wonder any of us survived."

That's all they were willing to say.

A few hours later the machine gun officer approached. He was a serious looking fellow, never smiling and always succinct. Two men trailed behind and I saw two gleaming smiles on their dirty faces. I had to fight off the urge to make a smart remark. After the formal introductions and a few brief instructions, the officer left so we could get acquainted, which was hardly required under the circumstances,

"How did you blokes pull it off?" I asked Mick and Frank.

"Easy," replied Mick, "We just used our charm!"

"So, you didn't do any of the talking then Frank?" I suggested.

"Very funny!" Frank didn't have much of a sense of humour.

It turned out they were members of another Lewis Gun crew at Passchendaele, and both asked to be placed with Bert, Dickie and me. I was surprised given Frank's concerns, but I decided not to open that wound again. I'd pushed my luck making a joke at his expense, but I wasn't going to let him get to me anymore and decided on a more aggressive approach from here on.

As a Lewis Gun crew, we were responsible for looking after the gun, pulling it apart, replacing worn out components, putting it back together and loading ammunition pans. I quickly learned that loading .303 bullets into the panniers was the most boring job you could get but it had to be done. When we were in action each man would carry bags of ammunition to make up for the gun's limited magazine. One pannier held forty eight bullets unlike the German Maxim machine gun which could rattle off hundreds of bullets from a belt before a reload was necessary. As a crew we seemed to coordinate very well, in training at least but we were untested in battle together. I was in no hurry to find out how we'd perform.

At night I often peered across to the eastern sky and watch the muzzle flashes, explosions and flares. The ever present rumble of the guns was impossible to ignore. By day, observation balloons and aircraft filled the skyline. We even got to watch the occasional dogfight between German and Allied planes. Anti aircraft fire followed German planes as they broke away and heavy artillery lobbed shells from behind our lines onto the German trenches and our boys were getting plenty of the same back. The sound of war was in the air day and night. I also learned who I could trust and who to avoid in our unit. Some of the veterans were very helpful with us new chums but there were others who didn't want to know us. To them we were a burden. Untested in battle, we were considered a danger to everyone. It would take a while to fit in properly.

Three weeks later the battalion received orders to move. The name of our destination was a town called Dickebusch, near Ypres. We would once again have to travel along the Menin Road and back around Hellfire Corner before reaching our new billets. This time it wouldn't be as easy. Instead of a handful of men the entire battalion and all our equipment had to go. The odds of us making it through undetected seemed very low indeed.

We moved out under the cover of darkness and the crunching of our boots seemed louder in the still of the night. As silly as it sounds, I found myself trying to tread softly but it was impossible with an eighty pound pack on my back. We soon approached the most dangerous section of the road, evident by wrecked machinery and cratered roadsides. The nervous tension was winding me up inside and I was sweating freely despite the cool air.

I thought I heard a whistle in the distance and stopped to listen. Everyone else heard it too and we all baulked for a moment. The whistle grew louder and before I could think men were barking orders and everyone scattered.

"Take cover!" someone shrieked.

I froze for a moment then Tom grabbed my arm and yanked me off the road. We'd run only a few paces when the first shell hit the ground. It was so close I heard the thud. In an instant there was a flash and a roar, and the air lit up momentarily. Tom and I threw ourselves to the ground. The shell had landed about fifty yards away, but I still felt the concussion and heard the shrapnel zing through the air over our heads.

Tom looked at me intently, "Stan!" he shouted, "We need to run, OK? Do you understand? We can't stay here; they have us pegged....STAN!"

I suddenly realised he was shaking me. I'd been mesmerized by the intensity of what was happening. It didn't quite seem real and certainly didn't resemble anything we'd been exposed to on the training grounds. The entire battalion had been caught in the open. Tom shook me again.

"STAN!" he yelled once more.

"Run. Yes, I understand."

We started moving into the darkness, away from the road as another shell shattered the soil. This time it was further away but more would come. Running with the full weight of a pack was incredibly difficult but we had no choice. There was no cover except for shell holes, and most were full of water and debris. We had to find somewhere to wait out the attack and the further we were from the road the better. We ran as fast as our legs would allow and I suddenly fell headlong into a shell hole. I landed heavily, halfway down the hole and tumbled the rest of the way. I hit the bottom, my fall broken by a pool of water which instantly soaked through my uniform and was cold against my skin. My heart was pumping and my nervousness has been replaced by something else, a surge of adrenaline. I crawled out of the ooze and made my way back to the top of the hole where Tom was already lay prostrate, watching the goings on. I looked out into the darkness expecting to see dead and broken men, but it was impossible to see much. Before long a few others found our hole and took cover.

"Five point nines," said Tom.

I knew what he was talking about. German artillery, big ones with plenty of range which explained the lack of flares and machine gun fire. They had quite a distinctive sound and I wouldn't soon forget it.

"What now?" I asked.

"Every man for himself. We find our way out of this mess and muster further up the road, away from trouble," explained Tom.

While we waited for a break in the barrage, the men hauling the heavy equipment had no option but to make a dash for safety along the road. I could hear the gallop of hooves and the clatter of limbers as shell after shell thundered down.

"How did they know we were here?" I asked Tom.

"Probably a listening post or something. The bastards always seem to know what we're doing."

Enemy shells were dropping at an alarming rate now and blistered the Menin Road with a mosaic of pock marks. Thankfully they were hitting ground we'd already covered, which was indeed miraculous. My heart was thumping against the wall of my chest and felt like it would burst out at any moment. While the Menin Road was ours the Germans liked to remind us that they were nearby and did so with their most devastating field guns, time and time again. We had nothing to match the 5.9 so none of the batteries in our sector returned fire. It was soon clear that the Germans had miscalculated and we were confident that waiting it out in our hole was probably our best option for now. As I lay there I began to calm down and my senses started getting back to normal. I soon became aware of the foulest stench coming off my uniform. It was then that I realised that we'd been sharing the hole with the decomposing body of a horse and I'd fallen into the rancid juices which had soaked my now stinking uniform and pack. Everything I had was enveloped in sticky, stinking ooze. Worse still, everyone else realised what was happening at the same time as I did,

"Ain't no aftershave in Belgium or France will hide that stench young fella," someone said and the rest of them laughed. Tom was laughing too,

"Sorry Stan...but he's right. You're truly putrid my friend!"

I didn't bother to reply and simply lay there, soaked in the blood and gore of a long dead steed. Now my fear was joining forces with mortification, if that was at all possible. It seemed like an eternity before the barrage broke off and after another fifteen minutes or so we emerged from the shell hole and made our way parallel to the road for a distance and eventually joined the rest of the battalion. I was forced to endure a lonely march and a series of smart remarks for the rest of our journey. The good news was that we hadn't lost a single bloke in the bombardment and counted our blessings although I felt a little less exhilarated than most.

After surviving the German attack, the rest of our march to Dickebusch was uneventful but very uncomfortable given the state of my uniform. On arrival we made camp. Dickebusch was another little farming village which showed evidence of past battles. It was only five miles from the front, but many locals had refused to leave despite the danger. As dawn broke villagers emerged from their dwellings and got down to the business of the day, tending their animals and vegetables. I quickly availed myself of their hospitality and did my best to get the rancid grime out of my uniform and kit. It took most of the morning and while I did the best I could, a lot of gruesome muck had ingrained itself into every woollen fibre and piece of fabric I had on me. I eventually gave up and hoped the smell would eventually fade. That hope also applied to the vast array of jibes I was being subjected to.

The 18th Battalion spent the next few days doing more training, resupplying and resting. Some were lucky enough to take leave and went back to England, but we all knew we'd be sent to the trenches soon enough. Tom used the time to write to his wife and others caught up on news with the delivery of newspapers from London. They gave us something new to talk about and broke the monotony for a while.

On November 1st the 2nd our division received orders to march east of the Passchendaele sector in Belgium. Despite the failed attack our blokes had made on Passchendaele Ridge, the Canadians had been successful in securing the position with the loss of over 3000 men. Better news was the follow. The brass had finally agreed to place all five Australian divisions under one command, something that most of the veterans had been hoping for. Our commanding officer would now be Field Marshall William Birdwood, an Englishman. Despite this he had gained a great deal of respect from the Australians. Up till now he'd commanded the Australian and New Zealand Army Corps and had done so since December 1914. He led our men through Gallipoli and earned the nickname of "Birdie", and it was Birdwood who approved the naming of ANZAC Cove. It wasn't long after that the soldiers started referring to themselves as Anzacs. The men were certainly buoyed by the news but soon we had other things on our minds.

One of the newer recruits overheard some men discussing our new destination, a place called Broodseinde Ridge,

"Where the Hell are we going now?" interrupted one of the newer chaps.

An older veteran leered at the young fellow then smiled, gaining the man's full attention before speaking, "The trenches mate!"

That was all he had to say. All the new recruits heard it and reacted the same way. Our stomachs knotted up and we turned white. The old veteran smirked; satisfied that he'd dealt with the young fellow for interrupting the conversation so rudely. A short silence ensued before someone finally blurted out, "Jesus Christ!"

The 18th Battalion would be relieving the 25th. It would be a clean swap giving some men from the 7th Brigade a well-deserved rest. We spent the next few days getting organised and set out in the pouring rain at around 2pm. It would take a few hours of hard marching to reach the trench system and a few more hours to make the transition. The rain was relentless for the entire march and kept up as the light faded, around the same time as we approached the rear sections of the main line. Voices remained hushed and I, like many, felt the tension as we shivered in our cold, wet uniforms. Our eyes were almost popping out of our heads as we strained to see through the growing darkness, made worse by the appalling conditions. The sound of artillery was louder than I had ever heard before and the muzzle flashes from Allied and German guns seems to clash in the low clouds like lightning bolts.

We moved forward steadily as flares hovered in the gloom. Every manner of bang, crack and stutter split our ears as ordnance exploded here and there with field guns, mortars, rifles and machine guns constantly exchanging a deadly array of projectiles. We were passing through the backblocks of the trench system now and I recognised a field hospital and supply station. Field kitchens were lined up beside the road ready for the next opportunity to feed the men who would soon emerge from their front line stint. We shuddered as we passed our own guns which were regularly answering the German shells...the noise was deafening. It was almost impossible to make out anything, but it appeared there was no cover ahead. Trees and buildings had been obliterated, replaced by a wasteland of craters and mud. There wasn't even a blade of grass in this horrible and foreboding place. We soon found ourselves treading on wooden duckboards which gave us a better fist of navigating this muddy ocean. Years of shelling and regular rain has turned the battlefield into a quagmire the likes of which I had never seen. There was nothing to do but keep moving forward and hope a stray shell didn't find us. As we moved closer to the trench system, we came across a station where each of us was handed a tin helmet to replace out felt hats.

Before long we were ordered to halt. It gave Tom a chance to check up on me,

"You alright Stan?" he asked.

I simply nodded, too cold and too scared to make a peep. He slapped me on the shoulder and gave an unconvincing smile. A patrol was sent forward to contact the 25th battalion. We stood in the pouring rain for another half hour absorbing the sounds and smells around us, many were pushed to the verge of panic, and I have to say I wasn't far behind them. The noise was relentless and uncompromising. 25th Battalion guides returned with our men to take us to the front. We were moving again and entered the rear most trenches, making our way along a series of saps which quickly had us walking below ground level. The duckboards here did little to protect us from the mud and only served to create a slippery surface which saw quite a few men on their backs in the slosh.

As we walked men of the 25th began filing past us as they headed out. I caught a few scraps of conversation, some wishing us well and others telling of how bad things were in this sector,

"I hope you've brought your gas masks fellas," someone remarked.

I found myself fumbling around for the familiar cylinder that contained my respirator as another twinge of panic tickled my stomach. It was exactly where it should be and I felt relieved. Another muzzle flash briefly showed us the silhouettes of dozens of men moving in the opposite direction, leaving this slush pit for some comfort and rest. Greetings were brief but most welcome; we had to make the exchange quickly to reduce any risk of a surprise attack. I looked at the faces of these men as they retired. They looked dead on their feet, some visibly haunted by their time at the front, others expressionless. I didn't speak to anyone as it took every ounce of strength to wade through the slop and keep my panic in check.

The German forward posts must have realised something was going on, just like that night on the Menin Road and opened up on our front line with an intense bombardment. The noise we'd struggled to get used to until now paled in comparison. We winced at the crack of every explosion and were showered in clods of mud and spray. The enemy had the line went targetted and I thought it only a matter of time before a shell landed amongst us or exploded above us and showered down a lethal blossom of lead balls which could tear a man to shreds. We picked up the pace and worked through the zigzag maze of hessian walls to find our posts. For me it was a matter of following Tom as I didn't have a clue what I was doing or where I was going. Guides pointed here and there, and men scooted into dugouts or onto fire steps, setting up their equipment as quickly as they could.

More flashes in the distance meant another avalanche of shells would be on us soon. Seconds later a fierce gang of explosions battered the area just ahead. More mud and clay clattered down, and a huge clod thwacked my helmet knocking me over. My head was ringing as I clambered to my feet and got moving again.

"Is it always like this," shouted one of the new blokes to anyone who might care to answer.

"Nah! This is nothing mate," came the reply.

As we moved the rain finally eased and then stopped completely. Within minutes more shells landed around us, but these didn't explode like the ones before. Instead, there was a popping sound that immediately resulted in the screaming of orders,

"Get your respirators on!" The words came just as the clang of a bell rang out warning of a gas attack!

My stomach knotted up even tighter than before as I groped at the canvas bag strapped to my chest. I fumbled at the flap and clumsily pulled the mask out, unfolding it and pulling it quickly over my face. The straps had to be tight to create a seal, and biting on a mouthpiece I inhaled the air passing through a charcoal filter attached to a tube that fed into the canvas bag. A small vale was all that kept the gas from backfilling into my mask. Breathing was labored though this contraption, but no-one dared take it off. I looked around to check on the others; it was hard to see much though the smoke haze of the goggles, but it appeared everyone was set. I tried to relax, just as we'd been taught but another series of pops nearby caused my breathing to quicken and it appeared my goggles had fogged up. I suddenly realised the fog was on the outside, a lethal layer of gas was settling in our trench.

All we could do was keep trying to move and find our stations. Spoken communication was almost impossible, so we had to watch for signals as we marched. Gas shells were mixed with explosive shells which were now jarring the ground above us. Shrapnel balls whistled overhead and spattered into the mud, some striking the inner wall of the trench. I watched as a piece of hot metal let off some steam as the mud cooled the fragment. The next shell struck about 50 yards ahead, splitting my ears as it burst with orange flame. The line of troops was brought to a sudden halt and when the smoke cleared men were digging frantically to save those who were buried in the muddy avalanche. By the time we hauled them out, two had smothered.

My mind was racing and I felt dizzy and near panic. I'd only been in the trench for about 15 minutes and already my nerves were frayed. Another shell exploded overhead and a man fell to the bottom of the trench. I couldn't see who it was. One of his mates plucked a smoldering fragment from his shoulder and tried to scream for stretcher bearers. We stepped over the poor fellow who looked as good as dead from what I could tell. We kept moving, straining at every step in the God awful conditions. After a while we reached our section of the forward trench lines. Soldiers moved left and right, guided by their platoon leaders. I followed Tom along the trench for a distance before we stopped. More shells burst all around us, some popping while others erupted with flame and shrapnel. There was no moving forward from here, this was the front line! Tom yelled out a muffled instruction,

"Stay down; we just have to sit this out!"

How long would that be? I wondered.

It seemed the more experienced men knew what to do. They hugged the trench walls while other risked their lives watching over no-man's land on the parapets, protected only by a pile of sandbags.

The exchange between the two battalions was finished around 10pm but the barrage went on for another hour. Who knows how many might have been killed or wounded in that time. It finally petered out and the gas cleared quickly after that thanks to a decent breeze. We didn't waste any time taking off the gas masks. The air smelt funny and everything around me strobed and spiralled as flares filled the night sky.

I saw Dickie on the fire step, "How far to the German line?" I asked him.

"Dunno Stan, I can't even tell which way is up!" he replied.

"That's because you haven't developed your night vision yet," someone said.

We looked around and saw our platoon leader, "Our what?" we asked.

"Night vision. After a while out here, your eyes will get used to the darkness and things will become much sharper. Just give it some time," he explained.

"Thanks sir," I said.

"Now, try to get some rest if you can. Not much for you to do tonight." He turned to Tom, "Look after them for me Tom?" He asked.

"Righto boss," Tom replied and Blue moved on up the trench, checking the new boys as he went.

Tom showed me a small dugout in the trench wall,

"This is where we sleep Stan. Try to make yourself comfortable," he explained.

It was a rather dank little space with barely enough room to roll over. I shoved my pack into one end to act as a pillow and lay down my great coat and blanket before squeezing into the space for some rest. I closed my eyes and hoped against hope that I could sleep but my senses were still very much on edge. I could smell the musty sandbags around me, the remnant stench of the gas attack and the wet clay. It was mixed with the odour of cordite and a hint of decay. Repulsive doesn't begin to describe it. I tried to remain calm, but it was impossible. I was soaked through, cold and the Germans kept sending over constant reminders that they were nearby.

I listened as orders were given, working parties organised and crews assembled to repair damaged sections of the trench line. I gathered that this was the normality of life on the front. After a good long while I drifted off to sleep. It was a restless, unsatisfying slumber but it was better than nothing.

A few hours later I was woken abruptly by violent shaking.

"What! What is it?" I blurted as I sucked in a big lungful of rancid air.

"Just me Stan," replied Tom, "Time to wake up."

"Stand to, stand to!" came an order from the platoon leader.

Tom smiled, "Come on mate, I'll show you what to do."

I learned that we had to *stand to* every morning before dawn and every evening at dusk, in case of a German attack. Every man stood at the ready, rifles and machine guns loaded, waiting just in case the German's decided that today was a good day for an advance. This was my first chance to look across no-man's land. My stomach felt like it was twisting inside me again as I stepped up to the gap in the sandbags, but my excitement was dashed by a heavy fog that had rolled in after the previous nights' rain. There was nothing to see but the dirt a few yards ahead. After an hour or so, the sun began to pierce the cloud and the order to stand down was given. Most of us returned to our sections, while others kept vigil.

Just then a shell dropped near our position, raining dirt down on the trench.

"What now?" I blurted.

"Just a wakeup call from the Germans. They do it most mornings just to say hello," Tom explained.

"That's just great," someone said as we fired back a volley from our own artillery.

Tom was smiling and I tried to smile back, "Don't worry Stan, you'll get used to it soon enough. Come on, let's have a cuppa!"

Tom boiled up a billy of tea as a few more shots landed in front of our line, raining down more clay. Our artillery boys replied in kind before things settled down again. Despite the added soil, I enjoyed my tea very much. It was the most civilised thing I'd experienced since we arrived. Tom even has some sugar which I certainly appreciated.

The veterans were relaxed and spent their time on post duty, preparing food, writing letters or resting. There was little else to do in such a god forsaken place. For those of us who hadn't been in the war until now, it was a very strange experience. The constant fear ate away at us like acid and the noises we heard from miles back a few days ago were now all around us at one hundred times the volume.

I finally had a chance to inspect the surroundings. The trench was about seven feet deep with a wooden duckboard floor. It barely kept the mud from squelching up and we were constantly coated in wet soil. From back to front the trench was approximately five feet across with sandbags lining the walls. It zigzagged along the front line, designed that way to make an enemy penetration more difficult because you simply cannot see around corners. Consequently, our view was limited in all directions. There were parapets every few yards where sentries took turns keeping watch and machine gunners waited for any sign of the enemy in no-man's-land. I thought it quite remarkable, despite everything that men were laughing and chatting, eating and drinking tea in the haven of a clay crevasse.

We found comfort any way we could, keeping to our tight little groups, cooking and eating together, sharing utensils, food, razors and other luxuries. Most of our waking hours were spent on watch or maintaining equipment. The smells were different during the day, death and hessian subdued by new aromas like sweat and body odour. After breakfast Tom took me to see Bert and Dickie. They were at the fire step with the Lewis gun set up strategically to repel any German advance, its muzzle poking out through a slot in the sandbags.

"How close are we to the German line," I asked Dickie.

"I don't know, hard to tell," he replied as he peered through the sandbags.

Just then the platoon leader, Bluey Wilton spoke, "How are you blokes feeling now?"

"Good thank you sir," we replied.

"OK then, good!" then he turned to Tom, "We'll muster in 10 minutes, can you pass the word. We'll get everyone up to date then, ok?"

"Sure Blue, 10 minutes," replied Tom.

"Oh, and take one of the new blokes with you. They need to know what's what around here," Bluey added.

"Will do," said Tom. "Come on Stan, I'll show you around."

I grabbed my rifle and slung it over my shoulder, following Tom down the trench line. He told everyone we'd be gathering in 10 minutes for a briefing. My first outing was all of 50 yards, but it was good to stretch my legs, and it certainly gave me some perspective on our environment. It was hard to imagine we were in a trench that stretched from the North Sea, winding south through Belgium and France ending at the Swiss border. All up it was four hundred and fifty miles of zigzagging trenches, dugouts and barbed wire facing a similar trench system on the German side.

We Aussies looked after the central sections of the system with other Allied troops from England, Canada, India, Scotland, Ireland and untold others. The Belgians held the line to our north right up to the sea while the French occupied the southern half of the line. A few minutes later around fifty men gathered to hear from the platoon leader.

"Alright, here we are again. Keep your eyes open and heads down. We should be out of here soon enough. The 25th suffered a bad gas attack yesterday, that's why we're here."

Most of us were very much aware of that situation as Blue continued,

"We'll need some work crews to repair the trench in our section and others to do some drainage work, maybe lay some new duckboards. As you can see it's no palace," he said, looking at the new lads," so let's make the best of it."

With that Blue started assigning tasks for the day. Then he added, "Some of the wire needs attention too, so we'll send out a patrol tonight to fix it. It'll give some of you new blokes a taste of things. My heart skipped a beat. Fixing the wire meant going into no-man's land.

After the business of the day was settled men got organised. Some ate or shaved, washed if they could. Tom and I shovelled down some bully beef and biscuits. Some of the more experienced amongst us feasted on a few nice chickens they'd liberated from Dickebusch. It wasn't encouraged but it never stopped a hungry soldier.

"I can't wait to go on patrol," announced Les Giles.

"You're joking," replied Bert which forced Les to glare.

"Beats sitting around in the mud," blurted Les.

"I'm going to bet that after tonight, you'll be wishing that having a muddy arse is as hard as this war gets," said Bert to which Les had no reply.

Walking around in no-man's land was dangerous but it seemed to keep the German's in check most of the time. Australians had a reputation for getting things done out there, whether it was fixing broken wire or hauling in prisoners. Headquarters was more than happy to let us stir things up a bit. At least that's what the vets were telling us.

Blue appointed patrol leaders then told them to pick out some of the fresh recruits to go along. There was a united groan from the veterans. Tom and I were allocated the task of deepening the trench in our sector and laying new duckboards, a filthy job but one that was necessary. It also kept us well out of sight which I didn't mind at all. By the middle of the day, it got quite warm in our trench and I was utterly exhausted. Many of us were catching up on sleep, playing cards or reading London newspapers that had been brought up earlier. They were several days old, but it didn't matter, it was something to do.

Observers kept watch over no man's land but didn't report anything unusual. In fact, they said there was hardly a sound coming from the German side. The rest of the day saw most of the jobs that had been allocated, completed, including the repairs to the damaged trench walls. Sandbagging was something we'd all get very good at it seemed. My first day on the line was routine when all was said and done.

Chapter 6

<u>The Enemy</u>

For the next two days we went about our duties, fixing duckboards, sandbagging and draining trenches. Any thoughts I had of escaping such work because of my position on a Lewis gun crew quickly evaporated. The gun didn't need a team of five in the line, and being the new chap, I was put on detail often. When we weren't involved in maintenance we were on watch. Bert, Dickie, Frank, and Mick would take turns on the parapet, watching over no man's land. Finally, I got my chance to have a real good look at no man's land. I had a few glimpses here and there since arriving on the line, but it was never a good idea to stick you head up or it could be the last thing you did with snipers always ready to have a crack but my first time on watch is something I'll never forget. It was like looking out over a wasteland. All I could see was mud and slush which had been fractured and tortured by years of stalemate. Pockmarked earth with the waste of war scattered all around. Through the wire I could see the German line, about two hundred yards away on a ridge. They had all the high ground it seemed. The Germans kept their heads down just as well as we did. Occasionally we'd hear a sound drift across from their side; a laugh or a shout but it was rare to see the top of a helmet or a face rise above the protection of the sand bagged walls. No doubt they had their Maxim crews on the fire steps too, watching for movement on our side and an opportunity to shoot.

I didn't mind the hard work that much. It was dirty and exhausting, but it passed the time. Life in the trenches could get very boring at times, so it was always good to have something to do. Tom was called on less often than me, but he always helped. He was 42, well-liked by the men and had become something of a father figure to most of the boys, me included. He was very reassuring and watched over us like a mother hen. On our third night at the front blue approach us,

"Thorn, Jones, Dunkley, Giles!! It's time you earned your pay. Join those blokes over there, you're going on fatigue," he announced.

Fatigue, we all knew it would happen sooner or later. They liked to send the new boys out as soon as they could to get a feel for no-man's land. Fatigue seemed to be the preferred option because it was the safest stunt outside of the trenches, if you could call it safe. It usually meant fixing broken barbed wire or sandbagging areas that couldn't be reached from inside the trench. It was always done at night.

I surprised myself by jumping up as soon as I heard the order; I straightened my helmet and walked up to the group. The lead man was allocating pliers and coils of wire. Joe Maxwell, the same bloke who'd welcomed me into B Company with the underwear avalanche would lead this patrol. He didn't remember me,

"Righto, no heroics out there. We stick together alright? It's dark and the German's are a little bit feisty after a raid earlier tonight," he explained.

"If there's a flare, do not move, don't event drop to the ground. Your best bet it to stay very still until the light is gone. Most important, be quiet. Sounds carries up there and the slightest clang or thump will bring merry Hell down on us, understood?" he looked hard at us new chaps. "Any questions?" there was no reaction.

"Good, grab a roll of wire if you haven't already got one and get some posts. Follow me and do as I say!" He ordered.

With that he slapped a wooden ladder against the sandbags and hauled himself up like he'd done it a thousand times, which he probably had. He hesitated momentarily at the top then slithered out of sight. One by one the others followed, disappearing into the darkness like rats on the prowl. I was the last to go, following behind Les Giles. My stomach was all in knots and my hands were shaking as I climbed the ladder. When I reached the top, I peered into darkness like I'd never seen before. The rest of the men were waiting for me as I stepped onto the mud of no-man's land. Joe made a hand signal and we all obeyed, following his every direction.

It smelled different out of the trench. The musty odour of sandbags and dirty men was replaced by a mix of clay and decay which was intensified by the cold night air. I looked towards the German line but didn't see anything. It was an overcast, moonless night which was certainly good for us. My legs felt like jelly as we scampered along our trench line making for a gap in the wire. We turned in and out following the maze until we were clear into no-man's land a good many yards from the safety of our hole.

Joe signalled again, pointing at a section of wire that had been torn apart by shelling. This was where we had to make repairs. Just as we started to make ready there was a pop. Joe warned everyone with a whisper,

"Freeze, don't flinch!"

The sky lit up like day as a flare burst above no-man's land. I could see as clearly as if it were summer on Bondi Beach. The light flickered and dance across the mudscape, the shadows moving like giant black fingers as the flare descended. None of us breathed, hoping we wouldn't be spotted. I was looking across at the German line and made out the dark edge of their trench line. Surely, they could see us, but all remained quiet. Then, like a spell was broken, I heard a terrible clang. Someone had dropped their metal posts and even though they only fell a short distance they rolled and clattered a few yards making the most awful din. Within a split second a fusillade of machine gun fire erupted from the enemy line. Our Lewis gunners immediately retaliated hoping to draw fire away. We all fell flat to the ground instinctively as another flare, then another burst above us. I heard bullets sizzle over our heads and others spatter into the ground several yards away. My heart was pumping so hard I could hear it between gun bursts. Another volley of shots came frightening close and spat dirt in my face. The instinct to run was overwhelming but Joe remained calm and didn't move, so we did the same.

The gunfire played out for only a few moments, but it felt like an eternity. It soon became clear that they didn't see us and were firing wildly. As the flare light diminished, we waited for Joe to give us all clear. In the few moments that the ground was lit up I saw dozens of shell holes, a helmet, bits and pieces of broken equipment and to my horror what appeared to be two bodies. I'd seen the dead on the Menin Road, but this was so much more terrible. They were once living, breathing souls and now they were laid to waste in the mud. There was no telling if they were Germans or our own. They were just out there in the middle of nowhere, caught by a shell blast or machine gun fire. I fought the urge to heave up my dinner as the darkness slowly enveloped us again. Joe ordered us to get to work but I was having trouble seeing properly. I'd forgotten to keep my eyes closed when the flares came and now, I was temporarily blind. It took a few minutes to adjust, but I knew I wouldn't make that mistake again.

We worked in pairs to fix the broken section of wire. I was with Les Giles and Bert and Dickey were close by. Posts were designed to be screwed into the ground by hand, to avoid the sound of hammering. Once the posts were in the ground, we had to string the barbed wire into metal loops, thus closing the gap in the defensive curtain. The German artillery had done its business well and it took a great deal of time to do the job, slowed by the relentless array of German flares. This process went on night after night on both sides.

It was now around 2am and we'd just finished stringing the last of our wire when there was yet another pop. Again, we didn't move. I closed my eyes to keep my night vision intact. This time the flare must have been well placed because the German Maxim opened up again. Joe shrieked out an order,

"Take cover!"

Men jumped and dived to find any cover they could. I had dived into a nearby shell hole while others made a dash for our trench. The Maxim just kept on pumping away *tak tak tak tak tak*! I rolled to a stop just short of a stagnant pool of water, taking in a lung full of the stench. I then scrambled back to the top of the hole and saw Les. He was flat on the ground and in sheer panic,

"Here Les, this way," I yelled.

He looked up and saw me, stood and sprinted for the hole. It was only a few yards, but it must have felt like a mile. He dived headlong towards me just as a spray of bullets spattered across the rim. I ducked and Les tumbled down on top of me,

"Blimey Les, are you alright?" I asked.

"I don't know, felt like someone threw a rock and hit me in the back," he explained.

I looked at his tunic and saw it was wet with blood,

"You're hit Les. We've got to get you back to the trench."

Machine guns exchanged fire from both side. Men were shouting in the din, but the voices soon faded as the rest of our group escaped back to our line.

"How bad is it, Stan?" Les asked as he coughed, spitting blood onto his sleeve.

I could see him going white as the shock set in,

"Don't worry Les, you'll be OK," but I didn't have the slightest idea how bad his wounds were.

I looked out of the shell hole and saw that it was dark again,

"OK, it's clear let's make a run for it," but Les didn't answer.

Blood stained his lips and his eyes lolled about like he was drunk,

"Come on Les, let's go!"

I grabbed him by the collar and heaved him up and out of the trench. I could hear that we was struggling for breath and felt his weight increase as he began to black out. I hauled him along the wire and back through the maze as the Maxim fired up again. Rifle fire rang out too and our side responded in kind. Just then I was met by others who saw our dilemma. They lifted Les and carried him the rest of the way, despite the incessant gunfire. I sprinted for the trench, falling headlong into it. Moments later Les was lowered down by his two rescuers, both unscathed. A few more shots were exchanged then nothing but an eerie silence as the light of one last flare evaporated.

I looked across at Les Childs. Blood drenched his uniform now; he was limp and crumpled up in an awkward pile.

"Bad luck fella, he didn't make it," someone said.

I just stared at Les's face. It was without expression, eyes wide open and all glazed over. His lips were blue against the stains of blood. He must have died in the short time it took to get him out of that hole and into the trench. Someone offered me a swig of rum as Joe Maxwell put his hand on my shoulder,

"I'm sorry about your friend," he paused then said, "You best get back to your station young fella."

Joe seemed to have accepted the events of the last few minutes with ease.

"Yes sir," I replied, barely able to form words.

I ripped my gaze away from Les's body and started down the duckboard track. I began to shake and felt my legs weaken beneath me. I stumbled and groped for the trench wall to stop from falling, paused and vomited into the mud on the trench floor. Somehow, I managed to make the remaining thirty yards and saw Tom.

"Jesus Stan, you're as white as a ghost," exclaimed Tom, "What happened out there?"

I looked up and saw everyone staring at me, "They got Les!"

No-one spoke for a moment, we didn't really get to know Les Giles that well, but he was one us. It was just then that I remembered him saying how much he wanted to get out there, into no-man's land. He got his wish and paid a high price for it.

My emotions were a mixture of anger, hatred and deep sadness but most of all I was exhausted. I crawled into my dugout just as the Germans sent over a few shells to shake us up. The thunder of the explosions shattered the last of my resilience and I wept, thinking what a terrible mistake I had made coming here. I thought of running but where would I go? I curled up into a ball and waited for the barrage to stop. Exhaustion finally got the better of me and I fell asleep.

A few hours after escaping the German fusillade I woke, feeling oddly better. Perhaps my purge after the stunt had released some of my fear. I sat up, said hello to Tom and talked about the nights' events. I managed to eat some breakfast. The mood in the platoon, however, was somber as Blue came along to muster the men and allocate tasks. I shouldn't have been surprised that we were to go out again after dark. I suppose it was the army's way of getting us back on the horse. We did our usual array of jobs around the trench, snatched some sleep when we could and geared up for another trip to no-man's land. This time we weren't on fatigue, we were on patrol. We would try to get a handle on the enemy's defenses and if we were lucky, take a prisoner or two. Tom joined this patrol and told me to stay close. I felt much more comfortable knowing he was there. We followed a route that took us a long way from our section of trench, checking on some of the more significant German defensive points. We could hear their men at times chatting and laughing. They seemed to be oblivious to the danger but that's how it was I suppose.

The experienced men knew what to look for and where to go while I was simply an extra gun on the task. We'd been out for a while and were making our way back to the trench when our lead man stopped us in our tracks. He made a hand gesture or two and everyone spread out. We lay prone on the ground, waiting. A few moments later a group of shadows appeared before us, creeping through the shell holes and debris.

I wondered who they might be, another of our patrols perhaps. Who could tell? Just then our lead man called for the password. The group, about forty yards away, all stopped as one. There was a pause, but no password came back. Then one of the men yelled,

"Uten!"

"Shit!" blurted Tom, "they're krauts!"

Before I could think, rifle fire erupted from both sides. I let fly with my .303, aiming at the scampering shadows. It was impossible to see if I hit anyone, there was so much confusion. As was their habit, the Germans lit up the sky with flares and machine guns started spraying our position. We scampered for cover in the nearest shell holes. Our Lewis guns replied to the German Maxim's and orders were barked out.

"BOMBS!"

I wretched a mills grenade from my belt and pulled the pin, throwing it without hesitation. Several of us got them away in quick time and they rained down on the enemy position. Most fell well short but one or two hit the mark given the screams I heard. I then heard a few thuds on the ground near us,"

"Stick bombs, watch yourselves!"

With that three explosions rained dirt down on us as the German bombs exploded. We kept firing into the smoky darkness. I wasn't sure if I was aiming in the right direction. My heart was fluttering and I gasped to catch a breath. Seconds seemed like minutes as the fight went on. It didn't see like there was any way of winning this skirmish, but as the flares died, I heard more gunshots coming from the German shell holes,

"Hand hoc you grimy bastards!"

Our experienced men had somehow flanked the Germans and got in behind them. They dropped their guns and threw up their hands. The machine guns stopped and we waited for a moment.

"OK, let's get these blokes back to our line, MOVE!"

With that we rushed forward. I expected the German machine gunners to start at us any second but that would have meant aiming at their own men. Better they are captured than killed I suppose. As I approached the Germans, I could see them more clearly. There were five of them alive, some with wounds. Two more lay dead at the bottom of the shell hole. We rounded them up at gun point and worked out way back to the line. They didn't seem too keen to make a run for it, but they were outnumbered and now unarmed.

We got back to our trench unscathed and I looked them over. Their white faces practically glowed against their field grey uniforms. I caught the eye of one fellow. He must have been 18 or 19.

"Zis is a terrible war!" he said in near perfect English

I was taken aback briefly but then replied,

"Indeed, it is, but you're out of it now."

He smiled as he was herded down the sap with the others. I'm not sure if he was relieved or knew something I didn't. It made me feel uneasy.

Tom slapped me on the back,

"Not so bad huh?"

"If you say so Tom."

Close up they were people just like us. They looked like us and spoke like us. Up close they didn't seem so horrid.

Headquarters had ordered regular night-time hops to keep the Germans on edge and disrupt their relatively secure hold on the Western Front. We were ordered to take prisoners and steal anything of value, and it seemed to be paying off. Over the nights that followed German soldiers surrendered regularly as we kept the pressure up. Our approach was an effective psychological tactic, but it had another curious effect on our side; our morale was high. Simply getting out of the trenches and moving about proved the best medicine for all of us. Yes, it was dangerous, but it was better than sitting in the bottom of a hole for days at a time bored out of your mind. We revelled in the opportunity to sneak about in the dark.

There was of course a price for our tactics; German shelling proved relentless and occasionally one would find its mark. One shell burst killed three men and wounded four others; such was the way of trench warfare.

On November 5th our battalion received new orders; we were to be relieved by the 19th battalion and were soon off the line resting in the town called Staples. I'd survived my first stint on the front line, and I can't tell you how relieved I was. From here we would keep supplies up to our sister battalion; duckboards, ammunition, sandbags, wire; we always seemed to be ferrying something up to them.

Some men took leave and headed off for Paris or London if time permitted. We weren't so lucky being new. We hadn't earned such luxuries. You had to be wounded to get a break, and I wasn't too keen on that idea.

After a few more days in reserve we got moved off again, this time to rest. It was a constant rotation between the front, reserve and rest that supposedly kept us fresh. One day some mail arrived. I didn't pay much attention but then heard my name ring out. I jumped to my feet and sprinted to collect whatever had come. There was a small package for me and two letters. I was delighted and quickly looked to see who they were from. One letter was from my brother Allan, as was the parcel and the other letter was from my good friend Harry Robson. I ripped open the letter Allan and began to read,

My Dear Stanley,

You must be surprised to hear from me? Dad wrote me and explained that you had joined up. It took me some time to track you down, but I hope this letter

finds you well.

I have great news, I am married! Her name is Eva Lambert, an English lass. We met when I was on leave in England. I have enclosed some wedding cake, which I hope survived the journey. We plan to return to Australia when the war is over and hope to see you when we get home.

Stan, I also have some upsetting news, Harold has been wounded. He is presently at Royal Victoria Hospital in the south of England. He may be there for a good while although I don't really know how badly knocked, he is.

By the way, your old friend Alex Ironside was sent home. He contracted meningitis and was declared unfit for active service. Truthfully, he might not have made it. I'm yet to learn his fate.

I'll close now Stan; Dad sends his best.

Sincerely,

Allan.

I felt mixed emotions, joy for Allan…married, fancy that but then I pined for my brother Harold. How badly was he hurt? Could he die? The thoughts spun around like a waking nightmare. One thing pleased me though; the postmark showed that Allan was in England, so I knew he was quite safe for now. I then opened the letter from my friend Harry Robson. I was shocked to read that he was still very much intent on joining the army at the first opportunity. He and another mate, Jack Billson. I immediately scrounged up some paper and a pencil and wrote back.

My Dear Harry,

Your letter of August 12 to hand. I am pleased you are well at home. Look here Harry old chum, both you and Jack had better get that idea of enlisting out of your head, for this place is no place for youngsters. I have found out how hard it is, for I can only just manage to keep up to the great strain, which is required of us. We're in the line and out of it too. Just let your mother see this and I know she'll take the advice of one who has found out what it is here.

You ask what it is like here. One cannot look anywhere but what he sees is mud. Although it wasn't too bad as we had fairly good weather. I dare say however, that shortly good weather will be a thing of the past for at least five months of winter is coming on you know.

Allan has been married to a pretty English girl. I had a piece of wedding cake.

I took the letter and put it with the rest of the outgoing mail. It would be some time before it found its way to Harry's address and I hoped he would get it before he had a chance to enlist, if he hadn't already.

Another few days passed by at rest before we were on the move again. We found ourselves once again at Steenvorde, where'd I'd first joined the battalion. We took up billets and were inspected by company commanders, including the Corps Commander General William Birdwood. He presented ribands to some of the men. We were then ordered to the Wallon Cappel area for training where the battalion organised a football match and spent the afternoon forgetting the war. For the rest of November, we continued training and marching from one place to another, Moorlenauere, Steenwerck, Pont De Nieppe and Westhoek Ridge. We played many sports and enjoyed concerts at the YWCA when we weren't in the line.

On December 12 the Germans attacked our battalion by air with a formation of Gotha bombers. They were slow, lumbering biplanes with huge, seventy foot wingspans. They were driven by two engines with the props behind the wings. A gunner sat in the nose while another was behind the pilot, both firing MG14 machine guns. A rear gunner had two more of these fearsome weapons, one for shooting at other aircraft and the other to strafe troops. I learned that these planes also carried fourteen heavy bombs which were either attached to the bottom of the fuselage or stored in a bomb chamber. The formation blundered towards us, and we hastened to set up the Lewis gun on an anti-aircraft tripod. Everyone who had a gun opened fire on the planes.

With bullets screaming toward the formation, bombs began to drop all over the place. A dozen of them exploded on the ground missing their targets but it would only take one or two to hit a prime objective and the Germans would have achieved their goal. I watched as bombs fell to earth, seemingly upon our men. The huge explosions sent shock waves through the ground and sent up huge plumes of smoke and dust. One bomb hit a small building which was blasted into splinters. I wondered if anyone had taken refuge there. Another came down where several men were clustered and even though they saw it coming they couldn't get clear before it erupted upon them. Bodies were flung in the air in all directions. I didn't have time to think about them as I reeled of shot after shot from my rifle while Bert hammered away with the Lewis gun.

It wasn't a one way fight though, with so many guns aimed skyward, some hit their marks. Bullets ripped through the flimsy fabric of the lead plane, right underneath the pilot seat. The Gotha lurched upwards, stalled and then spiralled to the ground, crashing a short distance from our camp. Another followed soon after and burst into flames. The attack ended as fast as it began. Their payloads spent, the remaining bombers turned for home. We kept at them until they were well out of range. Counting the cost of the encounter revealed the damage, seventeen dead and sixty seven wounded. It was a very dark day indeed. The only thing to be thankful for was that none of them were from our platoon.

We were ordered to work to start salvaging what we could and clean up. Others were put on burial duty while medics looked after the wounded. Some men checked the wreckage of the downed planes but the crew of both were dead. They did manage to salvage the machine guns and maps from one plane, but the other had been destroyed by fire.

After the clean-up we held a funeral service for our lost men and the Germans. Even well behind the line, the chances of being killed were clearly obvious to us all.

Chapter 7

Winter

The weather was changing quickly now. It went from plain cold to freezing with snow flurries, the likes of which I had never seen before. The landscape was alien to me now. While the cold was uncomfortable and something the new chaps really struggled with, it had one great advantage, the fighting all but ceased on the front line. Snow made it impossible to mount a full scale advance so both sides settled in for what would be a few months of boredom. It was mid-December when we were ordered to move again and we took over the line from the 34th at Ploegsteert, in Belgium.

Despite my best hopes the conditions at the front were, to say the least, miserable. The only saving grace was that the mud had frozen solid. Winter in the trenches was probably as bleak as things could get on the Western front. Australians were not well adapted to such harsh conditions, and everyone was feeling the cold despite our woollen great coats. Even the fine days were bitter and when the weather turned bad it was a frozen Hell! Between the snow, the rain and the mud there was little we could do but wait it out. The trenches still had to be manned, and patrols sent out but there was no concern regarding a major German advance; it was simply out of the question for both sides.

The Lewis gun crews took turns as usual at their posts watching no-man's land. It was too cold to move most nights, but we did our duty without complaint. I was well used to the routine now as were Bert and Dickie. We didn't see hide or hair of the Germans most days except for an occasional flurry of bombs or gas shells, which kept us on our toes.

About a week before Christmas a few of us huddled together, trying to boil up some tea and killed time by talking about home,

"Mum would be getting ready to cook up a feat right now," suggested Mick Hogg. "We always have a big family Christmas. Dad kills a cow and we have roast beef like you never tasted. No pansy ham at our place!" We all laughed.

"It's a bit different in the city. We sort of bounce around from one house to the next", explained Frank Curry.

Tom then chimed in, "Well Margaret, my wife, is a mighty fine cook. She can do anything with a chook, a lamb or a pig."

"Is that a pansy pig?" suggested Mick. We laughed again as Tom continued, "Me and the boys go huntin' for wild pig, so no, they're not pansies Mick. We bag a few rabbits too so there's plenty of meat for everyone. Wish I was there now…we'd be out in the bush for sure."

The conversation made us all feel homesick, even though Tom's way of life sounded wild compared to the city blokes. I thought I should add my tuppence worth,

"We used to have Christmas at home in Granville every year until Mum died. After that it just got too hard for Dad. He tried but it wasn't the same."

I looked up and saw three blank faces; I'd silenced the lot of them. Tom finally broke through for the group,

"Well, we're all here now, so let's make the best of it, who's for a Christmas carol?"

It sounded like a good idea, and we started belting out Silent Night. The rest of the platoon joined in and for a few moments we forgot about the cold and the trenches and revelled in the spirit of the occasion. Soon, for a hundred yards up and down the line, men sang, not caring who could hear. It was an odd experience to say the least.

Just then an observer watching out over no-man's land alerted us to something,

"Germans!"

Our groups stopped singing, but the rest kept it going.

"What are they doing?" Tom asked.

"They're just looking?!"

We poked our heads up to see, knowing what a risk it was with snipers so close, but somehow this didn't seem to be a concern. Sure, enough as we sang, German faces appeared one by one, until there were about a hundred of them.

Word quickly passed up the line, and we were soon all standing, peering at the Germans who were peering back at us. The captain ordered us to stop singing and it came to an abrupt halt, but then we heard something. It washed over no-man's land in waves, Silent Night in German.

"How would they know that song," someone asked.

"Because it's German you loon!"

"No, it's Austrian," said someone else.

"Same thing!"

It was an eerie feeling but one that was most welcome. Some of our men again began to sing and soon everyone chimed in.

"Jesus, they're human after all," someone said. I had to agree.

When the singing ended we all resumed our respective huddles. I took a last look across no-man's land and saw a single German wave. I waved back before we both disappeared into our respective trenches. That was the oddest experience I'd had so far.

"No-one's going to believe this", suggested Tom.

"Doesn't matter. We know it happened," I suggested and everyone agreed.

A short time later the monotony of winter in the trenches enveloped us again and life on the Western front was back to normal.

Next day the Germans gave us a double quota of gas shells. Perhaps they thought we'd be off our guard after the nights' proceedings, but they were out of luck.

Over the next couple of nights, we sent out of regular patrols but made no direct contact with the enemy. The adjutant took great pleasure in writing his daily report and concluding with the words, *casualty rate nil.* If we weren't on patrol, we were trying the keep the trenches in some kind of habitable order. One couldn't help but worry about how quiet things had become, were the Germans up to something? Boredom always gave wave to rumour mongering and word quickly got about that a major enemy attack was about to come down on us. There was nothing to substantiate the rumours, but I couldn't help but worry. Much to my relief we were taken off the line on Christmas Eve, 1917. A better gift we could not have asked for. As we made our way behind the line, we passed men of the 19th coming in. There were some good, spirited jibes delivered, and a few unsavory remarks fired back but for the battalion from Sydney, Christmas would not be spent in snow and ice.

While A and C Companies moved back to rest at Le Rossignol Camp, my company was put on support and spent Christmas as Fusilier Camp. Christmas Day was the coldest day yet. It had snowed lightly again, and we had trouble mustering for parade. Still, we were in good spirits and morale was high. We were given a little extra rum with our rations and some men even exchanged gifts. Most of us didn't have much to offer except good cheer. That night we feasted on turkey, duck, ham and pudding and then enjoyed a concert put on by the 2nd Pioneers. Unfortunately, there was no heating fuel, and the hall was bitterly cold. Despite the temperature it was the most fun we'd had in quite a long time.

A few days later we were relieved and given first use of the bathes at Pont de Nieppe. We had hot showers and a change of clothes. Our uniforms were washed and we discarded our old underwear. The new clothing, while clean, was infested with lice eggs and a few days later we were scratching and complaining again. I wish I had a schilling for every time I heard the words, "Bloody lice!"

The year ended with an odd occurrence. Someone had found a piano in a deserted village. The piano was almost unscathed despite four years of shelling. It was put on a stretcher and carried two miles to the front line so the men could celebrate the New Year. There was no shortage of optimistic players, some good but most well below par. It didn't matter and we sang the night away before the inevitable return to the trenches.

Back at the front we quickly got back into the business of patrols, trench maintenance and trying to avoid boredom. I couldn't help but wonder if this was all the war would be? How would it ever end if all we did was this? To add to the frustration those rumours of a major German offensive had not abated. Patrols were continually coming back empty, adding to the speculation. The word was that patrols up and down our section of the line were returning with similar reports.

Occasionally a prisoner or two was captured and took great joy in hinting at some great offensive, but they didn't know anything of substance. All we could do was wait and tend to our daily chores. The routine of moving back and forth from the line was monotonous. One night Tom and I were put on watch and took our positions on the fire step. I peeked through the periscope and tracked left to right across the macabre landscape of no-man's land. The entire region was devoid of vegetation and once again it resembled a reflection of the moon, a sea of grey with great craters. The only evidence of humanity was the jumbles of barbed wire and refuse of earlier battles. There was a body half buried in the frozen ground. Its decomposition delayed by the conditions I suspected.

As observers we worked in pairs and with good reason. It had been noted many times early in the war that men were often spooked by the shadows of flares in the dead of night. Many false alarms resulted when a man was startled by the face of a German, which turned out to be nothing more than star shells lighting up a rock. HQ quickly solved the problem by ordering that all observers work in pairs.

We'd been ordered to remain well behind our sandbags as the Germans had a habit of firing their Maxim's in the faint hope that that might hit someone. Snipers too were always looking for a clean shot if someone peered across the wasteland at the wrong moment. Our shift ended the same way as most, no movement. Working parties continued to improve the trenches and a new support trench was built while the ongoing patrols went out and came back with the same reports, *no enemy contact.*

A few days into our latest stint I heard a commotion a little way up the trench line. I couldn't help but wonder what was going on. Then I saw a few men carrying a stokes mortar. Their job was simple; set up, lob a few bombs at the Germans and move on. A Stokes Mortar crew couldn't stay in one place for long because they would become targets soon enough, so they moved up and down the trenches to keep the Hun guessing. The trouble was they were not popular with the infantry because we inadvertently became targets too.

"Come on you blokes, take it somewhere else."

"Geez fellas, it's nice and quiet down here…don't mess things up for us."

The Stokes crew would always say, "Sorry gents we're following orders."

They set up their mortar about twenty yards from our dugout. I noticed that everyone in the area scattered and I thought I should do the same. Moments later the mortar was firing projectiles across no-man's land and into the German line. They did this for only a short while but managed to send over quite a bit of ordnance before quickly packing up and moving on. The tactic was designed to disrupt German routine and stir them up a bit. The latter certainly held true as the German's always retaliated with their own mortar shells. Infantry was always on the receiving end of these counterattacks with the Stokes' crew long gone. To add to our misery, the German mortars were much more powerful, and we hoped they didn't have one of those dreaded Minenwerfers nearby. It was a weapon that resembled a small canon and sent the fear of God into us all. Its distinct sound was easily recognisable and had sent us scurrying for cover.

Within a few minutes enemy shells were exploding just over the bags in no-man's land. It was only a matter of time before one landed in our trench. The experienced soldiers had taught us to watch the sky because you could sometimes see the mortar shell falling, which gave you time to get out of the way. I watched as two men scampered right and left and a mortar exploded right on the bags above where they'd stood. That section of the trench simply caved in. After a few long minutes the Germans gave up, satisfied they'd answered their foe. No one was killed on our side, not this time but the damage to the trench was significant and would have to be dealt with quickly. Observers reported that damage on the German trench was particularly bad and so both sides would no doubt spend the night dealing with their own repairs.

Over the next several nights every single patrol that was send out reported no contact with the enemy. Some men even took to hiding in wait for a German patrol but saw nothing. It appeared that the enemy was simply manning their trench line and doing nothing else.

On the evening of January 10, 1918, we were relieved and moved back behind the line to provide support for the 19th battalion again. The next day our Battalion Commander, Lieutenant Colonel George Murphy conducted a full inspection of arms and ammunition. The men were then able to take some respite at the baths again. We washed away our aches and pains and got to talking with a few others who'd been in France for the last two and a half years. Wal Grayson spoke first,

Bloody quiet, never seen it like this before." Wal joined up in 1916 and had seen a great deal of action, "I don't remember going ten days without some kind of contact on patrol. I tell ya; the Hun is planning something big!"

"Yup, no doubt about it," came the reply from Phil Edwards, another 1916 veteran.

"How can, you be sure?" I asked naively.

They both looked at me for a moment before Wal replied, "Because none of us are dead mate!" The few vets sitting around us laughed and so did Tom. I just smiled, accepting the jibe but I wanted to know what they though. When the laughter died, I tried again,

"What do you think they're up to then?"

Phil was quick to respond, "A big push in Spring for sure. They'll try and break through the line somewhere. They'll have studied the weak points and they'll concentrate on that."

"And where might that be," asked Tom who was now as keen as me to get some answers.

"Who can tell?" replied Phil, which wasn't reassuring. "It's odd that patrols are coming back empty. It can only mean they're behind their own lines training for something."

"And whatever they do, it'll be big. You don't want to be on the line when the hammer comes down!" added Wal.

"How big is big," I asked, feeling butterflies in my stomach.

"Could be a full commitment. They might throw everything they've got at us and try to end the war in one fell swoop. They haven't tried anything for a long time, so when they do it will be huge," explained Phil.

"Why can't we hit them first?" asked Tom.

The veterans laughed again but I didn't see the joke. Neither did Tom and Wal could tell,

"Jesus, you blokes are too green. The people running the war on this side couldn't agree on what colour blue is, let alone stage an advance on the Germans. Just look at the Somme, Passchendaele, and..."

"Gallipoli," added Phil.

"Everything they've made us do so far had been a disaster. Even when we get through, the losses are too high. The madness of it all astounds me. I'd rather defend the line than push forward any day!" said Wal.

Tom was now champing to find out more, "How can you be so very sure they'll attack?"

"Easy," said Wal, "They have to finish us off before the Yanks can get here."

"So, the question isn't whether or not they'll attack but when and where, right?" I asked.

"That about sizes it up," said Phil.

"So, where the weakest part of the line?" I added.

They laughed one more time and eyed each other knowingly, "They'll hit the Tommies!" said Wal.

"And we'll have to clean up the mess," suggested Phil.

We pondered that thought for a moment before another question came to mind,

"When's Spring?" I asked innocently.

Everyone roared with laughter and a voice chimed out, "When the bloody snow melts!" and the laughter reignited.

A few days after that B Company was sent to Fusilier Loop to provide trench support yet again. The continuous rotation of line duty seemed to be endless. For the next several weeks we worked on and off the line doing more digging, duck-boarding and sandbagging than we did fighting. It was grunt work, but it was better than the alternative. The cold seemed to burn through our uniforms with ease, and I found that I couldn't feel my feet or hands most of the time now. Men suffered through the cold with little complaint. It was just something we had to endure.

After a few more weeks the snow and ice, at last, began to melt. It was still cold, but the melt caused a new and more immediate problem...slush! To add to our woes, it started to drizzle and soon the entire front was a miserable quagmire yet again. Trenches were soon flooded and all hands were needed to deal with the problem. Most of B Company was sent forward to help with drainage. We soon discovered that the line had collapsed in several place in our sector alone. The work was hard and relentless, and the showers escalated into driving rain. The only saving grace was that the Germans too were dealing with the same situation, so no-one was thinking much about being attacked for the time being.

The only people who got out of trench duty were those on patrol. They concentrated on an area known as Moat Farm which was considered good ground for a German advance, but as was commonplace these days, no enemy was sighted. The rumours and speculation about a major German push became the most common topic amongst the men.

The drainage and clean-up of the trenches took us many days, and we were exhausted when the job was finally done. Our uniforms were sodden and filthy and we were frozen to the bone. When the end of January came, we were sent back in reserve again. A few days after that, lorries arrived and the entire battalion was transported to an area known as Lumbres, about seventeen miles west of Hazebrouck. We marched the last few miles to our billets and finally settled down around 9pm. The billets were in a frightful condition and the next morning we were again put to work getting them into a habitable state. Some of the men were sent to battalion HQ to arrange for food and materials and I was lucky enough to be part of the group. About a dozen of us set out on foot for Seninghem, a round trip of ten miles. We were most surprised to be walking past beautiful meadows and farms, virtually unscathed by the war. We'd spent so long amongst the obliteration of the front line that seeing grass was quite a treat.

We reached headquarters in good time, and the head of our group divided us in to working parties. My group oversaw finding building materials for the billets. It proved to be a very difficult task as there was a shortage of everything and the quartermaster wasn't in the mood to barter. We'd have to employ other means to get what we needed. We decided to break up and scout around in the hope that we might happen across some supplies. I wondered how any army could win a war if we couldn't even find a bag of nails. There were people everywhere, all looking busy and important.

As I rounded the corner of a farmhouse I stumbled across a man in a very smart uniform. I immediately recognised him as Lieutenant Colonel George Murphy, our commanding officer. He was sitting on a wooden milking stool and was trying to pull on a new pair of boots, with little success. Just then he looked up and called out,

"You son, give me a hand, will you?" he asked.

"Yes sir!" I replied.

He braced himself against the wheel of a lorry and I straddled his outstretched leg and pulled with as much force as I could muster. The boot simply wouldn't budge. After a few more attempts I took a breath and relaxed my efforts.

"I'm sorry sir, it won't fit." I suggested.

"Blast it!" he shrieked, "They're too bloody small!"

I couldn't help but be a little amused by the man's dilemma, given what we'd been enduring for the last month. He looked me up and down,

"Thank you private. I appreciate your help." He paused then asked, "What brings you to HQ?"

"Supplies sir, our billets are in pretty poor shape," I explained.

"I see, well let's see what can be done...ROBSON," he yelled.

With that another officer appeared, looking suitably unimpressed when he saw me,

"Yes commander?!" he enquired.

Lieutenant Colonel George Murphy pointed at me as he addressed the Adjutant, "Help this young man with whatever he needs!"

"Yes sir," came the snappy reply.

"And find me some more boots for God's sake," boomed the commander.

"Yes sir," said Robson again.

"Thank you, sir," I said.

He brushed off my thanks without another thought, "How long have you been over here Private?"

"About four months sir."

"What are the men talking about son?"

"They're expecting a big offensive from the Germans anytime soon sir."

George Murphy pondered for a moment, "I think they're right, but we'll be ready for whatever they do." He paused again before he added, "Good luck to you son and thank you again for trying to help."

"My pleasure sir."

With that I set off with the Adjutant, explaining our needs. He arranged everything without a hitch and a short time later I rolled up to the rest of my group with a lorry loaded to the gunnels.

"Well strike me," said the squad leader, "It's always the quiet ones!"

The truck was loaded with all the food and stores that the men had gathered and they climbed on board, finding a seat anywhere they could amongst the timber and boxes. I opened the door to step out but the squad leader stopped me, "Keep your seat, you earned it."

As we set off the driver offered me a cigarette. I'd taken quite a liking to the habit. It was something to do during the monotony of trench life, "Thanks" I said as he lit me up.

"The name's, Jim...Jim Long."

He was a lean man and looked rather weathered. His receding brown hair suggested he was in his late thirties, but who could tell. The war had a way of ageing people beyond their years. His handshake was very strong and his gnarly fingers gave away his blue collar working life.

"Stan, Stan Dunkley. You been here long?" I asked.

"Since 1916. I was on the docks before this as a driver and joined up when they called for more volunteers. I figured it would be nice to drive through the countryside instead of the streets of Sydney, but I didn't reckon on the mud!" he explained.

"I know what you mean. I had no idea what I was in for. I wanted to come but I didn't really think we'd be wading through slush most every day."

"That's why I got me a lorry Stan," said Jim.

I smiled at him, not convinced that his lot was much better than ours, "You must have been into a scrap or two Jim?"

"Yeah, I suppose so. When there's a big push on you know? But most of the time we're doing this and that...no worries at all really." He smiled broadly and I did the same.

I drew back on my cigarette, "I could get used to this. Only problem is I can't drive!" Jim laughed heartily.

"I'll teach you if you like? Next trip, OK?"

"Really, that would be terrific," I said, "Thanks."

We enjoyed each other's company while the lorry trundled across the pot holed road. When we got back to the billets we unloaded and everyone gathered for a decent meal, our first one in quite some time. We had a stew and even managed to enjoy some crusty bread. Jim was invited to stay, and we all had a good time swapping stories. It was a very good day indeed.

Soon after I shook Jim's hand and saw him on his way, "Don't forget you owe me a driving lesson."

"Don't you worry Stan, next trip for sure! I'll bring something extra to keep you warm if you like," and he winked cheekily.

He jumped back in his lorry, started the motor and waved as the machine jerked away. I waved and turned to re-join the other men. I'd take only a few steps when a whistle spilt the air. A second later the ground erupted behind me. I spun around to see the lorry hurled into the air amongst a plume of orange flame. I froze solid as I watched the horror unfold. The lorry literally came apart as the explosion tore through it. As the smoke and dust climbed up, pieces of lorry rained down in all directions. My senses finally clicked in, and I dived to the ground. I heard a big thud nearby and looked to see Jim's tortured and lifeless body crumple to the ground about twenty yards away. His right arm was gone and his uniform in tatters.

As the smoke cleared and the last few fragments of truck spattered on the ground I stood up. Men ran from everywhere but could do little. They gathered around Jim's body with someone simply saying, "Poor Jim!"

A stray shell most likely did the job, or it may have been one of those speculative shots the German's were known to take. Either way, their luck was Jim's undoing. We doused the flames quickly so as not to give away our position and arrange for Jim's body to be returned to HQ for burial. No-one could find his arm.

The other men quickly accepted Jim's fate but for me it was a bitter pill. Despite everything, to see a life extinguished so quickly and easily was shocking. Memories of my mother and sister flooded in. The joy of a new baby coming into the world snatched away at birth, both dying due to some complication that I didn't understand. I don't know why Jim's death opened such a painful memory. Maybe the fact that I'd connected with him on a personal level only to have him die like that. I pushed the sorrow down as far as I could and tried to get on with things. I joined up to escape a horrible home and because I saw it as my civic duty while most had joined up to be with their mates. I felt like a fool now. There was nothing civilised about this, nothing at all.

We got back to our routine quickly and took advantage of our free time. We played football, wrote letters, caught up on news and visited local villages. The locals sold their wares to the diggers who were always keen to spend their hard eared pay whenever they could get away from the drudgery of drill practice. All too often I found myself in hand to hand combat drills, learning how to deflect an attacking soldier and reply with the stock of my rifle. Even though I was on a Lewis gun crew, we were all expected to keep up with the latest techniques and tactics. Under the watchful eye of Sergeant Bill Hanson, I was put through my paces along with the rest of the platoon. The sergeant didn't like what he saw,

"Dunkley, what the hell do you call that? If you want to survive this war son, you'll have to do better...a lot better. Now let's try it again!" I stood my ground as Ces Davis charged. He was a big brute of a fellow and I had no doubt he was handpicked as my opponent for bayonet drill. I didn't stand a chance.

He ran towards me, screaming like a crazy man. I raised my Lee Enfield with its blunt, wooden blade attached. Ces pointed his straight at my chest. We met head on and while I did manage to deflect his rifle, I couldn't counter his momentum, and we both crashed to the ground. My rifle went flying and Ces recovered quickly enough to fain a thrust to my chest. There was a momentary pause before the Sergeant bellowed again,

"You're dead as a doornail Dunkley, get up and try again."

And so, it went on, time and again. My mates were faring better and after a while everyone stopped to watch. It was becoming comical and I was the brunt of many laughs. As much as I tried, I was outmatched. I thought I was following the textbook, but it didn't account for his bulk and strength.

After several more "deaths by Ces" the sergeant, in an act of either pity or desperation, called me aside,

"Look son, it's a question of balance. You're seeing him as too big and too strong, but that something you can turn into an advantage. Big men are easy to over balance, as long as you time it right."

I'd never seen the drill sergeant in such a mood. Hearing him talk rather than scream was odd and, as it turned out, made more sense to me than red faced screaming. He went on to explain some techniques he assured me would do the trick...

 "Right then, let's have you," he ordered and he slapped me on the back.

I readied myself and Ces began his charge.

"Come on Stan, you can take him," called Tom with a few positive comments from Bert and Dickie. Ces raise his rifle and ran head long towards me with his usual screaming crescendo. When he got within a few yards, I crouched. Ces was surprised and baulked slightly but adjusted quickly and went in for the kill...again. In the split second that followed I thrust my rifle up and under Ces's and drove up with my legs as hard as I could and just like a coat hanger tackle in rugby, Ces came down flat on his back. I stood over him with the point of my bayonet bearing down on Ces Davis' chest. My mates cheered and the sergeant was smiling,

"You're a dead man Davis, dead as a doornail!"

Ces was unimpressed but accepted my offer to help him up.

"Right," yelled the sergeant, "let's do it again!"

It went well for me after that. I still hated the bayonet, but I was gaining confidence. I'd shown some metal and was well pleased with my efforts.

Chapter 8

Operation Michael

Early February 1918 and our respite from winter was short lived. Snow covered everything again and we huddled around stoves and wrapped ourselves in anything we could find to try and stay warm. We were enjoying a rest behind the line and thought it might be a bit longer than usual with our commanding officer, George Murphy and other higher ranks on leave in Paris. We'd arranged intercompany football matches when we weren't doing drill or working on our musketry. It was a much better lot than being in the trenches. Still, the sounds from the front were a constant reminders of why we were there and the rumours of a German attack didn't abate. Those rumours were confirmed by a communiqué from HQ; *prepare for rapid movement of troops forward should the necessity arise.*

Despite our fears, the rest of the month proved uneventful much to our relief. Front line patrols were starting to prove fruitful with prisoners regularly being rounded up. That saw our relative calm short lived with many of the Germans suggesting that we would all soon be wiped out. They were cocky but mostly tight lipped, only hinting at what was to come. Most were sent back to HQ for interrogation, the results of which weren't made known to any of us.

We were soon on the move again for more training. This time we were taught the latest techniques in dealing with a gas attack and then put through our paces making a mock attack on a hill. The scenario was based on some of the more common problems faced during an advance. The battalion had no support with flanking soldiers pinned down by machine gun fire from positions on the hill ahead. Our objective was to advance on the strong points which were marked by smoke in this instance. Normally there'd be machine gun nests full of Germans and artillery raining down on the advancing troops. Attacking a pall of smoke seemed ridiculous to most of us and we joked about the whole affair.

Dickie and Bert were ordered to fire on the German strong points with the Lewis gun, allowing bombers to get in close and clear the positions for the advancing infantry. The advance went well, or at least the men thought so. Bert and his fellow gunners enfiladed the targets with precision while Dickie kept up the ammo. I watched the right flank and kept extra ammunition panniers handy. In the end the smoke didn't put up much of a fight. After the exercise the commanders weren't happy. Observers reported that rows of hedges had hampered the attack and caused the infantry advance to move obliquely making them much easier targets for the German machine gunners who were experts at using crossfire tactics. At parade later that day we got an ear full and then received the news we'd be back on the front line by March 4th. So much for our extended holiday!

A day later we were route marched to Lumbres Station again, entrained and dispatched to the Messines sector. We knew of the area which had been the subject of an incredible battle the previous June, while I was still training in England. The distant thunder I heard that night was the result of a detonation the likes of which had never been witnessed before. I was told that about ten thousand Germans died in the blink of an eye as underground mines wiped out the enemy position. I shuddered at the thought of such power.

B Company was initially put in reserve and thus began another round of front line rotation. Patrols resumed and we finally made contact with the enemy. On one occasion a bomb fight ensued. The Germans were quick to withdraw leaving three of their dead and one wounded. None of our men were injured. The wounded German prisoner was eager to goad us about the upcoming offensive, and it had the desired effect. There was no denying that something was afoot but where and when it might happen was unknown. I'm not sure the Germans we captured even knew the details themselves.

Trench mortar activity was continuous and aircraft from both sides were regularly overhead. German planes occasionally strafed our line and there was an escalation in artillery fire. Allied reconnaissance aircraft were spotted and added further to the speculation of a Spring Offensive with rumours of huge troop movements and new guns being transported from the eastern front. This pattern of events continued for two weeks.

As the weather improved, activity on the front became more intense. I helped Bert and Dickie as they took aim at German biplanes with our Lewis Gun. We fired off the occasional burst, but we had little luck. Others took pot shots with their rifles, but the planes were either too fast or too far away. Still, it did have the effect by keeping the Germans at a safer distance much of the time. At least that's what we hoped.

Our group was soon sent on patrol again. We were hoping to surprise the enemy and capture more prisoners. We were deep into no-man's land in a diamond formation. Those at the back of the group faced the rear in case of a German ambush. It gave us a good chance to look around the Messines sector. The enemy trenches were about a half mile away, on the other side of the River Lys. As was the norm, the area was pockmarked with deep artillery craters and littered with refuse. Every hole was full of water and tree stumps were the only signs of what was once a forest. Sticky mud was all we could see whenever the Germans lit up the night with their flares. Ghostly silhouettes danced across the ground as the light descended but I'd grown used to it now. The mortar and artillery fire was constant, but we weren't too worried as both sides were targetting each other's trenches. We crept parallel to the German line when a voice rang out, challenging us. It was German.

Within seconds Blue was shouting orders, and we tossed bombs towards the area where the voice came from. The Germans immediately replied with their stick grenades and a flurry of explosions blossomed all around us. There was much shouting and we exchanged rifle fire. I tossed a mills bomb as Bert fired a volley from the Lewis gun. Shadows moved about as a flare lit up the whole area. It worked against the Germans revealing about twenty soldiers spread out only forty yards away. It was an even match, but the Lewis gun gave us an advantage. The flare dimmed and Bert blazed away into the darkness. The Germans, realising they were outgunned made a hasty retreat. It was almost impossible to understand how no-one received so much as a scratch. My heart was pumping in the aftermath of the skirmish, and I felt a weird exhilaration in my body instead of fear. Blue sent a few men forward to scout for German wounded, but it appeared they too had escaped unscathed. Our patrol returned to the line to avoid being flanked and Blue reported the contact to our captain.

A few days later the 18th battalion was relieved and sent further behind the line for yet more training. This time the focus was on counter attacking and quick reloading techniques. Our platoon was then ordered to conduct another mock raid on German positions. We were to provide support on the right flank while the other platoons moved up to the designated jump off point, marked with knotted tape. Zero hour was set at 3.45am. Everyone was allocated mills bombs and I carried two bags of spare Lewis Gun ammo and a rifle. At 2.32am forward scouts reported that all was clear and ready. By 2.45 the raiding party had moved up and found the tape. Our orders were to seek out and destroy the German positions. The next hour dragged monotonously. Even thought it was a drill; I felt butterflies but for most of the others it was all a bit of a joke. Frank and Mick were close by with spare ammo and I spotted Tom further down the line. We lay prone on the jump off point, rifles slung.

At 3.45 sharp the attack began with a smoke barrage on the theoretical German positions. We stood and walked forward. I trailed just behind Bert and Dickie carrying the precious ammo. I felt more relaxed now that I was moving and soon joined in the jibes about the silliness of the mock attack. "Watch out Robbo, that stumps' got you in its sights!" I heard someone yell and everyone chuckled. Robbo shot the stump.

A creeping barrage moved forward fifty yards every minute and screened us from, so called enemy fire as we moved forward. After fifteen minutes of dodging fake shell holes and chasing smoke, we reached our objective. The exercise concluded and all agreed it was rather pointless.

We went back to camp for breakfast and a rest. It was now 4.40am on March 21st, 1918. Talk of fresh troops arriving from the United States was very reassuring. We learned they'd already mustered five divisions which were in France but only one was up to the task of manning the front line. According to some of the chaps, the Germans would have to act very soon.

Over the next few days rumours of a huge assault started filtering into our ranks. We heard all sorts of stories about breaks in the British line around Amiens and masses of German troops routing our allies to the south. We soon learned exactly what was going on when we were mustered for parade. Our commander, George Murphy was back from Paris and addressed the men,

"Good morning gentlemen. Our suspicions have been confirmed. Early on the morning of March 21st the Germans attacked and broken through over a wide front. It also appears that they've been reinforced with men and equipment from the Russian front. They have achieved total surprise."

I realised that the exact moment we'd come off the training exercise was when the German offensive had begun. We'd been expecting this news, that was true, but as I looked around everyone appeared to be in shock. The commander continued to explain the situation.

"Their target, from all reports, appears to be Amiens. If they succeed, they'll quickly take the channel ports and starve us of supplies. In short, we will have lost the war *if* they get through. For the first time since the war began, we are outnumbered and out gunned. It also appears they've developed a new tactic. The Brits say that the German forward troops are lightly equipped and are moving fast, avoiding the heavily defended areas, leaving them to those behind. These storm troopers have swept forward sixty miles in only a few days."

The commander paused allowing us to take in the news. There were no flippant remarks, no smiles and a general feeling of foreboding,

"Men, the war will be won or lost on the events of the next few days and weeks. The Australian 3rd and 4th Divisions have been rallied and are already moving to intercept. The 2nd Division will dump nonessentials and go mobile immediately. We take over the line at Messines tonight. Thank you, men, dismissed!"

We were not to intercept the Germans. To me that was good news. We didn't waste any time and followed our orders expediently and replaced the 31st battalion on the line. The weather was fine and clear as we settled in. I was on watch with Bert ready with the Lewis Gun. We were much more alert given the news of the German advance.

"What do you make of it Stan?" he asked me.

"Sounds like some of the vets we spoke to were right. The Tommies were caught cold. It's grim from the sound of things."

Bert offered his customary response, "Yep."

Dickie joined us having overheard the conversation,

"I hear the Germans have sixty divisions!" he offered.

"I don't want to think about it," I replied and Bert just grunted.

The Messines sector wasn't quiet by any means. We were told the Germans were turning our own tactics on us with regular raids on the line. Patrols were challenged regularly and skirmishes were common.

The area was in a dreadful state after months of relentless bombardment and conditions were harsh. Heavy shelling every night made sleep impossible and by day men snatched naps whenever they could, me included.

On our second night the Germans sent up a strong raiding party. They were intercepted in no-man's land resulting in some heavy fighting. They were eventually beaten back and again we suffered no casualties. The next night they tried again and this time they made it to our forward trench line. Our posts raised the alarm, and we raked the area with gun fire. I emptied my rifle several times while Bert sprayed the enemy with the Lewis gun. Everyone who was able let fly at the Germans and they were eventually repelled. The next day they tried yet again were easily pushed back.

Another day passed and the weather turned bad. Rain began to fall and I wasn't unhappy to see it, hoping it might quell the Germans for a while. It rained for three solid days turning our trench into mush. Conditions were simply horrible, but the rain indeed did keep the Germans quiet.

On March 31st we were relieved, giving the line to the 10th Worcesters. We were ordered to head south and take up positions in the reserve line to protect a town called Villers Bretonneux. It was a vital position in defending the rail hub at Amiens and we knew the Germans wanted to take the ground.

Hill 104, just to the north of the town was also a key position. If the Germans won it from us, they wouldn't need to take Amiens. They could simply shell it into dust.

After being briefed on the German advance buses took us south to Caestre and we marched from there to Westhoek and rested for the night. Next day we marched to Godewaesvelde where we caught a troop train. It took us through Boulogne and on to Abberville then Roch. On foot again we marched through Amiens. The scene was vastly different to the one I'd observed months before. The city was crammed with refugees carry nothing more than what they wore. They cheered as we came into view but there was no time to rest. We route marched six miles east of the city and were ordered to round up any English soldiers who were retreating from the German advance. We didn't have to look far to find them, and they were only too happy to warn us of the coming wave. No-one could tell us exactly where the Germans would come from, but the hasty retreat suggested they were indeed close.

Artillery could be heard some miles ahead as we finally got a chance to rest. Day turned into night and with that came a strained silence. After a few hours we were marching again, closer to Villers Brett and seven miles closer to the enemy. We didn't have long to wait before things went awry.

Snipers were taking shots at anyone who moved with several men hit; we didn't have any cover. Australian artillery arrived next morning and started bombarding German positions. The enemy retaliated and both sides spend most of that day trading shells while we cowered within our inadequate holes. The noise was simply horrible and strained nerves of every man in the line.

Then, the German infantry attacked in force. Their barrage was concentrated on our line hitting the left flank very hard. German infantry swept into view as the artillery lifted and they were coming on fast. They took on one of our forward posts where a bomb fight broke out. Our men held their own until they were enfiladed by machine gun fire, forcing them to give up the ground. The Germans moved on with haste, using the same tactics that had been so devastating against the British 3rd and 5th Armies. Hundreds of Germans reached our line and tried to break through.

"God almighty!" someone shouted as the Lewis and Vickers gunners took a heavy toll on the Germans. Bert unloaded six hundred rounds in no time and the other machine gunners did the same. The crossfire was devastating and the Germans fell, dozens at a time. I could hear them screaming and saw others caught up in our newly laid wire, some in agony and others dead.

We moved from one hole to another to confuse the enemy as they advanced. It was then I noticed one of them with a strange looking apparatus on his back attached to a hose. A flame flickered from the tip of a long tube attachment. I thumped Bert's shoulder and pointed at the German as the flame thrower spat at our line. The horror was indescribable. I watched as one of our own men was enveloped in flame. His screams were hideous and seemed to last for an eternity until someone put him down. I don't know if it was a German or one of our men, but he was better off. Bert swung the Lewis gun around and squeezed off a volley. Bullets spattered into the German's backpack and about a second later his canister erupted in a small mushroom plume burning the man alive, along with two of his comrades.

"Three for the price of one," said Bert without batting an eyelid while he continued to enfilade the advancing troops.

Despite the horrific losses, the Germans kept on coming. Wave after wave threw themselves at our line. They kept probing for weak points but there were none. The success of their advance in recent days must have given them a false sense of security. It seemed to me that they expected to roll over us with ease given their tactics. And still they came, thrusting forward, probing and even crawling forward but they were shot down every time.

As the battle raged, I watched for more targets and kept Bert's supply of ammo up. Everywhere I looked I could see German infantry pushing forward. They were relentless and determined and if they broke the line and exposed our flanks we would be in dire trouble. The noise and the choking smoke made it more difficult to see what was going on. We simply had to rely on each other to hold our respective sectors along the line.

When one onslaught was repelled another soon followed. The Germans came on in regular waves and got close to use on several occasions. I could see their faces as they tried to break through our wire but every time, they came upon us we sent them scurrying with lethal doses of machine gun fire. The initial terror of facing the attack had been replaced by something else. Everyone was focussed on the job at hand with little time to think about much more. There were moments of anxiety when the Germans pressed at us, but I wasn't thinking about getting shot or bayoneted, just doing my job. There was no panic on our side and certainly no sign that we were faltering.

The German attack was repelled repeatedly and after a while it looked like the waves of men we'd faced initially had been reduced to a few small groups here and there. After a few hours the attack collapsed and the enemy stopped coming, at least for the time being. Dozens of German dead littered the battlefield, so we sent out a patrol to search for papers or maps and identity tags. Any information would be useful. The patrol came back with little more than a mouser rifle. Our mortar batteries sent over some gas shells to keep the Germans busy, and you could have cut the tension with a knife as we waited for their response.

Just then Tom came by. I was glad to see that he'd come through unscathed.

"What now boys," he asked.

"Just waiting for something interesting to happen," said Bert making Tom smile.

"They won't wanna come back or they'll get more of the same," suggested Dickie.

"Right" said Tom with a smirk, "Keep it together you blokes." He gave me a wink and a slap on the back before he moved off.

The rest of the night and most of the next day were uneventful. None of us had managed any sleep after the onslaught and struggled to catch any while our artillery hammered the German line to great effect.

Our CO was called away to headquarters for a briefing and left us with strict orders to hold the line at all costs. Fatigue parties had managed to lay more wire during the night, and it was just as well. At 1am the Germans attacked again. This time they targetted the centre of our line with gas and some heavies. Bert kept an eye on his sights while Dickie readied the ammo drums. I, as usual, scanned a wider area under the light of flares. Within a few moments the Germans appeared, about twenty five of them. They got to the Australian wire and began cutting. I aimed my rifle at them just as Bert opened up the Lewis gun. A fusillade of bullets hit the group and the man I was aiming at falling. I'm sure I hit him, my first confirmed kill. Guns were firing from all parts of our line now; Vickers and Lewis guns, Enfield rifles, pistols, mills bombs and mortars. The Germans were torn to ribbons before they could breach our barrier and those that could, ran back into the distance carrying their wounded. We fired until they were out of sight.

"Take that you bastards!" someone shouted.

They didn't come back again that night or the next.

We continued to send out patrols, sometimes making contact and getting into a scrap but after several days it appeared the German offensive was faltering. We took prisoners who were tired and hungry and seemed to have spent more effort looting French villages than fighting. Many carried or wore stolen clothing under their uniforms. It was a pitiful sight indeed.

We were eventually relieved and sent back into a reserve position, giving the line to the 3rd Division. We'd been fighting off the Germans in one way or another for almost three weeks now and we too were exhausted. The German advance had finally petered into another stalemate with bombardments and skirmishes the order of the day along the entire front. The Germans had been stopped only yards short of Villers Bretonneux. After a short time in reserve, we were ordered to move forward again. The news wasn't at all welcome and we grudgingly worked our way back through the maze of trenches and took up our positions from the 3rd Division men. Just for once the jibes were few and those that did come were mostly ignored. None of us were keen for another German onslaught. We were told there was a strong chance the Germans would be attacking again and the artillery that came down on us certainly added to our concerns.

The skies above us were very active too. I watched several dog fights between allied and enemy aircraft and saw a German plane crash into a field near our position. No-one emerged from the wreckage.

There was much confusion along the front line since the German advance; things had changed dramatically in a short time, something no-one was accustomed to. Then something curious happened. We were watching over no-man's land when a lone German soldier appeared. He was close to one of our forward observations posts and certainly appeared to in good health.

"This joker's lost," suggested Mick.

His actions caught the attention of almost everyone in the trench line. Hundreds of eyes were upon him and yet he seemed totally oblivious to our presence. Most of us were amused by his meandering until the spell was broken,

"Oi! Hand hoc Jerry!" someone shouted.

I'm certain the man would have stumbled right into our wire, or a trench had we not caught his attention. Realising his mistake the soldier panicked and chose to turn and run. He was shot dead after a few paces. I couldn't help but feel a twinge of regret but it soon passed.

A few days after the latest German attack was repelled, they managed to deal us a savage blow when they shelled Allonville and destroyed the battalion kitchen. For some it was a blessing but living off dry rations soon had them whining again!

On Aprils 6th we entered Villers Bretonneux. It was in a dreadful state with debris littering every street, buildings shattered and roads ripped up by artillery. The shops and houses had been looted of food and wine while dead horses and other livestock lay everywhere, unable to escape the German bombardment, which hadn't yet abated.

Our snipers were taking pot shots at the enemy for a change as we pressed forward, meeting up with a French contingent on the right flank. We settled into a new position just east of Villers Brett. The line was nothing more than a series of scrapes and potholes, so we spent much of the time improving our cover. It was an otherwise uneventful stay.

At 2am on April 8th we were moved again, this time to Gentelles where we finally had access to good lodgings and were looking forward to our first decent sleep in many days...but our respite was short lived. The Germans started to bombard the village giving us no choice but to find cover anywhere we could. They'd found the range and rained terror down on us to devastating effect. Most of the buildings we'd been using were turned to splinters as we huddled in shell holes hoping our luck would hold.

Smoke and flame erupted all around us and men could be heard shouting for assistance. After one sickening explosion the shouting turned to screams of anguish and pain.

I turned to Tom and shouted,

"I can't take much more of this!"

"Neither can I," replied Tom, "It's like Passchendaele."

The old crater we were in would keep us safe from everything but a direct hit, but it did nothing to stop the continuous explosions from ripping into every nerve. The shells fell like rain at times and forced me to curl up into a small ball while I pulled down on my helmet. We were continually showered in clods of dirt, and the ground shook every time a shell erupted.

Suddenly there was a lull, the shelling had stopped. The silence seemed strange after the relentless bombardment. My ears were ringing as I shook off the dirt and looked over at Tom. He too was brushing himself off and smiled when I caught his eye. He then poked his head out of our hole to survey the damage. At that very moment there was a loud crack as a shell tore into the ground right in front of our hole. Flame and smoke engulfed the ground all around us and I could feel the heat wash over me just as the ground caved in, half burying me where I sat. The spatter of shrapnel was very close, and I was again forced to cower under my useless helmet.

"Jesus Christ, give us a break," screamed Mick as the dust of one last shell cleared away, one final shot to make a point it seemed.

I extracted myself from the dirt that had fallen upon me and called to Tom,

"By gee that was close eh Tom?"

He didn't answer. I looked across and saw that he was lying face down in the dirt, his helmet missing and his body convulsing.

"Tom?" I called again.

I wriggled over to where he was as the fits subsided. I got to him first and rolled him over as others rushed to his aid.

His face was a mash of dirt and blood, and his left eye was missing. A piece of shrapnel had blown it out as the metal fragment smashed into his brain. His shirt too had been blown to shreds and his face and scalp looked like they'd been taken to by a butcher's knife. Blood oozed from his eye socket as I cradled him in my arms.

Everyone was in stunned silence as we looked down at our friend.

"MEDIC!!" cried Dickie, "MEDIC!!"

"Oh God," said Mick, "Tom, wake up mate...TOM!"

But I knew my friend was dead.

I felt the overwhelming need to cry out but fought it off as I held Tom close. Even when the medics arrived, I couldn't let him go. Frank, Mick and Bert had to tear me away and it was only then that I screamed in anguish. He was more than a mate and watched out for me like a father. I felt a deep hopelessness overwhelm me as the medics stretchered him away.

Our luck had finally run out with five killed and twenty six wounded. Tom's body was transported behind the line along with the other dead and buried in nearby graves. There wasn't time for a proper service, so we held our own in camp. That was the way of the war.

As miserable as I felt, there was a compulsion to write to Tom's wife,

Dear Mrs. Bower,

I wish to send my deepest condolences to you upon the loss of your husband Tom. He and I joined up on the same day in Sydney and quickly became close friends. He was a very good soldier and very much liked and respected by all of us. His loss has left us with great sorrow.

I was with him when he died. A German shell burst near our position in the village of Gentelles. Tom was hit by shrapnel and died instantly. Rest assured he did not suffer.

The spoke of you often and missed you terribly. I cannot offer any words that will lessen your pain. Just know that he was amongst friends at the end.

Yours sincerely,

Pvt Stanley Dunkley

A tear trickled down my cheek as I put the letter with the outgoing mail. I felt more alone now than ever before in my life.

Chapter 9

Attack and Counterattack

We soon learned that the enemy had opened another attack to our north in the Passchendaele sector. They again charged for the channel ports hoping to choke off our supplies. We were reminded that if they were to succeed, we would most certainly lose the war. Belgium would be cut off, and the allies would be left in no position to fight back. The Germans had very cleverly chosen to attack Portuguese positions and rolled over them with ease. We didn't have much time for the Portuguese on the occasions we ran across them. They seemed inept at best and now they proved to be just that.

But it wasn't all bad news; the British had managed to hold up the advance just to the south of Passchendaele and fighting was now concentrated on the village of Hangard, which the Germans now held about a mile to our south-east. The success of both the Germans and the British had created a huge bulge in the line.

Next day we heard that the Germans had taken the high ground back at Messines Ridge where so many of our blokes had fought and died. It was a very bitter pill to swallow after the success of the Australian attack there only six months earlier. The Germans were making inroads again and the threat of another major breakthrough loomed.

A message arrived from the Supreme Commander of the Allied Forces, Field Marshall Douglas Haig,

"Fight to the end!"

Haig wasn't much respected by an of us and Bert sized up our feelings, "His precious cavalry can't fix this one!" We all found great humour in the remark. It was well known that Douglas Haig thought honour and cavalry would win the war. Unfortunately, machine guns aren't scared of a brave man on a horse.

The 2nd Division was mobilised quickly, and we soon learned we were to attack the Germans at Hangard Wood. We were to secure the eastern sector while the French were charged with attacking the village cemetery. The enemy had dug in and looked set to stay put.

Plans were hastily laid down and the 19th and 20th battalions ordered to make the first attack immediately. None of us knew the ground and there was little information passed on when we were briefed. Enemy numbers were unknown. The attacking battalions were soon on the advance and were able to gain their objectives but couldn't dig in and quickly withdrew. With the retreat of the 19th and 20th we were sent forward. Our role was the make a push to the right of the wood, a feint aimed at drawing the German's attention while French and British units broke the Germans on our left.

We moved forward and were faced with total confusion. French and English soldiers were mixed in with our own units, and no-one seemed to know what to do. We shared our position with French troops, but the language barrier proved to be a major problem. We had no idea what they wanted of us and frustration soon devolved into anger.

Mick tried to break the ice with a greeting,

"Bons hello!"

It was somewhat successful with a French soldier smiling back at us but then he blurted out a string of words we didn't understand which was followed by an awkward silence.

"Tres beauty cobber," Mick spluttered, giving the fellow a thumbs up.

Despite the circumstances it caused a ripple of laughter. Even Bert expelled a small chuckle.
We were barely settled when our plans changed. Most of the English divisions were ordered to withdraw and made a hasty exit, sent north to deal with another threat from the Germans. That left just us and the French and a handful of English to make the attack. It was decided that the battalion should focus on a small section of the woodland near Hangard Cemetery itself and advance about sixty yards beyond it where the Germans were believed to be holed up. We would have to cross about four hundred yards of open ground before meeting the enemy. The French and some members of the 10th Essex Regiment would attack the cemetery itself. All the men were allocated two hundred rounds of ammunition and ordered to fix bayonets. I took some mills bombs and put them in my pockets and carried some extra Lewis gun panniers. Mick, Frank and Dickie also carried ammo for Bert.

It was impossible to ignore the French who appeared to be in disarray. I worried that if they failed to our left we'd be flanked by the Germans, but before anything could be said the attack was postponed. We remained in our position for the rest of the day while the Germans bombarded us with seventy-seven millimeter canon as well as 4.2 and 5.9 howitzers. That night it rained and soaked us through. We were freezing and couldn't sleep at all.

The next day things were quiet, and we continued to prepare for the attack. But again, we were held back and ended up spending the entire day in limbo. That night scouts were sent forward to establish three strong points for the attack. Once they were in place they signalled their success with flares. Another more strategic post was ordered but the ground proved too hostile and they withdrew. It was decided that the post would be established as part of the main attack instead. We were advised that each platoon would act independently instead of the more traditional wide scale attack formation.

At 3am the attack finally began. It took the form of two waves, the first aimed at taking out the German trench and the second ordered to clear the ground sixty yards beyond the trench line. Mortar and Artillery fire started hammering the German positions and continued for seventy minutes. After ten minutes platoons from B Company started moving forward. We were to take centre position and moved forward cautiously.

Hangard Wood was little more than a huge grove of saplings, most barely six feet high. The terrain was rough with small clearings and hills falling off the spur of a larger mount. Cover was minimal or non-existent. Air reconnaissance had provided information about the battlefield that was given to HQ who then translated it onto maps for the attack. We soon realised that the information was inaccurate.

A Company, now under the temporary command of Joe Maxwell took the right with D Company to our left. I could see a shower of flares lighting up the sky, but I couldn't tell if they were ours or the enemies'. We moved forward, pressing through a hedge line. Almost immediately German machine gun fire opened on us...tat tat tat tat tat!

We all instinctively dropped to the ground, but the cover was useless. Bert took aim with his machine gun, targetting the muzzle flashes. He squeezed off and entire magazine in a few second. Dickie replaced the pannier and Bert fired again. I could hear bullets sizzling just over my head and held my rifle tightly in one hand and the spare ammo in the other. I was scanning for movement and didn't have to wait long. In the darkness I saw soldiers to our right, but I couldn't tell if they were friend or foe. I called out,

"Australian?"

There was no answer. I fired a shot as they ran away from us. Bert swung the Lewis gun around and reeled off a burst. I saw two of the men fall.

"Good job Stan," said Bert, "Keep your eyes on em."

I felt a chill as a realised how close the enemy was to us. Bert trained his gun back towards the German Maxim, but it had stopped firing for the moment. A few of our men were wounded but there was little we could do. They'd soon be picked up by stretcher bearers in any case. Frank and Mick were blasting away with their rifles, but targets were difficult to pinpoint.

After a few more minutes the enemy fire evaporated and we were ordered to move forward again. We stood and pressed on.

"How much ammo have we got Stan? Dickie enquired.

"We're ok for now," I told him

"I hope so," said Bert. He'd used quite a large quantity of bullets to silence that one maxim and even now we weren't sure if he'd had any success.

We got the answer a few seconds later when fierce defensive fire opened up, slowing our advance yet again. It went on like this for a while; each platoon would press on only to be halted. We tried to move up in sections to confuse the enemy but every time we did there was a fusillade of bullets to meet us. The Germans were tactically withdrawing and only had to slow us down, which they were doing effectively.

By 4.30am the sun began to rise which improved visibility. I could now see about fifty or sixty yards ahead and scanned for enemy movement. Our artillery was falling behind the German line and doing very little to hamper their gunners. We were holding position in the tree line when the Lewis and Vickers guns were ordered to lay fire into a gully just ahead. They fired relentlessly for fifteen minutes, and we had our work cut out keeping up the ammunition.

"Jesus, have we got enough ammo"? screamed Dickie.

I checked the bags,

"We should be right," I told him, but I was only guessing.

Bert blasted the enemy position along with the other machine gunners. Thousands of bullets smashed into sandbags, trees and anything else between us and the Germans. It was like watching a giant slasher with everything two feet above the ground pulverised. And the noise! I swear my head was going to burst and I covered my ears at every opportunity but that just made it seem all the louder whenever I had to do something else. I gave up trying to protect my ear drums after a few minutes. The Germans were quick to reply to our onslaught. They had the better ground and managed to wound quite a few of our men.

As the minutes passed the morning twilight revealed the enemy position. There were dozens of Mauser rifles and Maxim machine guns firing on our position, but we held our ground. Bert was focussed on the enemy machine guns, trying to get a shot through the defenses which were doing their job too well for our liking.

Smoke and dust filled the air, constantly blotting our targets. It looked like a brown fog. The Germans too were finding it difficult to see, which probably saved many lives on our side. A battalion sniper, Joe Ryan was crawling forward of another Lewis Gun crew. They literally fired over the top of him as he took up a position that would give him a clean shot. He found a tree stump and settled quickly, squeezing off his first .303 bullet. I watched a German machine gunner flop back and disappear. The gun fell silent for a moment but was quickly taken over by another who opened up on Joe's tree stump. Bullets pulverised the charred wood, but Joe just curled up behind the cover and waited for the volley to stop. When it did, Joe cocked his rifle and calm as you like, aimed, squeezed and "thwack", down went another gunner.

Word came through that the right flank was stuck and that A Company had somehow been surrounded. More enemy troops arrived, many more than we had been expecting to face, which added greatly to the task. I realised my estimation of our ammunition supply had been way off. We were down to our last bag of magazines. I threw them to Dickie,

"That's the last one Dickie...there's no more."

"Christ where are the ammo carriers?" he screamed.

Our situation was starting to look dire. Low on ammo and pinned down with the enemy bringing up reinforcements. Forward movement was the last thing on our minds now and getting out of it unscathed was starting to look very unlikely.

Realising our situation, we decided it would be best to conserve the remainder of our ammunition, and we reverted to occasional bursts so the Germans would, hopefully, think we were still able to fend them off if they decided to counterattack.

We all took turns peeling of a few shots here and there to keep the Germans at bay. I fired off a volley of shots at nothing in particular. It was all about self-preservation now. As I reloaded a few German bullets screamed just over my head and careened into the skeletal remains of the woodland we occupied.

Our situation was really starting to deteriorate when men started to report they were out of ammunition. They were ordered to fix bayonets and stay put.

The Hangard Wood Offensive had stalled and our situation was dire. Reports spread along the line, the French too had failed to take the cemetery copse but before the news could sink our spirits further, we heard that D Company had breached the German line. We all cheered, loud enough for the Germans to hear!

More good fortune lifted us as the artillery corrected itself and started pounding the German line. The enemy fire dimmed significantly but we were still in a critical situation. Bert called me over,

"Go find Blue, tell him what's happening."

He didn't need to explain, and I was off in a shot, scrambling along the line behind rows of men. I spotted Blue stooped over a useless map,

"Blue!" I yelled

He looked up,

"What is it now!?" he said with exasperation.

"We're almost out of ammo and the Germans have reinforced their position. It's not looking good!"

"Shit! That's all we need. D Company just got tossed out and A Company is in big trouble. OK that seals it. Captain Cadle told me to call it off if we reached a point where the attack couldn't succeed. From what you're saying, we're buggered."

"That's about right," I replied.

"OK, Pass the word, we retreat, we're giving up this fight! I'll get word to Cadle, and he'll get the artillery boys to give the Germans a thorough going over so we can all move. Understand?"

"Yes Blue!"

"Right then, go and pass the word. Withdraw as soon as the shelling starts to increase."

I worked my way back along the line telling everyone we were to pull back as soon as the opportunity arose. We'd have to wait until the barrage came down. It would continue for as long as it took for stretcher bearers to get in and out with the wounded.

We waited for an eternity, taking fire from the enemy and only being able to reply with occasional bursts. Finally, the shelling on the German line doubled, then tripled and we took full advantage as the enemy gunners went to ground.

We worked our way back, through the smashed woodland, carry some of our wounded, leaving the severe cases for the medics. By the time we go back to our rally point it was 7am. A Company has somehow fought its way out of a sunken road where they'd been surrounded but reported several men missing, presumed dead.

By 3pm, twelve hours after the attack began the 20th battalion arrived to relieve us. It was only when I sat to rest that I realised I still had all my grenades, having totally forgotten about them.

In the aftermath of the battle, we learned that the ammunition carriers had become lost and blundered into German lines. When they were fired upon, they dropped everything and ran. That left us in a critical situation and the attack failed.

I'm not so sure it would have succeeded even if we did get fresh ammo, The German fire was dreadfully heavy, and I didn't imagine that too many of us would have survived an advance under those circumstances.

In the end the commanders blamed poor intelligence, failure to resupply and the German defensive strength for our failure. It didn't make any of us feel better. The most critical issue turned out to be our Company's failure to establish a fourth forward post. That led to A Company being flanked and cut off, suffering multiple casualties.

Our Captain and the other officers met with the Battalion Commander, George Murphy who was scathing in his criticism. It was concluded that if the fourth post had been established as ordered the German counterattack would probably have been stopped in the Cemetery copse. Losses amounted to eight dead, forty two wounded and thirty four missing. We got off lightly it seemed.

The attack, while technically a failure, wasn't a total waste though. Reports suggested that at least sixty four Germans had been killed in one sector and seventy four in another. Two enemy machine guns had been captured as well as scores of prisoners.

Even so it was our first failure as a battalion on the Western Front and the thought didn't sit well with any of us. We retired to the reserve line a few hours later and were then sent back to our bivouacs in Gentelles. As we made our way in silence a single German shell landed close to the transport column. The horses bolted and we had to chase them down. A bit more salt to rub into our wounds.

Gentelles was about halfway between Hangard and Amiens and was still well within the range of German guns. We'd barely settled down when a bombardment started, again reminding me of Tom's recent demise. Shells ripped into the remains of houses and shops, barely rubble by now but the Germans knew what they were doing, and they were twisting the knife into the Australian 2nd Division. We were immediately ordered out of the town and ran without hesitation leaving most of our belongings. The ground erupted all around as I sprinted past many others running to get clear. Brickwork was pulverised, glass shattered shells dug huge rifts into the roads. A few of us got well clear of the town ahead of the main body of men. It seemed there was an advantage to being so young...we had speed. Several of our men weren't so lucky, killed or wounded when they got caught up in the shelling. We couldn't do anything but wait until the Germans ceased fire, which they did an hour later. We went back into the town and buried the dead.

Sometime after we finally managed to get some sleep, but it wasn't restful. I, like many, had been awake for an interminable period under heavy fire. My nerves were stretched to breaking point and my body responded fitfully as I dozed.

Next morning we gathered up our equipment and had some breakfast. A runner came by giving us news that the German Offensive on Lys has been stopped in the north and the Channel Ports has once again been saved. Speculation continued about where the Germans might try to break through next, but I really didn't care. I was tired, filthy and ached all over. We'd deal with the Germans when the time came.

The 18th Battalion moved again, this time to Montingny where we acted as regular reserves. We moved again soon after to the Baizieux sector where we took up front line duties again. We were about six miles west of German occupied Albert.

On April 24th a message from Brigade Headquarters delivered the news the Villers Bretonneux had once again fallen to the Germans. It was another bitter pill to swallow after Australian units had cleared and held the town a month ago. On April 25th, Australians took the town back again. It seemed only fitting.

Two days later we were on the move again, this time to Warloy. It was only a mile away, to the north and many of us were under the impression that there were no plans to take us out of this region anytime soon. We remained there for the next two weeks getting as much rest as we could.

May 7th, the Germans were again shelling Amiens. We could hear the barrage and wondered if we'd be called into the fray. We didn't have long to wait, and we sent back to the line at Hailly with haste.

There was no time to be discreet, and we made the move in broad daylight. During the switch with the 25th Battalion, Captain Cadle ordered a platoon to go over the top instead of following the trenches. With the Germans only a few hundred yards away, Joe Maxell tried to talk him out of it, but he wouldn't relent. Joe eventually agreed and they climbed onto open ground in full view of the enemy. A firestorm of bullets immediately erupted as the Australians rushed for their trench. A few men were wounded, all but one making it to the trench line. Captain Cadle didn't live to regret his decision. Our company CO was dead.

The men felt terribly low as the news of Captain Cadle filtered through the ranks. No-one really understood what he was thinking. His attempts to be expedient were too costly. His body was retrieved and sent away for burial.

Our new trenches were in a terrible state and very muddy. The position was under constant shell fire, and the two sides sniped each other day and night. I helped with trench improvements, a filthy but necessary job. Morale was very low among the battalion, me included and it forced my thoughts back to Tom. I missed my mate terribly but had turned my emotional loss into something I could use...anger.

Mick and Frank were also channelling their emotions in a similar way. It seemed the only way to cope. None of us was ever taught how to deal with the horrors we faced so we just carried on as best we could. There'd be time to mourn when the war was over perhaps, if we survived.

Back on the front line we did our best to improve the state of the trenches, which were quite dilapidated. There was light shelling and machine gun fire from the German line, and we decided to respond by calling for an artillery barrage on our sector. Someone suggested that the Germans might take advantage and launch an assault after the barrage, and it was decided that the forward posts be reoccupied as soon as the artillery stopped.

The barrage was short but fierce. It was aimed at giving the Germans a shake down and put their snipers and machine gunners to bed, but as soon as the shelling stopped the Germans mustered for a counterattack. Around one hundred and fifty enemy soldiers were seen massing behind their own line. Within minutes they were advancing on our position. We let fly with Lewis guns and rifles. One group got to the wire, and I pointed it out to Bert. He enfiladed their position and the entire group fell. Others came, trying to breach our line only to be shot down. Another small group had broken off from the main attack and managed to work its way across the immediate front. They'd reached the wire and got through before I noticed them. They were intent on silencing the Lewis Gun. I raised my rifle and fire off a shot. One of the group crumpled and fell to the ground. Other rifles let loose on the men and two more Germans fell. Another managed to throw a stick bomb but was too far away to make the distance. The bomb exploded harmlessly, showing us in mud. Bert had swung the machine gun on the remaining members of the group and reeled off a few bursts when the gun fell silent.

"It's blood jammed," he shouted.

A single German, realising his luck, wheeled around and charged. He fired a shot which sizzled past me, grazing my tunic sleeve and sucking into a sandbag at the back of the trench.

Dickie fumbled with an ammo pannier as Bert worked on the jam. The German kept coming as I turned my rifle towards him. I squeezed on the trigger, hitting the man in the stomach. He loped a few more paces and collapsed into the trench right next to me. Blood was seeping into his uniform, and he struggled in the mud like a fish on a riverbank.

He looked up at me as I trained my rifle upon him once again. He'd lost his own in the fall and started groping around for something. I realised he had a stick bomb in his belt, and he was trying to work it loose!

"Don't do it Fritz!" I demanded but he didn't seem to understand or just ignored me.

He gripped the grenade and it popped loosed of the leather belt.

"For God's sake stop!" I yelled.

"Shoot the bastard Stan!" cried Dickie.

I looked at the German's face as he did mine. His ashen skin was draining of life, but he still managed to raise his other hand to arm the device.

I shot him in the head!

He stopped squirming and slumped to the floor of the trench, the bomb falling from his hand and sticking in the mud. Blood oozed from his forehead and a whiff of smoke trailed from the barrel of my gun.

I finally broke my gaze away from the man and spun around to see the rest of the Germans running off in the distance. I looked at Bert,

"Sorry Bert, I didn't see them coming. It won't happen again."

"That's OK Stan, you got him. No harm done."

I let out a sigh and Bert gave me a reassuring slap on the back.

"Easier when they're a long way off eh Stan?" suggested Frank.

"Yeah!" I replied and I knew he wasn't being critical for once.

I'd never killed anyone at close quarter before. I'd always believed in preserving life. As a child I'd try not to step on so much as an ant or I'd catch a moth in the house only to release it outside. What strange thoughts to have after killing a man.

"Mate don't let it get to ya. We'd be dead if you hadn't finished him off," said Bert.

But I wasn't feeling upset; I wasn't feeling anything much at all. I acknowledge Bert's remarks and smile but then my hands started shaking and there was a fluttering in my stomach as the events of the last few moments caught up with me. It was something I'd seen often after heavy engagements. Men vomited or shook uncontrollably, some even fainting but I didn't have time to think about it.

"HEADS UP!" shouted Blue.

The enemy was already sending a second wave, and we dealt with them just as savagely as we did the first. They kept on coming but their formations were breaking down with every attempt. Finally, they were only able to attack in small, disorganised groups and eventually made a full retreat. It seemed a dreadful waste of life.

The Germans had thrown themselves at our machine guns and I wondered how they thought to win against such odds. Perhaps they were given no choice. It was simply horrible to witness.

While we'd exacted a heavy toll on the enemy our own 17th battalion wasn't as fortunate. Word came through that their trench had been infiltrated. A company was sent down to assist. Around eighty Germans had taken the trench and couldn't be tossed out. They'd gained a foothold, forcing our men to withdraw. Artillery was quickly ordered to hit the position as our men counter attacked. They regained the position quickly taking sixty prisoners. They paid the price of being successful when the rest of their advance had failed leaving them stranded. It was over for them now.

The Germans didn't attack again. That night we secured our trench line with fresh wire. The situation had quietened significantly, and we felt satisfied that we'd dealt a timely blow to the Germans and redeemed ourselves after the debacle at Hangard Wood.

Over the next few nights patrols kept the Germans in their place. There were occasional exchanges of gun fire between the trenches and some sniping, but it appeared the regular routine of trench life had returned, at least for now.

Our spirits were buoyed further when news arrived that the Australian Corps was now under the command of Lt General John Monash. We all cheered. He was much admired by all of us.

Chapter 10

The Turning of the Tide

Most of May and June slipped by quietly in our sector, the Germans clearly with their tails between their legs after their disastrous advance. We'd heard of further attempts to break through elsewhere but again they were stopped.

There was light shelling from the enemy on the night of July 1st. One shell killed Bill Smith as he was sleeping in his dugout. It reminded us that you really weren't safe no matter where you were. If a shell found, you that was that. At least he went without any idea of what happened.

The front line had stabilised again but even, so we were on constant alert for another big push. Some thought the enemy was spent and that we would soon take the initiative now that Monash was in charge. Thoughts were divided amongst the ranks with other starting to think that the war couldn't be won by either side and that it could drag on for many more years.

By July the 3rd our battalion was again in the rear providing trench support. We were hearing all sorts of rumours about some kind of Australian operation, and a report soon came that gave us reason to be in good spirits.

There were a couple of places on the line that were a problem. We heard of one situation where the Germans were certainly taking advantage of a salient near the town of Hamel. The kink in the trench line gave them a strategic advantage and they used it to constantly shell our men. It was a thorn in the side of John Monash who worked up a plan to take the town in ninety minutes. The tactics he employed were impressive. The men moved quickly and easily because they didn't have to carry food, water or ammunition and were supplied by air drop. They were protected by a creeping barrage and in the days leading up to the battle the Germans were shelled with smoke and gas so that when the attack finally came, many of them were found wearing gas masks while the Australians did not. The ruse proved very successful with only smoke dropped on the enemy line on the day of the attack. Tanks were there to support the troops and proved highly successful. Most surprising, we were told the town was taken in ninety-three minutes only a fraction longer than Monash had predicted.

After hearing about the successful AIF attack on Hamel, we received new orders which involved the use of another new tactic. It was called peaceful penetration. Normally we'd be suspicious but after Hamel we were very keen to listen. Instead of making a full scale attack over a wide area we were to attack in smaller, more manageable jumps. The idea was to take small pieces of ground from the Germans in a more calculated manner. It was also designed to save lives. We listened to the briefing intently and liked what we heard.

A few days later we were back on the front line near Villers Bretonneux. We settled back into the usual trench routine, fighting off rats and trench fever while digging, duck boarding and keeping watch. It was quiet until the 4th Division was ordered to attack the Somme on July the 8th.

We were soon under some heavy German shelling and had no choice but to bunker down and wait it out. By that afternoon the 5th Brigade was ordered to advance the line. Australian artillery opened on the enemy to try and silence their guns. The exchange was brutal but by midnight the German guns had been put to rest. Reports came back saying we'd only suffered some minor hits on our left flank.

A and D Companies had successfully established forward posts under the protection of artillery cover. B Company was expected to do the same at the centre of the line, but we were slowed by the pitch darkness and some very hard ground. We somehow managed to complete the task before daybreak and spent the rest of the day rifling through care packages which had arrived, astonishingly during the bombardment.

We all got hot meals and a rum ration, but our good humour was soon subdued when it began to rain. Then, at around 2.30am the German artillery started again, this time they targetted the centre. We endured a sleepless night but their targetting was off, so not much damage was done. Even so, we were ordered to move before the enemy could correct and we stumbled off into the darkness. It was hard going and we were soon quite cold as the rain soaked through our tunics. We walked forward at a very slow pace, not knowing what the ground was like ahead. I spotted some movement, a shadow really but it was enough to be of concern, so I pointed it out to Blue,

"I see em. Ok Thorn, give em a burst!"

Bert didn't hesitate and fired the Lewis from the hip. Licks of flame burst from the muzzle and a spray of bullets speared into the darkness. Everyone hit the ground in anticipation of a reply from the Germans. About seventy yards ahead more shadows could be seen retreating but they didn't return fire. A few minutes later we were up again and came across a German forward post. It had been vacated only minutes earlier judging by the food that was left uneaten and the flickering candle, which somehow survived the drizzle.

We inched forward, alert for any contact with the enemy. We'd only taken a few steps when the crackle of rifles broke out. We dropped again and let loose with everything we had, firing at the muzzle flashes. The Mauser fire was followed by bombs, but they fell well short. We could see figures retreating further. It was clear they were trying to delay us so that the rest of their unit could get away.

"Geez they're sneaky beggars," someone said as the gunfire died away.

"Let's keep moving," called Blue but before he'd even finished giving the order the skirmish started up again. Bert remained prone, replying to the German gunfire while Dickie scrambled for a fresh ammo pan. The Lewis gun fired ceaselessly into the gloom. It was then that two Maxims started at us but most on our men had found shell holes and I was soon sliding into one myself.

We estimated that there were about forty or fifty Germans ahead, who again appeared to be on the retreat. There was no doubt they were buying time for the main body of troops, and it was working. We were only making what ground they gave up in small, staggered movements.

To our right things sounded a lot fiercer. A savage gun fight had broken out. The Germans had set up a redoubt, a defensive position that gave them a 360 degree field of fire with four Maxim machine guns. This was something new and a much more difficult prospect when advancing on open ground. They'd tricked out men into moving wide creating room for our company to be flanked. The Germans were able to silence a Lewis gunner, but his number two took over and with our superior numbers we were able to fend off a counterattack and bomb the redoubt. Others in our group soon joined in further along the right with several Germans cut down in savage crossfire, forcing the rest to retire from the fight.

We were up again soon after that and caught up to the 27th Battalion who had secured a section of the main German trench. It was obvious that they're evacuated with some haste and we quickly set up a defensive perimeter. We spent the rest of the night securing our position and fully expected a large counterattack. We weren't challenged for the rest of the night.

The next morning orders arrived from HQ.

"Exploit the trench line if possible."

Blue ordered patrols to move along the trenches and into the German saps.

"Weed em out boys," he ordered.

It was terrifying work. Our men had to sneak along the muddy trenches, checking every dugout for enemy soldiers, all the while hoping not to run across a booby trap.

Bert, Dickie and I had established a machine gun post in a good position. Our field of fire was excellent. All we could do now was watch for any German movement.

There were occasional flurries of gun fire coming from the saps and the bobbing of German helmets could be seen zigzagging away from us through the trench network. We dared not fire as we knew our own men were working their way through the same sections ratting out the saps. Before long they returned, confident that all the Germans had been accounted for. The enemy line was now ours. We'd been on the go for almost two full days without sleep. By that evening we were exhausted and relief was a welcome sight. We retired into a support position and slept where we dropped.

Over the next few days work details and salvage crews kept themselves busy. On July 15th news came though that the Germans had again launched a major offensive, this time to the south in the Marne River region near Mont Blanc. They'd successfully crossed the river only to be driven back by a massive French counter offensive. Two days later they were back where they started.

The weather was turning bad now and the front line conditions were oppressive. Sanitation had become a big problem and most of us were suffering constant bouts of dysentery. Adding to our woes was the fact that our gains were under constant bombardment from German artillery that had a bead on their former position, almost to the inch. The shellfire only got heavier as we went forward for another stint on the line.

Our guns did their best to silence the Germans who replied in kind with gas shells, but our artillery men kept up their counter battery work which made the transition a little more tolerable. By 3am on July 18th the changeover was complete, and we settled in while the exchange of shells continued.

On our right the 7th Division was ordered to consolidate its position. I watched the attack begin as flares slashed through the darkness. The incessant chatter of machine guns rattle our nerves and bombs exploded as the battle moved through the trenches. Mortar and artillery fire shrouded the entire sector in smoke. After an hour things were quiet again but then SOS flares could be seen coming from the Australian positions. There were concerns that the 7th Division may have failed in their bid to join up with us, so a patrol was dispatched to investigate and attempt to contact the Australians. Our Lewis gun crew was added to the patrol, and we were soon moving south, along the trench in the hope of meeting up with men of the 7th.

We soon found that the Australian line was indeed split between the two brigades. The good news was that the Germans hadn't yet exploited the opportunity. We sent word back to HQ and stood watch over the unclaimed territory. A few hours later, reinforcements were spreading up and down the line, plugging the gap. We'd only just managed to consolidate the line when about one hundred enemy soldiers approached in skirmishing formation. They moved on the 7th Brigade section. Again, we saw SOS flares and A Company was dispatched to counterattack. The rest of us were ordered to hold our positions. The Germans then let fly with a fierce bombardment. Gas shells exploded across Villers Bretonneux. Telephone communications were soon lost, so any changes in orders would take much longer to reach us.

The barrage had all the hallmarks of a full assault, but no-one came. As quickly as it began, the attack ceased. Whatever the Germans were thinking of doing, it had either failed or been called off. We didn't really care why; we were just glad that it was over for now and we took the opportunity to rest.

Having made good ground in recent days we heard news of a major offensive by the French further south which was an outstanding success. They'd taken twenty thousand prisoners and a hundred field guns. We were very excited by the news,

"Maybe we can head down there now boss," someone asked assuming it was now much safer than where we were. I didn't disagree.

We'd had some success too. Our artillery had made a significant impact on the German positions. German stretcher parties were reportedly picking up their wounded in great numbers right in front of our battalion. They spent the entire day in no-man's land but no-one on our side fired a single shot.

Suddenly two Germans approach to within forty yards of our forward post carrying a white flag. They didn't speak English and no-one could discern the reason for their approach. They were eventually waved away and returned to their own line. Ten minutes later a volley of shot from German rifle grenades slammed into the post killing one and wounding another. We returned fire with great accuracy and killed all the Germans who'd advanced on the position. They'd paid a high price for their ruse.

The next day there was much talk in the ranks. The Commander of the 18th Battalion, Lt Col George Murphy had been appointed temporary commanders of the 7th Brigade. His replacement was Major WRC Robertson. More news followed; an attachment of Americans Doughboys, were to be embedded with the 2nd Division for training purposes. The Americans were seen as a saving grace for the Allies who had been fighting relentlessly for four years. While the Germans were able to bolster their numbers after an armistice with Russia, we'd been losing men at a steady rate. Battalions that started the war with one thousand men were depleted to the point where some only had a few hundred left. The new Americans divisions swung the pendulum back in our favour.

When they arrived, it seemed to most of us that they were decent young men, if not a little too enthusiastic. Dickie reminded us that we'd been much the same when we'd first arrived. I'm sure I wasn't like that at all, but I knew what he meant.

We mingled with the new arrivals and tried to make them feel at home as best we could. I spotted a young fellow, who was white faced with fear and smiled at him as I reached out to shake hands,

"G'day, I'm Stan, from Sydney. Where you from?" I asked

"William Kowalski from Fargo, North Dakota sir!" he replied with a snappy salute.

I couldn't help but laugh.

"Mate...I'm no officer and for God's sake don't salute me. It's like putting a target on my head!" I instructed.

"Oh, sorry. This is all new to me."

I understood how he felt. I didn't know the man from a bar of soap, but that raw fear and inexperience was unmistakable and somewhat familiar.

"Nice to meet you old chap," I said in my best English to which Bert laughed but said nothing.

Bill continued, "So where are the Hun?"

"Just over there," I replied, pointing east, "We've been at em for a while now and they're darn good fighters."

"Well, we can't wait to help you guys out. Should be a hoot!" Bill suggested, clearly trying to mask his fear.

"A hoot? I suppose you could call it that," said Bert obviously annoyed, "You see any action yet sunshine?"

"No sir, but we can't wait to mix it up with you fellas!"

"Well, you won't have to wait long," replied Bert, holding a stare at Bill that dried up his next remark.

"Don't let him bother you Bill," I said, "He's a pussy cat when you get to know him." Bill didn't appear to be convinced.

The Americans stationed with the 2nd Division were shown the rigors of trench life. As Bert suggested the Americans were soon facing up to the reality of it all. Just after midnight the new arrivals got a welcome gift in the form of gas shells which pounded our line. The unmistakable thud of the projectile hitting the earth followed by the pop and hiss was all too obvious to us, but the Americans needed a little motivation to react at first. Most panicked and fumbled or dropped their respirators while we watched and even laughed. It was truly a bizarre scene.

By the end of the night thousands of gas shells had fallen in the Villers Bretonneux area, most of them behind the front line. For us the gas has no effect, but neighbouring units were savaged. The Germans engaged some of our forward posts with rifle grenades but were again repelled. A strong wind in the early morning cleared most of the gas quickly. The rest was diluted when it started to rain.

A few days later the front line was handed back to the 17th Battalion and so it went on. Trench routine, front line duty, reserve, training the Americans, digging, duck boarding, sleeping, writing letters and eating. It couldn't get much more basic than that. German shelling was regular but not too intense although the occasional shell hit its mark wounding or killing someone.

At the end of July, the Germans intensified their bombardment and sent over thousands gas shells. They followed it up with an infantry attack to our left and again they were repelled. The new American soldiers got their first taste of fighting and were reported to have performed well.

For the last week of July Allied bombers lumbered up and down our trench line, their bombastic engines no doubt causing some confusion on the German side of the line. The Australians too thought it odd, but whispers were starting to circulate about a major Allied offensive.

Chapter 11

The August Offensive

It was my turn to take watch. I scanned no-man's land for enemy movement, but a fog made things more difficult than usual. I feared that an enemy patrol could easily get in close and I wouldn't be any the wiser.

It was our last day on the line for a while, and it was certainly dragging. The landscape was unchanged, still muddy but with more gore. Crumpled, lifeless bodies produced awkward shadows in the meandering light of flares. My companion was Bill Kowalski; one of the Americans attached to our brigade and he was keen to learn about the Western Front.

"Seems quiet enough Stan, doesn't it?"

Bill was still quite nervous.

"It's quiet for the moment but it changes fast. *Stand to* is the most dangerous time, "I explained.

"Stand-to? That's when the Germans are most likely to attack right?"

"Yeah. Blue should be waking the men any minute."

Bill paused before asking another question,

"Do they attack very often?"

"They have lately," I replied.

Bill went quiet for a while but seemed to be paying much more attention to his observation duties. I smiled to myself just as the company started to be roused for the daily grind. It was then that I noticed a single flare shooting up from deep behind the German line. Bill saw it too,

"What's that?" he asked, but before I could answer the shriek of a 5.9 shell split the silence of the morning, smashing down on the trench line. It was followed straight away by another, then another, much more than the usual daily greeting.

There was no need to rouse anyone else now, the entire sector was wide awake and taking cover anywhere they could. The shelling soon became ferocious with projectiles coming from directly in front of us and from the right and left of the German line. Both A and B Companies were being hit hard, and it wouldn't be long before the casualty count started to add up.

Instinctively I opened up with the Lewis gun, firing into the fog as did many of the other gunners. There seemed no point waiting for the enemy to appear, they'd be too close by then. We were soon strafing no-man's land despite the heavy shelling.

German trench mortar and heavy artillery soon combined but still there was no sign of any infantry. Telephone communications with company HQ were lost so a runner was dispatched to report on the situation. Bert was beside me in a flash but left me to control of the gun,

"Where's our bloody artillery?" he screamed as he helped me switch to a fresh ammo pan.

A few minutes passed and the barrage kept on coming. Our trench had taken a few direct hits, and I could hear men screaming above the roar of explosions. The attack was so heavy that the ground shook and it rained mud constantly, but I still couldn't see any figures approaching our line. Then, at last our artillery sprang to life and answered the German 5.9s

"About time,' Bert announced.

I agreed, but now the noise levels doubled. It took every ounce of strength to stay sane under such an ordeal, and I thought of Bill facing his first heavy barrage. I looked over and saw him crouching down on the bottom of the trench. His arms were wrapped around his legs, and he appeared to be sobbing.

Our anti battery fire started to do the trick and the German shell fire slowly died off. We'd stopped firing and looked out over the pockmarked ocean of mud, but still there was no sign at all of infantry.

"See anything Stan?" asked Blue.

"Nothing," I replied.

"Well maybe they changed their minds," he mused. "Keep at em just in case," and we reloaded and emptied another few panniers into the foggy smoke.

The Lewis gun vibrated like a jackhammer with the delivery of every bullet. Pencil thin flame spat from the muzzle as we kept up a venomous defense. By 6am it was over, our howitzers having all but silenced the enemy guns. There had been no advance. It didn't even appear like they were planning to send troops across to engage us. It seemed rather pointless but then the whole war felt that way to most of us. The rest of the day was spent clearing the debris and bagging up the trenches, again.

That evening we were relieved and made ready to leave our section of the line and hand over to the 20th Battalion. The Americans were to remain, so I said my farewells to Bill. He was twenty five years old, seven years older than me, but age didn't matter on the front line these days, it was more about experience. I hoped I'd managed to teach him a few things during our time together and he'd come through this whole affair unscathed.

"Good luck Bill. Don't get your head shot off!" I couldn't believe that I was being so blunt, but what else could one say?

"Seeya Stan and thanks for everything."

We left the trenches of Villers Bretonneux and encamped in the Camon region not far from Amiens. Something was off though. Most of us noticed that there were no officers to be seen. It could only mean a briefing of some kind at HQ, and we started thinking about a new Allied offensive. Our suspicions were soon confirmed when orders came to keep quiet. We weren't even to chat about the possibility, which left us with little to discuss.

The men were very pleased to bathe and get a fresh set of uniforms. The one's we were wearing hadn't been cleaned in weeks. They reeked of mud and body odour and were starting to rot. Worst of all we were all covered in lice. They were the bane of life in the trenches, constantly biting their hosts and breeding in great numbers at our expense. Being deloused and donning clean underwear and clothing would give us relief for a short time at least.

We were soon on the move again, this time by bus. We were sent to a training facility to inspect the new tanks that had been commissioned, Mark V's we were told. After some spectacular failures in the past, we weren't sure what to make of these lumbering beasts. There was a short briefing before we were allowed to climb on them, inspect their engines and workings and even climb inside. Some blokes got to drive them! I was still a bit skeptical about how something so big and heavy could cross a muddy wasteland when the driver of the machine we were looking at came along.

Frank too was having doubts as usual,

"Geez mate you'll get yourself killed in that contraption," he said motioning towards the huge rhomboid monster.

The Englishman twirled one end of his moustache into a tiny point, "Maybe so, but we'll be through the wire over their guns before they can slurp their tea."

There was a momentary pause and then Dickie did what Dickie always seemed to do,

"Do the Germans drink tea?"

The Englishman laughed, "I don't know but if they do, they'll need a nice strong cup after we're done with them!"

With that he climbed into his machine and took us for a ride. The thick armour plating was very warm having absorbed the sunlight and was studded with giant rivets. The driver explained that it could carry a six pound gun or a Lewis machine gun, which certainly impressed Bert. The driver's praise for his vehicle was infectious.

We watched how they could roll over barbed wire and open gaps for foot soldiers and the way they dealt with a machine gun post. We also saw how soldiers could use tanks as a protective shield while advancing on the enemy. The only problem I could foresee was the noise. Their engines were incredibly loud, and we wondered how the Germans wouldn't be warned of a coming attack.

After a few days of familiarisation and tactical training we were all feeling a little more comfortable with the new machines. Even Frank had to agree that they would be helpful during an advance. Commanders had been briefed countless times as a plan was formulated to make a major thrust against the Germans. Once the plan was set, the details were spread down the ranks until we finally learned that we were to attack in force, and soon.

It had been five months since the British had been routed by the German Offensive and now, we were to turn the tables. Weather forecasts were favourable and, despite enemy aircraft being seen in the vicinity, the massing of troops went un-noticed.

The 18th Battalion was on the move. Everyone from the kitchen personnel to the commander were heading for the front. Artillery limbers brought up our big guns and hundreds of men marched east. On August 7 we reached out rally point. All was in readiness.

The Australians had been allocated the task of driving into the Germans to the immediate south of the River Somme. On the Northern side would be the British Fourth Army and to our south the Canadians and below them the French. In all we would employ seven Allied Divisions against the Germans over a front of ten miles in our sector alone. So much for taking those little bites.

Early that afternoon the Germans sent over some artillery shells as they tended to do from time to time hoping to hit something. Just north of Villers Brett a squadron of carry tanks, fully laden with food, water, ordnance and petrol sustained a direct hit. The plume of smoke could be seen for several miles, and the Germans concentrated a furious barrage on the position. In the end, fifteen tanks and all they carried had been destroyed. Fear rose that the Germans were aware of our plans, but when no more incidents were reported it was written off as a bit of bad luck.

Four of the five Australian Divisions would be used for the attack with two brigades held in reserve. The advance would take the form of a double leapfrog. Two divisions would spearhead the initial attack. They had four objectives. The first was to reach what was called the "black line" being the immediate trench line across no-man's land occupied by the forward German defenses. It was hoped that most of this would be cleared by artillery twenty minutes prior to the hop over.

After taking the black line, the first wave would push on for three thousand yards, their second objective being a position called the green line. This was well behind the German front line, and it too would be targetted by a heavy bombardment.

Once that objective was achieved the two trailing brigades would leapfrog their counterparts and push another four thousand five hundred yards to the red line. Only after reaching that point would a decision be made about carrying on to a final objective. If we were up to it and our losses were minimal, we'd try and make the blue line objective.

If we made all our objectives we will have taken a total of nine thousand yards from the enemy, which was way beyond our ability to observe. It was indeed a very ambitious plan and given the large scale failures of the past, many agreed it was a high risk venture indeed. Our only hope was that this time our commanders had done their homework.

As we settled down at our rally point, we learned that tape was already being laid at the jump off position and ammunition dumps prepared. Freshly printed maps were delivered to each platoon, and we huddled together to examine our part of the operation.

Each man had been ordered to remain silent and if captured by the enemy before the attack, we were to keep quiet. There was some talk of two

Australians who had been captured during a trench raid, but the Germans hadn't started bombarding any of our positions, so we guessed they'd followed orders.

We were encamped near Villers Brett and were briefed on our role in the offensive. The 2nd Division was to advance the first three thousand yards covering the right flank of the operation while the 3rd Divisions looked after the left. The 4th and 5th Divisions would stay back ready to leapfrog us once we made the green line. No-one said a word while Bluey explained the plan. Mick Hogg was the first to pipe up after the briefing concluded,

"So, this is it boys, the big one!"

"Yeah, let's hope the artillery is on target for a change!" replied Frank.

"And those blasted tank don't get stuck, "I suggested. Given the sarcastic comments that followed, I wasn't alone in my concerns.

Bluey Wilton looked around at our group,

"Are you blokes ready for this?"

Everyone nodded or gestured that they were.

"Right then, we've got a message from the boos so listen up",

 To the soldiers of the Australian Army Corps. For the first time in the history of the corps, all five Australian Divisions will tomorrow engage in the largest and most important battle operation ever undertaken by the Corps. They will be supported by exceptionally powerful artillery and by tanks and aeroplanes on a scale never previously attempted."

We all listened intently as Blue continued reading the words aloud. They were inspirational and spoke to each man as if written for him alone. No-one interjected and no smart remarks were conveyed.

"I earnestly wish every soldier of the Corps the best of good fortune and a glorious and decisive victory, the story of which will re-echo throughout the world and will live forever in the history of our homeland. Lt General John Monash."

Blue looked up at our faces. We felt proud and our confidence was boosted by the words of our supreme commander.

No-one spoke for a few more moment until the spell was broken by Bert,

"Right then, can I get some sleep now?"

A barrage of bully beef tins and anything available pummelled Bert who smiled widely, a rare display indeed.

Spirits remained high as we readied for the big push against the Germans. We all got a hot meal which was most welcome and then we settled down and began the long wait for zero hour. We were still a long way from our jump off position, but it would be six hours before we were to move again so we tried to snatch some sleep.

A few men chatted; others kept to themselves. Everyone had their own way of dealing with the emotional turmoil leading up to a major attack. No-one was sure how the leapfrogging maneuver would work on such a large scale having only been attempted by a single division in the past. The success of the new tactics at Hamel and the results of peaceful penetration added to our confidence. During the night the Germans sent over a few shells but nothing too serious. It seemed they were oblivious to the nightmare that was to come.

At 9.15pm it was B Company's turn to move out. I felt a bit queer as the fear began to fester in my gut. It had a way of making one feel cold and my hands were clammy and my armpits dripped with perspiration. Everyone kept quiet, absorbed in their thoughts as 4.40am, zero hour crept closer.

We reached our rendezvous point but A, C and D Companies weren't there. The promised extra guns were nowhere to be seen either.

"Another complete cock-up!" said Frank! "Maybe we can throw rocks at em?!"

A runner was quickly dispatched to sort out the mess. He was only gone fifteen minutes having caught sight of the other companies about seven hundred yards to the east. He reported they had the promised weapons which had been put in the wrong place. Even so it took another hour to sort out the confusion but eventually B Company was geared up, and we marched to our jump point, just north of the Roman Road.

As we walked a group of Allied bombers flew overhead. The same ones that had been flying up and down the line for the last couple of weeks. Their engines were loud and smashed through the darkness for all to hear, including the Germans.

"Jesus, they'll wake up the dead Krauts with that racket," someone shouted.

Before long we came across one of the new Mark V tanks which had broken down on the road and didn't look like going anywhere.

"Blood Hell!" said someone, obviously frustrated at the series of blunders.

"This could get messy real fast," suggested Mick.

"Yeah, but it's too late to stop now," replied Dickie.

It took us another half hour to find the start line, and we were the last to arrive.

We heard engines bellowing behind us and thought it was that same flight of bombers coming back but it turned out to be a pair of tanks moving up to the line. Uncanny how they sounded the same as the planes. I suddenly understood what had been going on with those planes all this time. By 3.38am we were all in positions. As we waited a heavy fog descended on our sector, much to our relief. It would help keep us hidden during the advance.

Over six hundred tanks and around eight hundred aircraft would cross no-man's land with us. It was to be like nothing I'd ever seen before, but the nerves were really eating up my insides as the minutes ticked away.

At 4.20am our artillery barrage opened on the Germans. Three thousand heavy guns blasted their deadly cargo on an unsuspecting enemy: the cacophony of explosions, impossible to describe. Multiple blasts continually overlapped one another, each signalling a massive hammer blow on the enemy. The orange and red flashes in the distance seemed unending and I heard someone say,

"Poor bastards!"

The Germans must have been caught napping because there was no sign of any counter battery activity. It seemed likely that they too had been picked off as a part of the onslaught. We'd heard stories about the Australian heavy guns deliberately targetting old German artillery positions to lull them into thinking we had no idea where they were. Now, at the critical moment I hope our ruse did the trick and that the German batteries were being wiped out, otherwise we'd be walking into a firestorm.

"Five minutes!"

I gritted my teeth and looked around. I was so nervous my hands were cold with sweat. Some men vomited, others prayed. We all kept our heads down and waited behind the tape.

"Two minutes!"

Butterflies swarmed in my gut now. I tried to push the thoughts of death out of my head, but it was impossible. Humming a little tune to myself didn't really help. My throat was dry and I couldn't swallow. I noticed I was shaking all over and found it hard to keep my last meal down.

"One minute!"

It seemed to be taking forever, but then it began. 4.40am on August 8th, 1918, the shrill of whistles was heard all along the Australian line, the signal to get up and advance. Tanks rumbled to life and took the lead as thousands of Allied troops lit cigarettes and rose from their prone positions on the start line.

Bert carried the Lewis gun in its sling ready to fire as the rest of us trailed with a supply of ammunition panniers. We were in attack formation and heavily laden, my rifle with bayonet attached pointed at the enemy as we stumbled across the pulverised ground. It was impossible to avoid the shell holes in the dark, and the fog made things more difficult. A few German guns finally replied to our own artillery with their familiar "wiz bang" sound. They were raining shrapnel balls around us but then a few 5.9s started barking moments later.

The Germans has taken too long to respond and most of their barrage landed harmlessly behind us. Still, some managed to adjust within a few minutes and began to drop shells amongst the forward formations.

A huge boom and the concussion of a blast hit me from behind. I stumbled as a man screamed and went down close by. I looked back but couldn't see who it was through the smoke, dust and fog. Another explosion followed immediately and I heard the ping of a chunk of metal as it ricocheted of Mick's helmet, causing him to reel to his right.

"Shit!" he cried as he regained his footing.

We soon heard the clatter of machine guns as we approached the German forward posts. Not all of them had been silenced by the barrage. Bangs, clunks and thuds of metal and mud could be heard as shells and bullets cascaded into our platoon.

A tank veered toward a German machine gun, slowly closing the distance as the maxim emptied hundreds of rounds into the methodical fortress. I couldn't tear my eyes away from what was happening. The muzzle of the enemy gun flickered, emptying everything it had into the metal beast, but it kept on rolling, straight over the top of the gun crew. The tank screwed around in a vicious circle, crushing the gun beneath it. The two surviving gunners ran into the fog but were quickly dealt with and fell into the mud.

We were finding it hard to navigate through the thick fog. While it shielded us from the Germans, it also hid them from our advance. All we could do was move forward and deal with anything we saw as it emerged. Mortar shells occasionally thundered around us, but they were few and far between.

Another machine gun strafed our line and we dived for cover. I watched as a figure crumpled in front of me. I got up and rushed over to see that Frank had been hit.

"Stretcher Bearers!" I screamed.

We were under orders to move forward, stopping for no-one but I couldn't leave Frank like that. I grabbed a bandage and pad from my pocket and put pressure on the wound. Frank groaned as blood leaked from his lower abdomen. I could tell from my training in England that it wasn't a fatal shot as the blood appeared dark and was only draining slowly.

"Don't worry Frank, help's on the way...STRETCHER BEARERS!" I called a second time.

I did what I could for Frank and was relieved when two men appeared in answer to my shouts. The red cross patches on their arms were very reassuring.

"We've got this mate...you best catch up to your mates."

"Righto," I replied. "Good luck Frank. See you soon"

He nodded through the pain as I moved off; I wiped the blood off my hands. My heart was thumping out of my chest when I realised I'd lost sight of the rest of my gun crew.

Helping Frank had cost me valuable ground and now I was well behind the advance and lost in the fog. I thought about going back to Frank and the medics but decided against it in case I might face a charge of cowardice.

I was beginning to panic, like a schoolboy late for class and started running headlong into the fog. A whistle then a *whiz bang* sound descended followed by an eruption of lethal lead balls which I managed to evade thanks to a nearby shell hole. A muffled grunt to my right gave away someone's position and I saw the man slump as the shrapnel slice into him from above. He was dead before he hit the ground.

I kept running forward and spotted a tank to my left and decided to catch up. It was easy to locate given the racket it peeled off, and I joined a small group of soldiers trailing behind the machine but didn't recognise anyone. We were firing blindly towards the enemy, and they were in the same situation but had the advantage of being able to enfilade us with machine guns.

The fizz of bullets was all around us and the tank certainly took some hits as we kept it between the Germans and ourselves. Those that got past were having an impact though and men fell to my left and right. The sound of bullets hitting flesh and bone was hideous. The man right next to me gasped and then flopped silently to the ground.

Another enemy shell screamed through the air but before any of us could dive for cover it erupted amongst us. I was flung sideway by the concussion effect and landed heavily in the ground. Briefly stunned I just lay there for a moment and then shook my head to clear the stars in my eyes.

"Are you alright fella?" someone asked?

I felt for blood on my uniform found none,

"Yes, I don't think I'm hit!" I replied as I groped for my rifle and ammo bags but couldn't find them.

They must have been flung away into the fog by the blast.

I stood and looked again at my uniform for signs of bleeding and was relieved to see nothing. I'd lost even more ground and was now unarmed. Could things get any worse? Panic welled up inside me again and I started jogging forward, almost tripping over a dead German. His throat was sliced open by shrapnel from one of his own mortar shells. I picked up his Mauser; bayonet attached and checked the ammunition. It held an adequate number of bullets, and I cocked the thing and got moving yet again.

Figures were bobbing up ahead, but it was impossible to see who they were in the smoky mist. The chatter of machine guns grew louder as I edged forward. My breathing was heavy and I could hear my heart thudding right up into my eardrums. Mortar shells slammed down spraying dirt in my face, the zing of metal passing to my left and right. Another massive boom and I was flat on my back again. The German barrage was being corrected and had no doubt caught up with some of us. Again, I raised myself from the rancid soil, my ears ringing. My face stung and I wiped blood from a small cut while spitting a wad dirt out of my mouth.

I managed to hold the rifle this time, got up and started moving once more.

"FORWARD!" came an order and I chased the sound, catching up to another group of men. I soon realised they were from the 17th Battalion who were supposed to be on our left. Had they strayed or was it me? It didn't really matter now, so I stuck with them and moved on.

"TRENCH! At em!" came the cry as the ground opened ahead. The wire had been cleared by artillery and tanks giving the Germans no protection from our onslaught. We'd reached the black line!

Germans were scurrying left and right as machine guns spat death at us from everywhere it seemed. I raised my rifle and aimed at the rushing soldiers. Firing once I watched a man stumble and fall, slumping into the mud on the trench floor. I fired repeatedly as did those around me. Germans fell like rag dolls joining their comrades who had already been pulverised by our initial barrage. Torn and tortured figures were mixed in with the living many cowering against the sandbag walls while others ran off down their saps to escape.

The first wave swept across the German trench like a giant broom and kept moving forward while those who were instructed to do so stayed to mop up and file prisoners back to our side. I ran across the edge of the trench to my right, hoping to find my own battalion again. It appeared that many Germans had retreated before we arrived in this section given the lack of dead. I came across more 17th boys and realised that I had been unknowingly traversing to my left after being split off from my team. I decided then that I should work further to the right along the trench and find my battalion before re-joining the fight. That plan was soon put aside by a lone German who saw me and started running off. He was only about fifteen yard away when I fire but the bullet sizzled over his head. I squeezed again only to hear a click. I'd emptied the gun and cursed my bad luck.

I then heard an awful guttural cry and felt a moment of terror as I realised that the German had turned and was charging towards me through the thinning mist. He was mere seconds from me, and I could see that he was a big brute of a fellow, not unlike the recruitment posters portrayal of Gorillas! I flinched at the glint of his bayonet and made out the ripples of a serrated edge. A flash went through my mind of the thing sinking into my gut but then my training kicked in. The man was only a few yards away, teeth gritted and bright white behind his filthy face. He was running hard as I propped onto one knee. He came down upon me and as he did, I thrust my rifle under his, glancing it to one side. I kept the thrust going, smashing my gun into the man's face. He fell away to my left as I recoiled the rifle to my side. As the fellow landed next to me, with a heavy thud I thrust again and sank my bayonet into his chest. There was a hideous cry, his face crumpling in agony. I tried to pull the bayonet, but it had lodged in the fellow's ribs, and he again shrieked at the pain as blood burst from the wound. I jerked, releasing the blade and was about the jam it in again. The man gasped and shuddered, clutching his chest, blood squeezing out between his fingers and running liberally down his tunic and onto the dirt. A few seconds later he relaxed and rolled over onto his back, one final breath leaking from his lungs.

I stood for a moment and stared at the body before the shock took hold causing me to shudder uncontrollably. I threw the Mauser down and started moving again. My mind was racing as I processed what I had done. I decided to move forward and rejoin anyone I could catch up with. I jumped into the enemy trench, working along the muddy broken walls, passing by dead enemy soldiers. I found a sap and again started towards the rear of the German line.

Machine guns still clattered up ahead and I realised the fight was far from over. I emerged from the rear of the first German trench, relieved not to have encountered any survivors or a counterattack. Machine gun bullets spat up the dirt around me, and I leapt for a shell hole. Two Australians were huddled in the bottom on the hole looking more terrified than I was.

"Hey mate...where do we go?" asked one of them. I looked them over and recognised their 17th battalion insignias. They were clearly new recruits judging by how clean their uniforms were, as well as the intense fear on their faces.

"Just follow me but spread out. Makes it harder for their gunners!"

I waited for a moment to catch my breath,

"Ready?"

The pair nodded and we all rose from the shell hole together. At that instant came the tat tat tat of a German Maxim followed by the unmistakable crack of bullets hitting flesh and bone. The two lads crumpled and rolled back into the hole, splashing into the murky bottom.

I instinctively dropped to the ground and looked back at the boys. Both were dead.

"Oh God!"

I then looked ahead for the machine gun but couldn't see it in the smoke and mist. It was clear that they could see me as dirt, ripped up by another volley, stung my cheek. I knew where they were now. I fumbled for a mills bomb, but before I could pull the pin another grenade erupted in the machine gun pit obliterating the crew before they could peel off another shot. It seemed I wasn't the only one pinned down and, thanks to my untimely arrival; someone took advantage of the distraction to deal with the problem. It was too late for the pair in the bottom of the shell hole though and I felt a pang of regret as I stood and moved forward again.

Disorientation and confusion got the better of me, and I simply forgot to pick up another weapon. Unarmed I began traversing the rear sections of the German trench system, still searching for my battalion.

More German wire soon appeared despite assurances that it would be cleared by the tanks, which I hadn't seen for a while. I decided to cut through rather than risk getting caught up trying to zig zag through the stuff. By the time I got to the German support trench I found it occupied by Australians. 17th Battalion personnel were ratting out the position while others moved on to the green line past the village of Warfusee. This seemed like the best chance I had to get back to my battalion, so I followed the trench line right.

Looking down I saw dead and mutilated Germans, brown mud blending with blood to create a dark bile. Our artillery had done a hideous perfect job here. It was then I heard a voice,

"Kamerad, Mercy, Bitter!"

A wounded German begged for help, but I kept moving, ignoring his pleas. He wasn't my problem. Bits of human bodies littered the entire length of this section, and I could smell the stench of blood mixed with cordite in the cool morning air. It was repulsive and I gagged.

I kept walking; looking for my own men, passing deep German dugouts and hoping that no survivors were suddenly inclined to fight back. I moved on and spotted two Australians as they moved to another dugout. They didn't bother to go in, and tossed two bombs deep inside...*boom, boom.*

"That sorted em out I reckon!" one remarked as they moved off for another dugout. It seemed that some of the enemy weren't willing to surrender.

I kept moving. The Germans who'd been captured were now being marched back behind our line. I lost count but there must have been at least two hundred that I saw in this sector alone.

Finally, after an eternity struggling along the top of the torn up trench line I recognised the shoulder patch of an 18th Battalion man. He was sitting in a fresh shell hole.

"Where you been sunshine?" blurted Jimmy Taylor.

"Nowhere special'" I replied as I spotted a large patch of blood on his tunic, "Are you alright Jimmy?"

"Right as rain mate!"

I looked at Jimmy's face, his broad smile giving away the joy at gaining a Blighty wound.

"So, I see," I replied as I stopped on the edge of his hole, "Have you seen Bert or Jonsey?"

"Nope, most of em kept moving. You best high tail it yourself...that way." Jimmy pointed beyond the German trench.

"Righto thanks Jimmy. You need a medic?"

"She's right Stan, already on their way I expect."

"Good oh. I see you then."

I turned and leapt across some jumbled wire then struggled along the edge of the trench until I found a sap. I then hopped into the enemy trench and walked until I came back up at the other side. I really had to hand it to the Germans; they knew how to build a trench. Despite the damage it was clear that their structures were far superior to ours, but then they never intended to leave.

It was still foggy, but the sun was high enough to improve the visibility. I spotted more prisoners being led back and shouted for directions from their captors. They just said to keep going and waved in a general direction that didn't really indicate much.

The gunfire had died down significantly now. In fact, I could only hear the occasional clatter and even those sounded a distance off. I decided to step it up and started jogging taking in more of the damage as it unfolded from the soup. Our big guns had been devastating along most of the German line from what I could tell. It looked like most of the prisoners had given up without firing a shot in this zone. I saw another group of Aussies and ran towards them.

"Stan," came a call. It was Mick, "Geez I'm glad to see you mate! We thought you got knocked."

"No, just lost in the fog. Where are Bert and the others?"

"Nearby. Dickie got a bit of a scratch but nothing much. Have you seen Frank? He wasn't with us when we looked."

I glanced up at Mick and paused, he sensed that it was bad news,

"He got one in the stomach. I called for stretchers and left his with them. It didn't look too bad!"

"Shit...poor Frank," replied Mick shaking his head, "You reckon he'll be alright?"

"Couldn't really tell, he was in a lot of pain."

Mick paused for a moment, processing the news then snapped out of it,

"Come on Stan, this way. You can tell us all what happened out there."

I followed Mick well beyond the enemy line coming across more of our men, many dealing with our wounded or sending captured Germans back. Our boys had really done their job, the area had been cleared swiftly, and we didn't appear to have suffered a great many casualties.

The trek to Warfusee Village was without incident and we stepped into the shattered streets, passing more German prisoners. They were all relieved of their personal possessions by opportunist Australians. The price for seeing the end of the war seemed to be something most were willing to accept. We walked through the village and out the other side where I was finally reunited with my platoon and the first person to spot me was Blue,

"Well, well...looks who's here! Get a bit lost, did we?" His sarcasm was clearly noticeable.

"Sorry Blue...got knocked about a couple of times." I thought it best not to say I stopped to help Frank. He looked at me for a moment, but I offered nothing more,

"Well, you weren't the only one, men a spread all over the place. They've been stumbling in for a while now. Can you account for anyone?" he asked.

I told him about Frank and a few others I saw fall, but I couldn't be sure of too many. Bert and Dickie were visibly shocked when they heard about Frank. Blue then made an announcement to the platoon,

"We'll wait a bit longer for the rest of em then we'll move out! Don't get too comfortable!"

I sat with Bert, Dickie and Mick and explained what I saw and how I got lost. They peppered me with questions about Frank, and I did my best to explain. They were pleased when I told them I tried to attend to Frank before the medics arrived. We all knew that it was against orders, but I had to do something for him. I knew the boys wouldn't mention it.

It seemed that most of our blokes came through the advance without too many problems. In fact, it sounded to me like I got it much worse than the rest of my platoon. They swept through the German defenses with little resistance and reported that the enemy trenches had been pulverised and most of the Germans they came across were dead or surrendered without a fight. There were pockets of resistance, but they were dealt with swiftly.

When Blue was satisfied that everyone was accounted for, we got the word to move again,

"Well done boys, we made the green line. Now let's move forward and dig in. Our orders are to wait there in reserve and prepare to repel a counterattack."

We pressed on for another few hundred yards and found the rest of the 2nd Division digging in feverishly while others set up machine gun posts. Bert came through it all without so much as a scratch, but Dickie had a wound to his left arm. I'm sure it was worse than he made out and it appeared to have bled freely for a while, soaking the sleeve of his uniform.

The fog had finally lifted which gave what was left of the German artillery a chance to target the tanks, which they did to good effect. Most were soon out of action in our sector, and I imagined it was much the same elsewhere.

As B Company and the rest of Division consolidated, the first leapfrog maneuver took place. The 5th Division was moving though our sector and were expected to press forward for another four thousand yards. Their goal was the red line just near the town of Harbonnieres. It was now 8.20am!

Looking ahead I saw a wasteland of abandoned enemy equipment. Lorries, field guns, wagons, limbers, you name it...they'd left it for dead. Word quickly passed that all the Australian battalions had successfully executed the first phase of the attack. Apparently there had been a tough fight to the extreme left where a spur gave German machine gunners a clear field of vision. The outcrop was to be taken by the 3rd British Corps, but they'd failed to do so, exposing our left flank. Casualties were high but they fought on and took their objective. Snipers were still taking pot shots at our men despite the gains.

The German front line seemed to have totally collapsed. There was talk of whippet tanks and even cavalry getting as far as nine miles into German territory. Our gains turned out to be much more than the ground we crossed. Our battalion took two hundred and fifty prisoners, three 5.9inch guns, four 4.2s, ten light minenwerfer mortars, seven 77 millimeter guns and ten machine guns.

"Well, I never," I remarked after hearing the reports of our success.

"Eh" enquired Dickie.

"Who'd have thought it might be that easy?"

"Yeah, we sure caught em cold." suggested Mick.

"That'll just make em harder next time," said Bert, the voice of reason.

Bert was getting used to having things thrown at him by now.

We spent the rest of the day watching from our new position, waiting for a counterattack but as morning became afternoon, we heard that the red line had been reached and by late afternoon the blue line had also fallen with little resistance. Our advance finally halted. We were ordered to stop digging as our advance had been so successful there was no need for a secondary defensive line. We rested and at 7.30pm, field kitchens brought up food and water. We were starving and everyone tucked in to a well-deserved meal. We were finally able to relax and most of the men fell asleep where they sat. Despite being put on notice to move at any moment we got a full nights' sleep.

On August the 9th we received orders to head down the Roman Road. We were split into our respective platoons and started marching. The road was thick with horses, mules, lorries, men and equipment trying to get here or there. There was great urgency in capitalising on our gains before the Germans could muster any kind of retaliation and push us back again. All was quiet until we reach a crossing which was being heavily shelled. We decided to move south to avoid the avalanche, crossing Morocourt Valley only suffering one casualty.

We spent most of the day moving across the battlefield and forward to the Old Amiens Line. The entire area was littered with refuse from the fight. Obliterated tanks smashed enemy guns, dead horses with their limbers still attached and small weapons strewn hither and thither. Some of the men snatched up a few souvenirs like the odd pistol or a dagger, anything they could find lying around. Prisoner were still being filed back, having spent the night under guard. They were eagerly relieved of their belongings, but no-one dared go near those killed. It didn't matter which side you were on, you didn't go through the pockets of a dead man, unless ordered to do so.

I looked at the bodies as we passed. Burial details were already busy. There were proper protocols to follow, even with the enemy. Their faces were drained of any colour; some obviously dying in agony while others simply appeared to be asleep. One fellow even looked like he had a smile on his face.

Tanks had done much of the damage here with many of the dead torn apart by six pound shells at close range. Several bodies were missing limbs or torn in half. Some had been completely flattened by the weight of a tank grinding them down. It was almost impossible to avoid treading on a body part, a finger here, a leg there with the boot still laced up perfectly. A few men had to empty their stomachs at the sight of it all, but no-one spoke. I somehow managed to avoid emptying mine despite to still fresh smell of blood. It was like I'd walked into a butcher shop.

These men might have been in enemy uniforms, but we all knew that it could have been any of us. It was hard not to feel a little shame. The long, sickening march finally ended at a railway line which was the starting point for out next advance. The few remaining tanks were also moving forward, and we were told they would begin their attack at 4.30pm.

Bert checked the Lewis Gun as always while the rest of us stocked up on ammo and cleaned our rifles. Just then a runner came bounding through the group who Dickie recognised,

"Hey Roberts, any news of the wounded?"

"Not that I've heard," he replied as he hustled off with some important message.

"Frank'll be OK," said Mick, "Right Stan?"

"I hope so," I replied.

Bluey Wilton called us all together,

"Righto you blokes, get it together. We're moving out!"

"You reckon you can keep up Stan?" asked Bert with a wry smile.

I just winked and looked ahead.

"Forward!" called Blue. The same command rang out all up and down the line and we stepped over the railway and started moving, again in battle formation. Our orders weren't nearly as complicated today. We were simply told to take as much enemy territory as possible.

The ground was very different here. It hadn't seen battle for about two years. It was farmland mostly, with crops growing in fields, surrounded by grass and scattered woodlands. It was quite a change from the muddy shell ridden muck holes we'd called home. Walking was much easier and we made good progress. We were all feeling much more confident than the day before, even cocky.

This, we thought, would be easy with the enemy in disarray. Initially resistance was thin with just an occasional shot heard from the Germans, but the relative quiet was smashed by an almighty boom and an enemy shell exploded in the centre of our line. Several men, including some officers were blown to smithereens flying through the air line store mannequins.

Our lackadaisical attitude had been well and truly knocked out of us, but we soon found that the line was getting scrappy as some got pinned down while others pushed on. The artillery was coming from an area known as Crepey Wood and they certainly had our position well targetted.

Small arms and rifle fire became more intense, and we responded while still moving towards the enemy. Bert fired the Lewis gun from his hip as it hung in a sling. It caused many Germans to up and run while others surrendered as we came upon their positions. But there were many more that wanted to fight this day and we had to work for every yard.

I spotted Mick pointing his rifle at a group of Germans and heard the exchange,

"Hand hoc you blokes" It was as good as his French from what I could tell.

"Kamerad," replied two of the men as they raised their arms but the other three refused. They kept hold of their rifles which caused some of us to turn ours in their direction. Bert too stopped and trained the machine gun on the quintet.

"Don't give it a thought Fritz," said Bert. The lead German leered at Bert for a moment then dropped his rifle. The other two followed suit immediately.

"Thanks Bert, they didn't seem too keen for a moment," suggested Mick.

"Send em back to HQ, see if you can give em to someone else and get back here fast as you can, " ordered Blue.

"Righto, come on you lot. Schnell schnell!" demanded Mick motioning for the group to start walking.

The advance continued and the artillery was replaced by Minenwerfer mortar shells as we moved north of the Roman Road. I heard a shout watched a few men scatter, then *woof*, a mortar exploded on the group. One man had his uniform blown clean off while another's stomach was slice open. His innards spilled onto the dirt. Both were killed instantly while a third rolled around in agony.

"Stretchers!" came the familiar cry.

This time I kept on walking, making certain I stayed with my crew. We soon came across a huge ammunition dump where a German post was firing on one of our tanks. Five men crept up on the enemy position and using bombs captured an officer and twenty one Germans. They seized three machine guns in the process.

We'd stumbled on the first of several machine gun posts and, with our flank exposed, took heavy fire from one of them, another of those redoubts. Our ranks were thinning out quickly and we took cover anywhere we could, but there were few shell holes to protect us here.

Our line became more fragmented, and we moved forward so fast we had no flanking support. Up ahead we saw a factory of some kind and Blue called a halt.

"I think we've come too far. That isn't supposed to be there!" he yelled pointing at the brickworks. "Dig in boys; we'll have to wait it out."

We'd wandered too far into enemy territory it appeared and were taking heavy fire. Realising our plight a group of tanks headed for the ruined buildings but before any of them could strike, two were hit by artillery. Shells came from an area called Froissy Valley. Another battery started firing from the Rainecourt region hitting two more of the machines as they crept into view. One tank survived and circled the brick factory despite the obvious danger. Plumes of dirt billowed as shells exploded all around it. With series of rapid shots, the tank hammered the German position sending up red brick dust. They fired relentlessly and it soon became too much for the Germans inside. They were spotted rushing off away from the rear of the building.

"Hoorah" we cried.

The tank completed it circuit of the factory and once the crew was satisfied it was clear they moved off. Even so, we decided it best to stay where we were for now. The Germans had barely started building trenches here, only managing a random array of shallow scrapes.

To our right the 17th battalion passed through Framerville and occupied a huge orchard while the Germans retired to Rainecourt. A few Australians scurried after them, encouraged by cheers and shouts but after a while we realised, they weren't coming back.

Despite our scattered formation and our left flank still exposed, we held the position. The next several hours were very tense as German artillery and machine gunner harassed us. We couldn't do much until dark, so we stayed low and kept watch.

Darkness finally fell on us and with that the arrival of the 45th battalion, who plugged the gap on the left. The line was now secure with the Germans had been pushed back another three miles. The towns of Rosieres, Lihons, Framerville and Vauvillers had been liberated. Bert has established a machine gun post as we readied ourselves for a counterattack, but it seemed the Germans were spent for now and the night was incident free.

Next morning our commanders accounted for most of the casualties and sent their reports to HQ. After two days of fighting the strength of the 18th Battalion had been savaged. In all, fourteen officers and one hundred and seventy other ranks were lost, leaving the battalion with a fighting strength of six hundred and ten, a far cry from the original one thousand and the scores of reinforcements that had joined since the battalion was formed in 1915.

We expected to push on given the inroads we'd made to date, but we were ordered to hold. Commanders disappeared into meetings discussing, who knows what? It was clear that something was amiss, but we didn't know anything.

"Jesus, why are we just sitting around?" Bert mused. "They're buggered; we should finish the job!"

Most of the platoon agreed but Blue had some inside information,

"It's the number gents. We're running out of men. They're talking about waiting for reinforcements and going at it again next year!"

"You're joking!" blurted Dickie.

"Afraid not," replied Blue.

"Well, that's just a load of rot," said Mick. "Giving us time to reinforce means they can do the same!"

All the men agreed.

"Well, if it were up to me..." replied Blue but he didn't finish the remark. He didn't need to.

And so, we sat, waiting while our commanders considered a strategic pause.

Chapter 12

What Next?

It was now early on August 10th, 1918. We'd moved several miles in only a few days and the Germans were reeling, so we thought. We were awaiting orders while our commanders contemplated our options. The offensive had cost every battalion a good deal of men and there were very few coming to bolster the ranks now.

We were on ground that hadn't seen fighting since 1916, where over one million had died. Grass had grown over the fields here and, while there were telltale signs of past conflict, it was more like farmland than anything we'd seem in quite a while.

While the hierarchy contemplated our next move the Germans attacked. They opened with a huge barrage, which rained down on the 20th battalion, about five hundred yards to our left. They were still moving up having been slowed in their advance. Flares turned night into day, and D Company was released to help the 20th after an emergency message came from their commanding officer. The rest of us were to hold the old German line while the 19th battalion moved forward to try and cut off the Germans at Rainecourt Valley.

We waited, listening as the battle unfolded, not having much of an idea what was going on. A few hours passed when word came that the Australian 3rd Division was in trouble. They'd been pushing past Lihons when the Germans counter attacked. It seemed our artillery had miscalculated their barrage which had fallen short. It did nothing but wake the Germans who made it to their machine guns unmolested and with plenty of time to deal with our blokes.

As the daylight broke, we watched as a lone German aircraft strafed the Australians while our supporting tanks were knocked out. The 37th battalion was reported to have suffered heavy losses, including the death of their commanding officer. The advance quickly declined into a shambles. Machine gunners were being taken out by German snipers and only the bravery of individuals and small groups kept the advance moving, despite the odds.

More news came back which indicated the 20th battalion had also been hit hard, and the men of our own D Company were trapped in a roadside drain.

They were only saved when a fog rolled in giving them time to consolidate their position. Finally, stokes mortars and Lewis guns quelled the German attack but it was clear that we'd lost quite a few more when the men of D Company finally returned.

At 4pm new orders came through. The entire Australian Corps was to move forward and line up with the Canadians. Commanders visited the front line and decided when the time was right to move. Enemy artillery had all but stopped and the machine gun fire was sporadic. It appeared the Germans were retiring north of the main road. The 5th Brigade would be relieved, and an attack carried out by the 6th. Despite regular bombing raids by enemy aircraft, we were in the line by 11pm.

We were met by field kitchens and a supply of fresh water and settled in for a good feed. Afterwards we managed to get some sleep but were soon roused again and marched to the support lines. Our commanders had been sizing up the cost of the advance and decided that the battalions needed to be reorganised. It was unsettling news and had many seething at the possibility of being split up.

I watched as a medic returned with a wounded soldier. The medic's uniform was soaked in blood, his face white and eye bloodshot, telling the story of the last few days. I doubted that he'd slept a wink by the look of him. He deposited the wounded soldier at a clearing station and set off for the front line again.

"We should ask someone about Frank," suggested Dickie.

"Good idea," I said, "Why don't you get em to patch up your hand while you're in there?"

Dickie, realising he dobbed himself in stood and made his way to the clearing station. He was gone for quite a while but finally emerged sporting a bright white bandage. As he came back Bert couldn't contain himself,

"Better not wave Dick, that bandage on your hand might be mistaken for a white flag!"

"Yeah, real funny!" said Dickie.

"Any news on Frank?" but before Dick could answer someone else chimed in,

"Hospital and surgery!"

It was Mick, returning from wherever he'd been for the last day or so. Blue spotted him and strode up immediately,

"Where the blazes did you get to? I told you to offload those prisoners!"

"Sorry Blue, but no-one wanted the responsibility. Couldn't just leave em wandering about," he explained with a wide grin.

"Yeah right, I should do you for going AWL!" With that Blue turned and walked off.

"Where did you go Mick," asked Dickie.

"Well after taking those prisoners back, I went looking for Frank. I finally found someone who looked up some records, and he told me they sent him off to hospital. He needed an op and wasn't in good shape. Don't know any more than that...but at least we know he was alive!"

We were only slightly relieved.

Blue then called to the platoon, "OK you lot, listen up. We're going forward again. Get your gear ready and wait for orders."

"Gee thanks for the rest," said Dickie wiping his brow with his clean white bandage.

"Bloody hell, what's that Dickie," asked Mick, "You are joining the signal corps?"

With that we laughed and got ready to move out again.

We'd only had a day behind the line and weren't feeling too keen to get back into the fight, but our spirits were buoyed when some mail arrived. It seemed almost ridiculous that amongst all this death and gore, a bag of letters had come through unscathed but there it was.

I heard my name called and literally bounced up and grabbed the letter. I tore it open and started reading...

Dearest Stanley,

I hope this letter finds you well. Young Harry Robson has been stopping by and shown me the letters you have sent. I hope you don't mind. We've heard so much about the war, but no-one really knows what's happening. Your letters paint a very sad picture of France at the present moment. I cannot imagine what you have been through. It's hard to believe men could be involved in such a horrible conflict as this. I imagine the truth is worse than we're being

I sat their gob smacked for a moment. Pangs of homesickness and regret surged through my gut. The letter was like a revelation to me as if my father had awakened from a coma and recognised me. Perhaps Agnes Vaughan had been good for him after all, although it was difficult to ignore how she felt about the younger children. Maybe Harold had given him a new perspective about the war and shaken the anger out of him. That would explain why it took so long for him to write. I've been away for almost two years, and this was the first time I really *wanted* to go home. A tear welled in one eye, and I wiped it away before anyone noticed but it was clear that I was emotional. For a moment I was a boy again, wishing I was sitting at home listening to one of my father's stories or helping in the shop. No-one interrupted me; these reactions were common when the mail arrived. I scrambled for a pencil and paper when the order came to move out. It was a cruel irony that I would have to carry this news without any opportunity to respond. I felt a terrible urgency, which was eventually replaced by anxiety, frustration and finally submission. There was really nothing to be done now and what difference might a few days make?

As we kitted up Mick came over, "You Ok Stan?"

"Yes, I'm alright." I didn't say any more. I stuffed the paper and pencil back in my pack. I would write to Dad later if I could.

We were briefed about the coming operation. Our battalion would take over from the 20th and set up a defensive perimeter. The 20th would move forward and establish posts along the road to defend the flank. The 10th Brigade would then advance beyond a strategic crossroad where most of the recent hostilities had taken place. They would then turn north and press for the River Somme. At the same time the British on the other side of the river would push south also aiming to reach the river. It was hoped that the Germans would be caught in a pincer movement and be quickly mopped up.

We settled into our new position around midnight, and I took up the role of number 2 on the Lewis gun because of Dickies hand wound. The bandages restricting his ability to grip. I helped Bert set up the machine gun on the left of our line while others were placed at the most strategic and, as was common, the most vulnerable positions on the line. The 17th battalion did the same on our right and we were soon ready. Once again, the enemy seemed to have caught wind of the movement on our line and started to dump a barrage, this time it came down on B and C Companies and Battalion HQ. Thankfully their targetting was off and they didn't appear to have many guns left in the area now, adding more evidence to suggest they were pulling back further. We heard machine gun fire in the distance followed by a huge bombardment from the British sector around 1am. Our big guns opened on the Germans with a barrage that lasted six hours. Thankfully we spend the night well away from the action and by noon the next day were told that the operation had met little resistance and achieved all its objectives.

After a short snooze we were woken again. This time they were looking for volunteers to go out and collect booty from the battlefield. Mick and I were chosen, and I felt somewhat excited by the prospect. We joined the others and headed out onto the newly gained ground. We'd been ordered to check the German dead and see if we could identify any units.

Our party moved north, passing the now infamous crossroad, then turned east along the road for several hundred yards. Again, the accuracy of our barrage was evident. German dead were scattered here and there, and we checked their uniforms for insignias and papers that might help our commanders. I came across a man who appeared to be asleep. There were no obvious wounds and no traces of blood on his uniform.

"Concussion most likely," said Mick

I bent down and looked him over, tearing off the insignia from his shoulder. I rifled through his pockets looking for papers and unhitched a pocket pulling out a wad of documents. When I opened the first page I saw a map. It appeared to be incredibly detailed with colour coding and topographical features. I'm sure it would reveal much about the units in this area prior to our advance.

"Struth, that's a bloody good find Stan!"

"I reckon...wonder what else he's got?"

Just then a photograph slipped out from between the pages and dropped to the ground. The face of a beautiful young woman looked back at me, no doubt his wife or fiancé. She was wearing a fine hat, and her skin was pale and she was smiling slightly. I stared at the image, knowing that she would soon be a broken hearted woman. I slipped the photograph back into the man's pocket.

"Gee Stan, they said to bring everything," Mick reminded me.

"I really don't think they meant personal effects and you know the code."

"True enough." He replied." Come on let's get this stuff back to the CO."

We gathered up the rest of the papers and handed them over. We continued to scout the areas for loot and managed to secure several Minenwerfers, quite a few machine guns, some field guns and an array of telephones, rifles, periscopes and specialist equipment. There was simply too much for our group to carry. We took what we could, deposited it with HQ and returned to our section.

When we got back the men were abuzz with news of another big push. That night we heard field artillery and tanks moving ahead of us and there were reports that Germans were setting up a machine gun line. There was some shelling from enemy 5.9s but most of the shells were falling well behind us. German aircraft passed overhead and dropped a few bombs focussing on the heavily laden roads.

Our section of the line was quiet which enabled me to scratch out a few words to my father. I made a point of apologising for running away and it struck me at that very moment that it took a war across the other side of the world to wake both of us from our manic state. I shoved it back into my pack intent on depositing it with the outgoing mail first chance I got. I was feeling better for having put my thoughts on paper.

We rose next morning to find the British 17th Division nearby. We also discovered that our commander, Lt Col George Francis Murphy was back in charge. Orders instructed us to stay in close contact with the English 50th Infantry Brigade to our immediate left. At 9.35 a German plane flew into our sector about eight hundred feet above us. Lewis gunner, Andrew Johnston opened up on the machine. Tracer fire streamed at the aircraft and bullets clearly cut through its fabric, somehow passing the armour plating. For a moment nothing happened but then the plane rose suddenly and flipped over before spiralling into the ground near Richmond Wood. We all cheered and Private Johnson received several slaps on the back for his marksmanship. We'd all grown very used to watching people die and even celebrating a kill. There was no remorse or second thought these days. It was only when we got up close to the carnage that our spirits were subdued.

We were soon able to bathe and receive a change of clothing, a rare thing indeed and something we were grateful for. A few unlucky men then had to go out on burial detail, an unpopular job which was particularly unwelcome in this instance as the men were all clean and didn't want to soil themselves on bloody, decaying corpses. You weren't guaranteed a safe passage either. The Germans were only too willing to shoot at you whether you carried a rifle or a spade.

We spent the rest of the day and the next night behind the line. All was quiet until 4.45am when German gas shells landed amongst us and rained down for an hour. We had to keep our respirators on for quite a while after it stopped. When all clear was given, someone cried out,

"They got the mess!"

The news was welcomed with a huge cheer.

Observers had pinpointed the source of the barrage, the town of Proyart and a message was dispatched. Shortly afterwards our artillery snarled to life, shelling the area only to be answered by the German guns. The exchange continued for the entire day and into the evening. No infantry movement was ordered and the Germans too sat tight.

The next day came and went with no change in our situation until orders arrived in the evening. We were immediately bussed to the Fuoilloy sector, east of Amiens. The journey was interrupted by shells on the Villers Bretonneux Road which we managed to avoid. On arrival we settled into new lodgings in the form of tents.

"This can only mean we're being rested for another huge push," Dickie suggested.

"I'm surprised we haven't been at it already," replied Mick.

For several days we waited around at Fuoilloy near a pretty section of the River Somme. We wrote letters, held swimming races and some improvised concerts. The weather was perfect and we were all in high spirits. Training, weapons instructions, hot bathes, delousing and practice at the shooting range took up most of our time but we managed to get in some sun baking too.

We seemed to have a good share of luck as well. The Germans were sending over regular bombing raids, but they always seemed to leave us be. Of course, the good times couldn't last and on August 26th we climbed back on our buses and left for the next stunt.

By 1am, after the bus drivers had been lost for a few hours, we settled into the trenches of Mericourt where the River Somme began a series of "S" bends leading to the big turn which came up from the south. We rested for the night, getting only a few hours of sleep before we ate, gathered our equipment and with full packs began to match. The road was crammed with men and all manner of appliances in long, slow columns. This was a general advance, and everything was moving forward now, taking over the ground that the Germans had vacated without a fight. It could only mean they were going to make a stand somewhere and we all knew that the river made for a natural barrier, so the big bend in the Somme seemed like an obvious place.

It took us most of the day to get to our rendezvous point, but none of the battalion guides were there to meet us as it turned out.

"Gee look at that!" called Mick. The Germans had left two huge coal dumps behind when they retreated, one of them was burning. As we looked around, we saw vast quantities of material that had been discarded during the retreat.

"They certainly left in a rush," I suggested.

"Yep, I wonder what scared em off," replied Bert and we laughed.

Another quiet night followed and then more marching as we continued to press forward. There was still no sign of the Germans who continued their retreat. The only soldiers we sighted were the unburied.

Just after lunch we were to rendezvous with the 21st Battalion. Preparations were made to relieve them but there was a lot of confusion about their exact location. None the less we were ordered to move forward and attack Mereaucourt Wood in the Chuignolles sector. The 6th Brigade would lead the advance, and the 18th battalion would follow and occupy the enemy trenches after the first wave had swept them out.

"Oh great, rat patrol," someone yelped. It wasn't a popular role and exposed us to booby traps and poisoned food.

On August 28th the entire 2nd Division was mobilised, and we trudged east for several hours without incident. The terrain wasn't too difficult and didn't exhibit any recent battle scars. We saw the occasional abandoned lorry or broken down tank but nothing else.

The River Somme snaked east to west here and the terrain opened before us like a picture postcard, revealing a beautiful river valley full of forests and hills. The Germans had retreated from the area without a fight, so our advance was once again without incident.

We finally managed to find the 21st battalion in an area between the river and Boucher Wood. Once again, we got comfortable and waited. Up ahead we heard gunfire followed by explosions and soon after, plumes of smoke were rising. We fully expected to be called up at any second to occupy the ground that had been gained and just after 7pm a message arrived, *all objectives taken.*

Three companies from the 18th Battalion were immediately sent forward to attack Mereaucourt Wood. We stood and walked, Bert at my side. We were all laden with extra bombs and with bayonets fixed. I carried Bert's side arm and Dickie carried the extra ammunition for the Lewis gun.

It was approaching dusk when we came upon a wooded area. Machine gun fire burst from the trees pinning down A Company but we were able to enter the remnant wood without incident as did C Company. We started working our way through and an eerie feeling crept over me. The trees were starting to grow back and provided some sort of cover. It was a far cry from the skeletons that were so far behind us now. We kept in touch by making a lot of noise, despite the presence of the Germans. When we emerged from the wood, we saw the enemy occupying a trench line near the town of Feuilleres, near the crest of the great bend in the Somme. This was where the river flowed north before the terrain forced it to swing to the west on its journey to the sea.

After a quick assessment, patrols were sent forward. They reported enemy soldiers on the northern side of the river who appeared to be behind the Allied positions. Word was sent back and an artillery barrage was organised to deal with them. B Company was ready to move beyond the town and establish a new front line, but it would have to wait until the next morning. We were ordered to secure our current position and hold.

Chapter 13

The Battle of Mont St Quentin

At 1am on August 29th, 1918, we settled into our new position, with nothing more than a series of holes rather than a trench line to hide us. Cover was scarce and even though there was no enemy fire we set about digging in to improve the situation. The *great bend* in the River Somme was still about six miles east of our location, much of the area still held by the Germans. Some of the enemy was still in Mereaucourt Woods where we'd lost contact with A Company after their little skirmish. A patrol was organised to mop up and clear the way for A Company to join us. I was glad not to have been chosen for the job. We'd been on the move for quite a while and most of us were ready to sleep where we sat. I could hardly muster the strength to hold my trenching tool as it was. Soon after, we heard some gun play to our rear and eventually saw the patrol returning with the stranded men. As luck would have it they all came through without a scratch.

We sat in our holes for around two hours waiting for new orders. I managed to snatch about an hours' sleep but was abruptly woken by a shake from Bert. He was as talkative as usual and smiled as I swore at him for bothering me. My mood changed when I realised that our orders had arrived and we were going back into action immediately.

"Push forward vigorously!" came the order from High Command.

The boys were all in good spirits. We'd made much progress since August 8th and had been chasing the Germans for twenty one days. It looked now like we'd come across the site of their rear guard, and it was indeed formidable.

Our new objective was the stronghold of Mont St Quentin; about one or two miles beyond the great bend. Mont St Quentin was where the river hooked west after meandering from the south. The Somme provided a natural barrier with its swamps and canals while the hill itself swept up from the river to a height of over four hundred and fifty feet. This hill gave the Germans a panoramic view of the ground we were to cross and a perfect field of fire. The news only got worse when we learned that it was defended by hundreds of machine guns, dozens of howitzers and endless rolls of wire. We'd only had time to absorb that news when someone explained how the area was held by the 2nd Prussian Guard, one of Germany's elite units along with several divisions of infantry.

"Bully for them!" said Bert, but it didn't make me feel better. Suddenly, our enthusiasm was gone as we realised what we were up against.

We couldn't go around the hill because the Germans held the town of Clery to the northeast and Peronne to the south. A coordinated attack would be needed to take all the enemy strong points in one operation. The task seemed monumental with our numbers having been savaged by recent actions. Many were already talking about failure. I looked at Bert but couldn't tell what he was thinking,

"You reckon it can be done Bert?" I asked.

"Dunno," he mumbled and cast a half glance towards the hill, "Maybe."

Dick, who was never short of words made his feelings clear,

"Suicide! There's no cover from what I can see, and they'll be all over us long before we get there. It'll be a slaughter," he suggested.

Usually, such remarks would receive a tirade of criticism, but the men were tired and most didn't disagree.

We were soon mustered for a briefing about the upcoming attack on the hill, Mont St Quentin. We listened intently while studying the newly printed maps. We'd try a traditional front on attack while other units attacked Peronne and Clery. We were told that if Mont St Quentin could be taken, the Germans would have no alternative but to retreat to the Hindenburg Line, several more miles east.

"Success is vital," the orders concluded.

The message was clear enough, but lots of men had died failing to deliver vital success before, why would this be any different? Then we got some news that gob smacked all of us, the summit of Mont St Quentin would be taken by just three infantry battalions. Our sister battalions could barely organise enough men to make up the numbers for one battalion, despite the recent reshuffle. There would be little artillery support and no tanks, and the men would have to wade through the marshes and canals before crossing the river and making the climb.

"Madness," Mick whispered.

The 18th had been allocated the task of finding a way across the Somme Canal south of a town called Ommiecourt. Once across we would have to get over the river before advancing on the summit. The 19th would provide us with support. We checked our packs in with the quartermaster and took our allocation of ammunition including rifle bullets, Mills bombs and bags of Lewis gun panniers. Despite my fatigue I slept restlessly and had some terrible dreams about getting stuck in the mud with machine guns firing on me. I don't think I was any more rested when I rose the next day.

At 5am the battalion started to move east, along the south bank of the Somme. There was little sign of the Germans over the next few miles, so we guessed they'd made for the high ground that we were charged with taking from them.

We pushed on, passing Feuilleres. Just ahead the river turned slightly to the left before curving back dramatically, creating a large natural peninsular. Ommiecourt sat at the tip of this spit of land with Clery on the opposite bank to the north. Our hope was that bridges beyond Ommiecourt were intact, making for an easy crossing. If we could take the town quickly the Germans might not be able to do much damage. However, it soon became clear that the enemy had done much to hamper our progress. A major bridge crossing at Feuilleres had been blown up stopping anyone from crossing to the north bank. That meant we would reach our target before Clery could be attacked, leaving our left flank open.

We moved down a slope towards the peninsular and found the Ommiecourt Road and saw that the bridge over the Somme Canal had also been blown too. The canal stretched about three thousand feet across the base of the peninsula and had to be crossed before tackling the town and then the river. Beyond the canal was about four thousand yards of land leading to Ommiecourt. The area was terribly exposed with Germans occupying all the ground ahead and to the left.

We saw a loch and were ordered to make toward it. It seemed like the best way to cross the canal, but as we got closer the shrieks of artillery shells spilt our ears and the loch was obliterated before our eyes. The shell fire continued and the clatter of machine guns soon chimed in. The area around us erupted and tiny plumes of dirt spat up as machine gun bullets danced amongst the men. We were in trouble!

"This is bloody hopeless!" I heard someone shout and I had to agree.

Our engineers had worked hard during the night to establish crossings over the canal, but these had all be destroyed as soon as they were spotted in the morning light. We decided to make our own bridge and gathered anything we could for the task. The engineers had brought up duckboards, so I grabbed one and made for the canal, only moving about thirty yards before there was a thunderous roar. I spun around to see a group of men flailing on the ground, their duckboards shattered by the blast. All died within seconds.

Machine gun fire followed immediately, spitting up more dirt. We were suddenly in a dire position and wide open.

"Jesus, Blue. What now?" I screamed.

"MOVE! Just keep moving or we're mincemeat!" He screamed.

I made for the canal holding the duckboard like a shield in the misguided hope it might catch a bullet that would otherwise find me. Plumes of smoke and dust burst all around us, some shells hitting the canal, one spout soaking me. I slapped my duckboard down on the bank and turned to get another. Despite the enemy fire, very few hits were being made. The Germans machine gunners were firing from quite a distance, which impeded their targeting. Still that artillery was relentless and hampered us constantly. Bert fired off the Lewis gun to try and slow the enemy Maxims, but the Lewis gun struggled to find targets just like the Maxims. The rest of us kept up with the duckboard relay.

By 10am we'd managed to create a small bridge, and men began crossing the canal. The Germans concentrated their fire on the position, and it seemed just a matter time before our work was to become matchwood. My turn came to cross and I slung my rifle and ammo bags over each shoulder. As I stepped onto the first duck board I slipped on the mud and landed on my side, falling on the bombs in my tunic pockets. It knocked the wind out of me and I gasped for air.

"Move Dunkley, get the hell over there," screamed Blue.

I struggled to my feet as more bullets sputtered around. I took a deep breath and stepped up again. It was a terribly rickety structure, and it took all my strength to keep balance. It seemed to take an eternity to make the twenty yard crossing, and I was very relieved to step onto the mud at the other side. I wasn't the only one having trouble; everyone slipped and slid across in one way or another while Blue screamed and cursed at them.

There was a cutting in the peninsula just ahead and B Company personnel crowded into the space, which provided some cover from the machine guns at least. I tried not to think about an enemy shell falling into the gap where we stood. Blue decided this was a good place to wait, at least until the machine gun fire abated. We were hoping that units to our north could take out some of the German guns.

Our first objective had been achieved; we'd crossed the canal. Now we had to get across the Somme before climbing the Mount. Blue peered through a pair of field glasses, trying to pinpoint the German positions. He counted twenty enemy soldiers in a trench. Field guns kept up their bombardment on the canal as the stragglers came across. Our duckboard bridge was defying the odds and remained intact.

We watched as an Allied cavalry unit thundered towards Clery to our immediate north about fifteen hundred yards away, across the river. German machine gunners clattered a fusillade into the men and their horses and cut them up badly. I saw only one of the men escape. Without warning a massive explosion shuddered our position as a shell hit the front of the cutting. We were showered with debris but were otherwise unscathed.

A runner arrived and told us that D Company has successfully pushed a group of Germans across the river and had reached Rooghi Trench. At first, we were elated by the news, but it soon became clear that their success and the fact that we were pinned down created a huge gap in the line. Men were scattered all over the battlefield, most unable to make any forward progress. The boys from D Company captured a few prisoners who were taken back to headquarters. They wore the uniforms of the 4th Bavarians, a division we hadn't come across before, but certainly respected as they were proving tough adversaries.

We were stuck in that cutting for the rest of the day, German shells and machines gun bullets making certain we couldn't move. Blue finally blew his stack,

"Bloody Hell! I'm fed up with this!"

He split us into three groups and sent us out for a look around. We ran out of the cutting and dashed forward looking for a crossing over the Somme. It was hard to see much with all the dust and smoke in the air. I hoped the Germans too were finding it just as difficult. We stumbled across the peninsula and moved towards the great bend in the Somme. Ommiecourt was about one thousand yards away when German machine gunners in the town sighted us and started firing. We had no time to look for a bridge or any other way across the river, so we withdrew to make our report.

New orders had arrived while we were on patrol requiring us to advance where possible or at least hold our gains.

"Hold what?" Bert asked sarcastically.

"Either way we're buggered," Someone else remarked.

"I know," said Blue, "Let me think for a minute."

I looked at Bert and saw his shoulder was bleeding where some fragment had penetrated. He just smiled at me and winked. He was a tough bugger.

Just then the other patrols returned with no good news. Waiting until morning would not change a thing. As soon as there was light the Germans would be all over us again. Blue decided to send a message back to HQ,

"STAN!" cried Blue above the din of gunfire.

"Yes Blue?" I replied.

"Run back to HQ. Tell them we're pinned down and need help. Forward progress impossible. Guns in Clery and Ommiecourt need to be silenced. You got all that?"

"Yes Blue!"

"OK, get moving," Blue ordered.

Mick, Bert and Dick looked at me. I could see they were worried. I was nervous but didn't want them to know it, so I mustered up a grin.

"Back in a jiffy," I said in a less than convincing tone.

"Be sure that you are," demanded Bert.

I slipped out of the cutting and ran for the nearest shell hole. I didn't have to go far. I thought it best to run from one shell hole to the next and take any cover available until I was in the clear. The hard part would be crossing the canal again. The ground was pockmarked with gaping holes and clods of dirt from the artillery. It was almost dark now, but the Germans were sending up their usual light show. If the war was a contest for turning night into day, they'd win for certain. I was caught in the flickering light as I dashed for the canal. The clatter of a Maxim rang out and a split second later bullets spattered into the ground flicking up little plumes of dust. I weaved left as the maxim corrected its fire and jumped into a shell hole just as another stream of bullets danced along its rim. I waited there for the light to diminish knowing the Maxim crew would be waiting for me to emerge. I decided to get out of the hole the way I came in assuming they'd be looking to the canal side, which might give me a slight advantage. Should I crawl out or run? If I crawled and they saw me, I was a goner. I scrambled out and started running.

I swerved to my right for about thirty yards before cutting back towards the duckboard bridge. My timing was perfect as there was a period of darkness between flares, so I was well clear of the shell hole when the next flare lit up. The maxim crew must have been fooled because it took them a while to pick up my movement, but I was soon zigzagging across the ground as the dirt burst around me again.

"Run you bugger!" someone screamed from across the canal.

Engineers had returned to try and do some bridging and saw my dilemma. A few more voices started urging me along.

"Go mate," "Come on!"

 I could see the duckboards and leaped onto the rickety structure. How it had survived the day I'll never know, but I was certainly glad. I didn't have time to worry about being careful and thought my momentum might carry me across before I lost balance. Sadly, that wasn't the case. I'd barely put my foot down when a shell exploded in the water. I watched in horror as dark wave swept down on the bridge. It hit me like Bondi surf, and I was suddenly sucked down into the canal. I rolled a few times before the water settled and I surfaced, coughing up a load of muck. I scrambled for the side of the canal as the Maxim crew again trained their sights on me again. Just then I felt the grip of a strong hand, then another. I was hauled out of the canal like I was a feather and immediately saw the smiling faces of the engineers.

"You alright sport?"

"Good as gold," I told them, "Which way to HQ?"

"Quarry Wood!" one of them replied and they all pointed.

"Thanks!"

I started running again. The maxim crew fired of a few more useless volleys before I disappeared over a hill and out of sight. I ran all the way to Headquarters and went to the first officer I saw,

"Sir, Stan Dunkley, B Company." I advised.

"Report son," said the officer.

"We're stuck on the northeast side of the canal, forward progress impossible. Guns in Clery and Ommiecourt have us pinned. They must be dealt with sir!"

I waited while the officer processed the report.

"What shape are you in?" he asked.

"We're OK for now, but the Germans have our position and we're dead ducks if we wait for daylight sir."

"Understood. Wait here," he ordered.

The officer marched off and disappeared into a small farmhouse. He was in there for about ten minutes before returning.

"Go back to your CO. Tell him we'll try to clear those guns. As soon as we do you are ordered to push forward. Go!"

"Yes sir!"

I saluted, turned and started running. Shell fire was flashing in the distance, and the ground seemed to shimmer in the red light of their explosions while the coloured flares signalled this and that, mostly SOS signals from our blokes. The engineers cheered as I ran headlong into the canal and waded across. It was about four feet deep and quite cold. I pushed a few duckboard fragments out of my path as I lurched out onto the mud and rested for a moment to catch my breath. Running was very difficult with my uniform drenched but I got going again after a few more seconds. Thankfully the machine guns were trained on other areas but I still I jumped from shell hole to shell hole just in case and finally made it back to the cutting. I was panting heavily as Blue approached.

"Well? What's happening?" he demanded.

I struggled to speak, "Artillery to hit Clery........we go forward when the German guns stop!"

"Right then, we wait until those guns are dealt with then move on Ommiecourt, clear it out then cross the river. Everyone got that," Blue yelled.

No-one answered which was an affirmative response under the circumstances.

Almost as soon as he'd finished speaking the roar of artillery started pounding Clery. Plumes of smoke erupted from the town with flashes of red strobing the shattered buildings. The 3rd Division men then started their advance on our left flank. We watched and waited as they entered the town. Machine guns were still buzzing along with the familiar crack of Lee Enfield rifles and Mills bombs. With the Germans now busy we high tailed it out of the cutting and made for Ommiecourt, looking for a bridge. Despite the guns in Clery being dealt with there was still plenty of artillery coming down from Mont St Quentin with machine gun support. We pressed on, maintaining artillery formation as best we could. This time we made it to the river. Ommiecourt was so close but could still be occupied. It too was under a heavy bombardment from our artillery. At least it kept them from firing on us.

We found what cover was available and set up a covering position while others started scouting for a crossing. They set off along the only road to the town then worked their way around the outskirts. They weren't gone long and reported back that all bridges had been destroyed and crossing here was out of the question. The Germans had no doubt vacated the town and destroyed the crossings as they went. Holding the peninsular now became pointless.

"OK men, back to the cutting," ordered Blue.

We sat in the cutting and waited. There was no hope of us moving forward even if other units broke through on our flanks. In other places men tried crossing the river using a weir but it too had been destroyed and was still under fire. Another group found an old punt but that proved fruitless. Those trying to cross the Canal Du Nord were stopped by thick marshes. The entire advance along the southern side of the river was literally bogged down. The enemy had the area well targeted and did a good job of impeding us at every opportunity. Nature did the rest.

We cowered between the earthen banks of the cutting for several hours until new orders arrived. They were now telling us to move back over the canal, head south and prepare to take the town of Halles about fifteen hundred yards southwest of Mont St Quentin. We gathered our equipment and moved out. It was still dark and the enemy machine gun fire was sporadic, however the artillery kept at us constantly. We crossed the canal and started for the new rally point. It took almost all night to get into position. Zero hour was set for 5am on August 30th. We waited as time ticked away, ready to move forward as soon as the order was given. Then at 4am the attack was called off. We learned that most of the units that were to join us simply couldn't make it to their starting points. Everything was going wrong and if we'd advanced without support, we would have been slaughtered. I'm thankful for the wisdom someone showed in calling us back.

Once again, we withdraw, returning to Quarry Wood where the cooks served us a hot breakfast. Only the 19th Battalion remained on guard near the canal.

"Well, that was a right royal cock up," suggested Bert and no-one disagreed.

"What now?" someone asked.

"We'll probably try again tomorrow. That's usually what we do isn't it?" blurted another.

We snatched a few hours of blissful welcome sleep. I reckon I could have slept twenty four hours without any trouble, but we were soon roused again.

"B Company fall in! Come on you lot, nap time's over!" ordered a Sergeant.

"Does he ever sleep?" enquired Dickie"

"Yeah, with his eyes open I reckon," said Mick.

We fought off the daze and assembled for a briefing. Clery had been liberated so we were to move northwest and cross the river then swing east and attack Mont St Quentin again. The 5th Brigade would take the lead but then we were relieved to hear the 18th Battalion was to stay in reserve. I didn't imagine for a moment that we'd stay out of the thrust for long.

The 5th Artillery Brigade had been moved up, and the 6th Machine Gun Company was split up amongst us to give the attacking units extra fire power. The rest of the day was spent marching, collecting ammunition and rations. We crossed the Somme at Feuilleres where engineers had repaired the bridge, turned east and marched into the rubble of Clery sur Somme. The attacking battalions continued through the town and turned south stopping on the eastern bank of the river. We waited just outside Clery.

August 31st 2am, German artillery started targeting the roads to try and slow us down and managed to hit some ration parties, wounding several men. Our counter batteries did their best, but they were hopelessly outnumbered. The Germans didn't seem to know what we were up to because most of their shells were landing in places well south of our new position. The darkness provided excellent cover.

At 2.30 the enemy shelling stopped and the rest of the night passed quietly, although sleep was difficult knowing what was soon to come. Others, like Bert slept like babies. I envied him being able to sleep regardless of what was going on.

A few hours later we moved up with some supplies for the 17th Battalion men who were taking the lead in this attack. Then the rum ration arrived early which many saw as a bad omen. Most refused to take a drink before a fight just in case it dulled their senses.

Mick was handing out dry ration packs and trying to reassure our comrades as he went,

"Good luck fellas. Don't make me come up there after you!" He ordered.

"Don't worry your pretty little head mate," came the reply.

I looked at Bert and saw the blood soaked shoulder of his uniform,

"How are you feeling?" I asked.

"Just a scratch!" he replied. If anything, every bothered Bert if never showed. It was comforting somehow.

The renewed attack on Mont St Quentin was about to begin. Dawn was starting to break, and I realised we had a great view of the battlefield. It was easy to see why the German's had stopped here, the territorial advantage was excellent. No matter where we came from, we'd be in the open. Mont St Quentin was two kilometers away and looked daunting. We could see Peronne to its south and a few other towns here and there. Many blokes were still having serious doubts about taking the objective. My gut twirled as I realised just how huge a task had been landed on us.

At 5am our artillery opened up. Fingers of flame scratched the sky as our guns roared to life, around ninety of them delivering shrapnel shells and high explosives onto the German front line, Gottlieb Trench. Some were aimed at breaking up the coils of German wire while others were firing on targets considered by our observers to have strategic value.

"I pity the poor bastards under that," I heard someone say. It was an awful spectacle indeed, but I was very hopeful that we'd make it across with no resistance when all was said and done.

Suddenly hundreds men from the first attacking wave stood and started walking. Most lit up cigarettes and strolled along like it was Sunday in the park. If they were scared it didn't show. The 17th Battalion was in the centre and would take the summit; the 19th was to take Uber Alles and Ott Uns trenches on the right while the 20th went for the village of Feuillaucourt on the left. This would enable us to make a flanking attack on the hill, hitting it from the side, rather than in front. We hoped the Germans would not be expecting such a tactic. We had no idea how many of the enemy held the hill, but it was clearly a significant number given the resistance we experienced the day before.

As smoke and flame rose into the air and the gunfire chorus rang out, the sun started to rise behind the mount. All three battalions ran into stiff opposition within a few minutes, every platoon coming across German forward posts. Savage gun fights broke out all along the front and all we could do was watch. The fighting was brutal, but the Australians pressed on relentlessly, wiping out the posts with bombs and bayonets. Then the 17th made its charge on Mont St Quentin. They literally ran up the hill, screaming like a mob of man men. The tactic was designed to make the enemy think there was a great force coming their way and it certainly sounded like it. The Germans were startled by the noise and panicked. Some surrendered where they stood, while others ran into our barrage. Those who bravely fought on were cut down in quick time.

Prisoners were soon filing back without escorts, following directions from Australians as they passed. Most were just boys with terror in their eyes. One group we noticed had a high ranking officer with them and he protested about how he was being treated. Lieutenant Joe Maxwell wasn't in the mood for good graces and relieved him of his field glasses and sent him on his way.

"This is where you get off mate," Joe said.

The 20th Battalion headed for Niche Trench. They attacked both flanks at once using speed and noise to confuse the enemy. Again, the Germans surrendered in large numbers. They took the trench in no time.

Word came for us to move up and support the 17th Battalion who were rushing up the hill. We moved further east and halted. More prisoners were streaming away from the fight. We could see Khaki uniforms chasing grey figures all over the side of the hill. Germans were literally jumping out of their trenches and running up the mount to escape the Australian juggernaut. Lewis gunners chased them, propped, fired a volley, picked off a target then ran again. Huge gaps in the German wire made the going easy and the Australians took Gottlieb trench in no time. Some stopped for a smoke while others carried on up the hill. Our barrage had lifted and started on other targets all over Mont St Quentin. Reports were coming back that lifted our spirits, *Casualties slight, troops awfully bucked*, said one.

The 17th quickly passed through the shattered remnants of the St Quentin village and across the Peronne road. They worked in small mobile groups, moving in quick bursts, selecting targets and timing their runs to perfection. The tactic was very effective in eliminating German positions with few casualties. To the astonishment of everyone, me included, the 17th Battalion reached the summit and occupied the German line. It was a wonderful sight and we all cheered.

Not everything was going to plan though. On the left the 20th Battalion's attack had become fragmented and their left flank was suddenly exposed. The German's were quick to realise they had an opportunity and counter attacked, using earthworks along the Cana Du Nord to conceal their movements. They strafed the Australians who took quite a few casualties. To their credit the 20th men pressed on and eventually overwhelmed the German strong points. They then focussed on Gottlieb trench and caught up to their barrage.

With one problem solved another soon developed. The attacking formations had moved apart during the advance causing large gaps to open between the 17th and 20th battalions. The Germans, ever vigilant massed for a strong counterattack. Within minutes they advanced on the Australians using a pincer movement hitting the left and right of the now isolated Australians. Their field of fire was perfect, and they used their guns to incredible effect, many from point blank range. Men of the 17th Battalion were falling all along their front and were suddenly in dire peril. The momentum had swung against us very quickly and runners were sent back asking for help.

At Noon we were called into the fight. Company Commander, Alex Irvine yelled,

"Let's move!" and we stood and started walking towards Mont St Quentin.

We soon heard the zing of bullets around our heads, and all kinds of ordnance began to drop around us. Smoke filled the air and the acrid taste of cordite stung my mouth. Wads of earth thudded down, hitting us like we'd challenged the playground bully. I tried to keep my head down to avoid getting dirt in my eyes. Some men were felled by shrapnel, others by machine gun and rifle bullets but we couldn't do anything for them as we pressed on. Our job was to get in and help the 17th secure a position on the hill before all the ground they'd gained was lost. We were to wait with them and fight off German counter attacks until relieved.

Before we got a chance to get into the fight the situation changed again. The 19th Battalion was making a good fist of the situation on their front, so B and C Companies were ordered to halt upon reaching Galatz Ally, a sap in the German trench system. We were ordered to stand by. Bert immediately set the Lewis gun up to defend the ground, as did the other machine gunners. I was close by with Dickie and Mick while we waited.

Four hours passed as the wrestle for the hill continued. We were under constant machine gun and rifle fire. A lone German howitzer had our position perfectly targetted and dropped a shell on us every few minutes. I watched as a shell curved towards us then ducked as it smashed into the ground thirty yards away. When I looked up again the side of the trench was gone. Several bodies lay bloody and limbless in the soil. It was shocking to see life snuffed out so quickly. Then I witnessed one of the most macabre things I've ever seen. We were close to a cemetery with headstones, crypts and statues all around. In the mayhem some of the men took advantage of the opportunity and found refuge in vaults. They even took to playing cards using coffins as seats while the battle raged outside. I don't know why but that seemed more horrifying to me than being shot at.

Another explosion lifted the earth very close to us, followed by shouts for stretcher bearers. Lieutenant Irvine had been hit and was unable to carry on. As he was carried away, signallers managed to establish a phone line to HQ. Lieutenant Joe Maxwell assumed command of B Company and reported the situation.

There was little we could but hug the trench walls and hope there wasn't another direct hit from a high explosive shell. Shrapnel wasn't a problem if you stayed below ground level and neither were the machine gun bullets that strafed us regularly. Luck was against us though, as another shell slammed into the sap exploding with a thunderous roar. I covered my face as chunks of soil crashed down on us, inhaling the acidic air. When the dust settled, I looked up to see the twisted body of a digger on the trench floor. Limbs were missing and blood oozed from the stumps, but it was his face that shocked me. He looked straight at me, as if he was wide awake but it was clear that his life has been brutally extinguished.

We received word to move to Moinville Alley, located somewhere else in the German trench system. Moving about was always risky, especially when the battle ebbed and flowed so much. It took a great deal of time to work our way through the now shattered trenches. When we arrived at our new position the Germans were massing for a counterattack against the 19th Battalion. We hadn't even settled in when we were ordered to assist.

Before long the enemy was throwing everything our way, mortars, whiz bangs, 5.9s, grenades, machine guns, rifle and pistol fire. They were all focussed on our position, and we were soon in trouble. Front line positions became very confused. At one point German soldiers were behind some Australian positions. A ration party died while retreating, running into a group of Germans. The Germans were mopped up very quickly.

My ears were ringing from the incessant noise as explosion after explosion cracked all around us. I watched Bill Phelps crying and calling for his mother. I was in no shape to comfort him; I too was about to succumb to this great pressure. Just then Father Frederick Tugwell, the 17th Battalion padre appeared and gave comfort to poor Bill. I was astounded by how calm and reassuring he was under such hellish fire. It renewed our confidence. Father Fred then moved around the trench offering cups of tea to everyone, oblivious to the danger. It was by far the bravest thing I'd ever seen.

German soldiers soon pushed the 17th battalion men back and retook St Quentin village. Germans were now probing for weak points along our dishevelled line. The counterattack finally came down on the 17th and 19th battalions, and we were stuck in the middle. We were barely hanging on to the rim of the mount as the enemy used their knowledge of the trench system and superior numbers against us. German counter strikes were hitting the entire defensive line, trying to break through. We knew that if they succeeded there'd be a rout, so we took the fight right back to them. Bert fired relentlessly at the attacking formations, while others covered the communications trenches where the Germans were sneaking up on us. Bert flicked off another pannier and I wacked another on the breech. I could feel the heat coming off the barrel and hoped the gun wouldn't cease.

Mick was firing at the flanks, and Dickie was doing his best despite the pain of his wound. He tossed me two more ammo bags, and I rifled around for another pan. A fusillade of bullets hissed into our position and miraculously missed everyone. I looked up to see a German rushing towards us, no doubt aiming to take out the Lewis gun. He fired his rifle at the same moment as Mick, the German falling in a heap only a few strides away from us.

The arm wrestle continued well into the afternoon. The enemy push and we repelled, repeatedly. Runners reported the progress to HQ, orders returned but we simply couldn't move. Ammunition was hustled forward and I was truly relieved to get some fresh panniers for the Lewis gun. We managed to hold on until darkness came.

Not long after sunset the fighting suddenly quietened, and then someone launched a flare and lit up the ground in front of us. Scores of Germans were caught in the open and Bert started firing, as did the other machine gunners. The rifles chimed in and I watched as, one after another, the German soldiers fell. Those that didn't die turned and made a hasty retreat. Stick bombs rained down to stem the hail of bullets. One exploded in front of our gun, blasting us with dirt. The remaining Germans slipped away into the darkness before we could fire another shot.

Another counterattack had been beaten back, but we knew more would soon come. Within an hour a flare revealed another group of Germans readying for the next attack. Australian artillery was ordered to help and sent a barrage down on their position. Again, they fell, one after another until the counterattack was called off. German artillery in Anvil Wood and in an old sugar refinery started on us again. They were doing their best to stop us taking Mont St Quentin and with good effect.

By midnight September 1st all of us were again running low on ammunition and the losses were adding up. Three fresh brigades were ordered to relieve us, but it would be a few hours before they came. At the same time the Germans were bringing in their own reinforcements; we could see them moving about on top of the hill, following the lanterns of their guides. The next push on the summit would be even more difficult.

The German counter attacks had ceased for now, replaced by gas. The distinct pop, pop, pop of the shells had us quickly donning our respirators. German aircraft buzzed us constantly while we received a meal of cold stew that had been brought up. We hadn't eaten in nearly two days, but the gas made it nearly impossible to risk taking a bite.

While our troops had made huge inroads into the German defenses, we still hadn't taken the summit. We learned that Peronne was still in German hands too, so there would be much to do when dawn broke. We were in no state to spend another day on the front line and hoped that relief would arrive soon.

Sporadic fire was ringing out here and there and we assumed the Germans were preparing to mount a fresh counterattack. The 17th Battalion had suffered dreadfully, while we had lost twenty eight men killed with another thirty eight wounded. Four others were missing. All three battalions managed to hold on for the next few hours while Germans again probed our line. Mortar and artillery fire started to come more readily again, and we knew the next counterattack was about to fall on us. All we could do was stay down until the barrage lifted, then try to repel them.

The 6th Brigade had been given the job of retaking Mont St Quentin, and the 14th would attack Peronne. Bouchavesnes Spur, eight miles north of us would be attacked by the 3rd, but it would all be for naught if we didn't hold the enemy back. Bert was trying to conserve ammunition, and we all hoped the Germans would not try our section of the line again.

"Ammo," cried Bert and I slapped another pannier onto the Lewis gun.

"Go easy Bert, we haven't got much left," I explained.

"Sounds familiar," said Bert in his usual dismissive tone.

The enemy artillery lifted and we readied ourselves to again repel a counterattack. We waited but they didn't come.

"Maybe they went home," said Bert and despite the tension a few of us laughed. We spend the next couple of hours waiting and watching as the occasional shell burst nearby.

At 6am we were ordered back to Gottleib Trench and completed the move by 8.45. An hour later the 6th Brigade boys began to move up for their push on Mont St Quentin. We were to provide cover fire. Germans were scurrying here and there as they saw our troops massing. Our snipers did their best to terrorise the enemy in the face of the new attack. Artillery was dropping on A Company as the 23rd and 24th Battalions passed through their position.

An hour later the order came *resume the attack.* Australians scampered up the hill, moving from shell hole to shell hole to avoid the machine gun fire. We provided cover fire and I watched as our men reached the German wire. Hand to hand fighting broke out as the 6th Brigade edged forward and soon prisoners were again filing back towards us.

The German defenses slowly but surely relented as the Australians continued their darting runs. When the enemy soldiers realised, they could no longer hold their positions, their line collapsed. Germans dropped their guns and fled while many stood with their hands raised. Confusion soon radiated up and down the enemy line. The momentum of the 6th Brigade increased, and they pushed beyond the German wire.

Defeat was now imminent for the Germans and by midafternoon Australians had retaken St Quentin Village and held the summit. This time the Germans would not be taking it back. The enemy was pushed further away and couldn't muster their customary counterattack.

We were well behind the fight now and exhaustion soon started to well up inside us. We were still being hounded by enemy artillery and found cover in an abandoned German blockhouse. These were solid concrete constructions and provided good cover except that their entrances now faced the Germans shelling. We'd been in the blockhouse for only half an hour when a shell lobbed outside with a huge thump. It rolled through the entrance and plopped on the floor of our dugout. We all looked at it, frozen with fear, anticipating the worst. After a few moments we realised it was a dud and someone simply picked it up and tossed it outside.

Two thousand six hundred prisoners were taken during the battle and despite being outgunned and outnumbered we prevailed. The 18th Battalion Adjutant tallied his casualty report and was shocked by what he found. In the three days we fought on Mont St Quentin we lost seventy two men, killed or wounded including four officers. Across all the divisions that took part the casualty count passed three thousand on top of the two thousand lost in the days before the battle.

I felt an incredible sense of relief because, despite the horror of such losses, I was still alive. My eyes were stinging due to fatigue, and a dreamless deep sleep soon engulfed me.

Chapter 14

The Beaurevoir Line

All of us were utterly exhausted. We'd been fighting without a break for three days and expected to be withdrawn to recuperate but no; an advisory from HQ ordered the battalion to *Stand by, ready to move.* It wasn't welcome news and two hours later we were sent forward again.

"They've got to be joking," screamed Mick.

"It's no bloody joke," replied Blue, who was clearly angry about the order.

We were to occupy Radegone Trench near Halle; the town we were supposed to take three days ago. It felt like a real slap in the face. German aircraft buzzed our position and enemy artillery kept peppering the area. Sleep was difficult amongst the continuing din, but we took a nap at any opportunity.

On September 2nd at 12.30am we readied ourselves to go into support for the 5th Division, but it wasn't until 5.30pm that the next phase of the advance began. The 7th Brigade took over the attack and pushed on well beyond Mont St Quentin, liberating several towns. We took up positions in the vacated trenches and settled in.

Peronne finally fell and two hundred prisoners were taken along with scores of guns. It soon became clear that the Germans were making another hasty withdrawal.

Taking Mont St Quentin most certainly forced the Germans into retreat and we were again pursuing them to their next stronghold, the Hindenburg Line. It was twelve miles from the front line, but that line was moving rapidly east.

The Germans had lost every inch of ground gained during their March offensive and much more. We were holding our position in the line, taking on a fresh supplies of ammunition as field kitchens arrived with food and water. No-one had eaten anything substantial in well over thirty six hours and we devoured everything like animals.

A roll call revealed that the battalion was down to a fighting strength of six officers and one hundred and fifty eight other ranks. We'd lost one-third of our number in less than two days. Command was forced to dissolve D Company and place its men within the three remaining companies to sure up the numbers.

At 6pm we were again ordered to stand by. We'd already spent the entire day waiting for orders, so this new communiqué only added to the frustration.

Enemy shelling finally eased and soon became sporadic. Bert's shoulder was still sore, but a medic had done a good job of cleaning the wound. Dickie was still nursing a damaged hand while Mick and I had somehow come through unscathed.

"You two must be blessed," suggested Dickie.

"I don't know about that Dick. Look at my helmet," and Mick pointed at a few dints.

"It's just luck, isn't it?" I suggested. They looked at me, compelling me to continue.

"Well, you either get knocked or you don't. A step this way or that could be the difference, right? It's just luck in the end."

We started adding up a tally of our losses.

"I saw Clarky go down," said Dickie.

"Thommo copped it too, so did Charlie and Wazza," added Mick.

We pondered the loss of good mates and then Bert chimed in,

"Well, I saw at least fifty blokes go down!"

We all looked at him with shock on our faces, as did a bunch of others who overheard the remark!

"What the hell are you talking about Bert?" asked Mick.

"Yeah, who were they," added Dickie.

Bert was rolling a smoke and answered in his famous dry brevity, "They were all named Fritz!"

No-one said anything for a second and then someone started to chuckle. It slowly escalated and soon became infectious laughter. Before long we were all in an uproar. We weren't laughing about killing the enemy; it was just the pressure valve releasing after surviving such a huge battle.

We didn't really hate the Germans. They were as fed up with the war as we were and just wanted it to be over. At least that's what a lot of the prisoners were saying. The war was certainly taking its toll on both sides.

We spent the next two days holding our trench until we were finally relieved and ordered back to Mereaucourt Wood. Salvage parties were sent out to gather useful items; rifles, bombs, food...anything that still worked. Our group spent its time cleaning the Lewis gun and loading panniers with .303 bullets.

The hours ticked by when Bert suddenly interrupted the monotony, "Jesus Christ!"

We all looked up to see what was going on.

"Bloody Hell!" added Mick.

Pretty soon most of the men in our battalion watched speechlessly as hundreds of wooden crosses were unloaded from a lorry.

Burial detail was about to begin. We all knew about it and some of us had helped on occasion but seeing that many crosses sent chills up my spine and I wasn't the only one feeling uneasy. After the fight we'd just been through, going out on burial detail was the cruellest irony.

That afternoon, when the dead had all been buried, we were on the move again. We travelled further away from the front at last, to the town of Frise which was nestled into one of the Somme's "S" bends. We were now fifteen miles west of Mont St Quentin and very pleased to see we would be staying in huts. They weren't palaces by any means, but they had wooden floors and they were dry.

We stayed for three weeks resting, enjoying sports, and attending church services. There were regular parades, plenty of training and gunnery practice too. We were in the middle of a game of cricket and, as usual, A Company was giving us a run for our money. In fact, we hadn't managed to beat them once since the battalion was formed in 1915 and this match was going downhill rapidly. Being the youngest in the team and of unknown skill I was battling at number 11.

A Company had scored a useful 139 on a pitch that had more lumps and bumps than a bush track and the B Company wickets had fallen regularly. Bert and Joe Maxwell were at bat with Bert facing a rather fiery character named Riley. No-one was sure if it was his first name, surname or his only name and they weren't game to ask. He was a big brute and only knew one way to bowl....fast!

Someone suggested he once played in the Sheffield Shield for Victoria, and it didn't surprise me. Bert stood inside a makeshift crease and patted his bat on the dirt, a cigarette hanging from his bottom lip. Riley pounded in off a ridiculously long run and was about to release the ball when Bert's cigarette dropped off his lip and fell inside his shirt! A split second later Bert screamed out in pain, dropped the bat and danced about groping for the burning cigarette. Riley didn't stop, releasing the ball which whistled down the pitch at pace. Bert had turned around and was bent over the stumps flailing away inside his shirt when the ball hit him square on the left buttock. The pain made him flinch and his knee knocked over the off stump. Riley appealed while the rest of the fieldsmen roared with laughed. The umpire lifted his finger and declared the batsman out!

"Arse before wicket Thorn!" someone shouted.

"Best shot you've played all day!" added someone else.

Bert pulled out the crumpled, smoldering remains of his cigarette and inspected the burn on his stomach. He then retrieved the bat but resisted the temptation to rub his aching buttock to avoid further embarrassment. I was already walking to the pitch and met Bert near the centre,

"Cocky bastards!" he said as he passed me the bat.

I just smiled but said nothing because I thought I would burst out laughing too. Joe Maxwell came up to give me some words of encouragement, and I strongly suspected that his focus was on winning the purse that was riding on the game.

"Three balls left and we need five to win. Why don't you push a single and leave the rest to me?"

I nodded and took guard. Riley was back at his mark and I inspected the field. I'd been watching Riley for a while and thought I'd picked up on his bowling pattern. If I was right, this delivery would be a bouncer. He stormed in again and flung the ball which bounced short and flew past my head. I ducked out of its way, lost my balance and landed flat on the seat of my pants. As the laughter waned, I stood and brushed myself off and there was Riley, leering at me.

"Got you scared have I son?"

I just smiled and checked the field again while he walked back to his mark. I took block again as he turned and started running in. This one should be a Yorker I thought and I was right. I barely managed to get the bat down but stopped the ball which simply spun in the dust. Riley retrieved the ball and gave me a wink in the process. I ignored him again.

"GO STAN, HIT HIM OVER THE FENCE" came cries from my team-mates. There was no fence but there was an agreed boundary, and I focussed on the line of men at long on.

Joe Maxwell strode up the pitch,

"Last ball, just hit the mongrel and run like hell!"

I nodded again and took guard. I tried to anticipate Riley's next ball. It should be just short of a length but being the final ball he might go for another Yorker.

As Riley came upon the crease I called out,

"This one's for Bert!"

Riley let go and the ball came down exactly where I expected it. I marched two paces and swung as hard as I could, barely grazing the pitch with the tip of the bat. I struck the ball on the half volley. It sizzled straight back down the pitch and over Riley's head. It arced its way up and over the long on boundary and disappeared into the mess tent. The umpire raised both arms signalling six while Riley protested.

We won by a single run on the last ball. Riley stared at me red faced, unhappy at being baulked. I winked at him as huffed off, refusing to shake hands with anyone.

"He must have lost a few bob on that delivery," suggested Joe.

"I'm sure you're right," I replied.

Joe slapped me on the back, "Well done son. I didn't know you had it in you."

"Me either!" I replied.

I accepted the congratulations of my teammates and saw Bert smirking at me with a thumbs up. But my good cheer was short lived when I saw Blue's face. He looked intensely in my direction and beckoned me over.

"What's up Boss?" I asked.

"Stan, you're being redeployed!"

I didn't quite hear him at first but then the penny dropped,

"Sorry Blue, I'm what?"

"Being redeployed. They need medics and I recommended you."

I was gob smacked, "But why?"

"Your young, fit and you're qualified...I'm sorry Stan."

"But I haven't done any medic training for over a year; I'll be useless to them."

"Well, that's more than the rest of us have had. I realise this isn't what you want but it's an order. They put blokes where they're needed the most and right now, they need medics!"

I was in total shock as Blue continued,

"Look on the bright side Stan. Next time we go over the top, you won't have to."

I understood the words but didn't feel relieved. A medic, I was going to be a medic working behind the main body of troops patching up the wounded. Yes, I'd been given intensive training before I left England, but I'd forgotten most of it. We all carried field dressings during an attack, but this was different. This would be my primary role from now on. Blue could see that I wasn't happy,

"Stan, we've lost a lot of blokes, and I don't really want to lose another, but I have no say in it."

"I know sir, but I don't have to like it," I replied.

"No, I don't suppose you do." Blue paused then repeated himself, "I'm sorry mate, I really am."

"When do I go?"

"As soon as you can son!"

I accepted the order without further comment. I should have been grateful that Blue didn't write me up for questioning an order, but he was a decent bloke and understood his men. He didn't stomp on us like some of the others.

The hardest part was telling my mates. Most of them took it in their stride and tried to make me feel better about the decision but everyone knew that the life span of a medic could be very short. They were right behind the action but spent much time immobile making them easy targets while they tended the wounded.

I could tell that Bert was none too pleased with the decision.

"I'll sort this out Stan," he suggested as he scanned the area for Blue.

"No, don't! You'll just get yourself in trouble. It's OK," I replied.

"Jesus mate, I need you. No-one changes ammo as fast as you."

"That's true," I said with a smile, "But it's all cut and dried Bert, you can't do anything."

Bert pondered for a moment and then said, "Well I'm glad you'll be the one watching my back then," and he gave me a genuine smile and shook my hand.

We spend one last night together sharing stories and enjoying each other's' company. Next morning I said my goodbyes and joined my new unit. It wasn't a huge journey. The medics were camped nearby with the rest of the battalion, waiting for orders. I met my news CO, handed over my file and joined and the rest of the medical corps men. There were quite a few new chaps from other platoons, and they too were feeling as displaced as I was. For the next few days we trained and studied, freshening up on the skills required.

On September 27th our battalion's little holiday was over. We were route marched to Bussu which put us well east of Mont St Quentin. It took us twenty four hours to reach the town, and it rained most of the way. A day or so later we moved forward again, catching up to the advance at Villers Faucon.

While we'd been resting, the big push had continued. Thousands of Germans had surrendered while the rest had withdrawn. It dawned on me that the thought of calling a halt to war and waiting until 1919 had been discarded, otherwise why were we pressing on? It could soon be over.

Only two Australian Divisions remained active on the front line at this time, the 3rd and 5th. Despite their obvious fatigue they were ordered to attack the Hindenburg Outpost. Resources were low with only a handful of tanks at our disposal, too few to do the job. Fakes were built from wood and hessian to give the illusion of a massive force and dragged to the front in the dark.

The attack opened with about two hundred and fifty Vickers gunners pulverising the German trenches. Australian troops then over-ran the enemy with ease. It appeared that most of the Germans were simply waiting to be captured. More than four thousand of them gave up the fight leaving scores of machine guns, field guns and even a few anti-aircraft guns for us to loot.

From what we'd heard about the Hindenburg Line itself it was a formidable defensive complex. Much more than a simple trench line system, this was a fortress the likes of which we'd never dealt with.

Taking the Hindenburg outposts was nothing compared to the line itself and led to controversy with new orders arriving from the British command. We heard that the AIF battalions were to be reorganised to sure up the numbers for the main attack against the Germans. This meant that some battalions were to be disbanded and absorbed into other units, not unlike what we'd done with D Company after the battle of Mont St Quentin.

The idea was repellent to everyone, including our commander in chief, John Monash. We heard that the negotiations went as high as Prime Minister, Billie Hughes until some kind of compromise was reached. The word was that John Monash was forced to accept the order of his Prime Minister. In the end, seven battalions were disbanded. But it didn't end there. Mutiny soon followed leaving our commanders with a dilemma. Eventually the battalion that held out was convinced to disband on the proviso that they could keep their original colour patches.

We had to laugh when, the very next day, John Monash deferred the disbandment order, leaving six battalions untouched. We were all certain that it was designed to send a message to the Brits and were pleased with our commanders' resolve.

We learned of other successes across the front with the Americans and French pushing the Germans back in the Argonne Forest region while the English took Cambrai. We were very pleased to hear about a breakthrough by Belgian troops at Ypres, where we'd spent so much time. The German retreat was happening right across the Western Front. Our guess was that the Germans planned to hold position in the Hindenburg Line until winter set in and then rebuild and wait until the spring of 1919. It seemed like the logical thing to do. The thought of another year out here filled us all with dread.

The Hindenburg Line was a formidable system of deep trenches, rows and rows of barbed wire, hundreds of machine guns and field artillery which stretched along both banks of St Quentin Canal. Crossing the canal alone would be a very difficult task without considering the enemy's fire power. The Hindenburg Line was six miles deep and twenty miles wide and the prospect of attacking such a fortification was terrifying to us.

As we were briefed, we learned that our attack would be concentrated on the only section of the canal that was covered, over a width of three and a half miles. This was called St Quentin tunnel, and we would push through this section before spreading out. No-one was under any illusions, the enemy defenses here would be heavy, and we would take significant casualties.

The entire plan had to be perfectly coordinated. If any one group fell behind, someone else would have their flank exposed, which could lead to a major defeat. We didn't need to be reminded of that. The attack would happen over a front of ten thousand yards. Engineers would have to work under fire to create crossings for the canal on each side of the tunnel. Companies of men would have to be maneuvered with a series of obliques to get into the proper positions.

Preparations took several days all under the watchful eyes of enemy soldiers. There was no doubt that the Germans knew exactly what we were planning, which would make the task that much harder. There would be no surprise this time. It would be more like the attack on the Somme in 1916 beginning with an extensive bombardment followed by an infantry assault and we all knew how that turned out.

The Germans were doing their best to disrupt our preparations and were holding a few key positions around Gillemont Farm, Quennemont Farm and a place called The Knoll. The Americans were sent to mop them up two days before the main attack was to be launched. The next day we learned the attack had failed. They become lost in the fog and rain.

We expected that the main attack would now be delayed, but it wasn't. Another Division of Americans was dispatched to deal with the pockets of German resistance with the main attack set to begin the next day as scheduled regardless of the outcome. It was a relief to learn that the 2nd Division would not be making the initial attack; that would be left to the 3rd and 5th Divisions.

Very early the next morning I woke to the sounds of hundreds of Allied guns as they sent a firestorm upon the Hindenburg Line. I climbed out of my bunk and joined the other men who had gone outside to watch. The lightning storm that was unleashed was beyond description. I'd never seen it from such a perspective before, having always been in the forward lines or well back when the whistles blew. From our semi advanced position, we got a new understanding of the tactic. A curtain of shells rained down on the enemy, pulverising, we hoped, most of their defenses. After some time, the barrage lifted and was concentrated on protecting our advancing troops. Of course, most of what I was looking at was darkness, with silhouettes appearing in front of flashes of white, orange and red. German flares could be seen rising across the line as they tried to repel the advancing formations.

The Germans replied to our artillery, lobbing a few shells our way, but most of their fury was concentrated on the advancing troops. As dawn broke the battle continued to unfold and we could only guess how the whole affair was going. Plumes of smoke and dust rising into the sky were common and the sound on our artillery blasting away and the regularity of explosions invaded our minds and threatened to send us all mad.

Initial reports suggested that our men had made inroads into the German defenses, but we soon learned that things hadn't gone so well. The American push to clear out the German resistance had failed again and our men were now mixed up with the stranded Americans. All of them, it seemed were now hopelessly pinned down. Reports of their success had proven totally false. We learned that the push to our south was going quite well but the attack in the north has stopped dead. We were stuck in the middle of it all, barely holding on. The breakthrough we had hoped for appeared to be beyond us.

The fighting continued into the night and on through the following day. An attempt was made to push the 3rd and 5th Divisions to the north-east to try and smash through the Hindenburg defenses. Pitch battles were being fought all along our front. Everything was in a state of confusion, the Germans resisting with more zeal than anyone expected.

For two days our men fought their way forward, inch by bloody inch. Reports of hand to hand fighting, bomb fights and point blank shootouts were filtering back but again, no breakthrough was achieved.

On October 1st, some hope. The 3rd Division was still crawling forward while the 5th Division was reported to have taken Jonocourt. It wasn't a complete breakthrough, but the enemy line was beginning to fracture at last. The 2nd Division was immediately ordered into the fight to try and exploit the success.

Instead of panniers and bombs I would carry field dressings, iodine and morphia. A white canvas band with a red cross was now wrapped around my left arm providing only a vague hope of protection, but bullets and shrapnel wouldn't differentiate. I had time to do one more thing before we move forward and I tracked down Bert, Dickie and Mick,

"You jokers take care of yourselves!" I ordered.

"That goes for you too Stan" replied Mick.

Bert's face didn't reveal much but his grip did. He shook hands firmly but didn't say a word. He looked me in the eye and gave me a quick nod.

At 8.40am on October 1st, 1918, the battalion moved forward to Villeret. The village had been destroyed giving us nowhere to stay. We made ourselves as comfortable as possible and waited for instructions.

At 6pm we were sent to Riqeval where we were to take over the front from the 8th Brigade. The going was painstakingly slow. The road was in a terrible state and thick with traffic. The area has been savaged by artillery and close quarter battles. The darkness made it more difficult, and we struggled along through the smashed up fortifications and the mud, regularly having to maneuver around shell holes and enemy block houses. It wasn't until 4am the next day that we finally reached our designated position. A and C Companies went forward and found cover under the bank of the canal while B Company was held back. The Medical Corps was even further back, our unit positioned somewhere between Jonocourt and Etricourt, about a mile short of the Beaurevoir Line. It was the very last trench line in the Hindenburg system, six miles behind the forward most enemy trenches and about fifteen miles wide.

The weather was cool and the rain had cleared and we were welcomed by a barrage which homed in on B Company's position. A Company moved into Jonocourt while an English division began an assault on the German line. Once again, we sat and waited, constantly harassed by German shells. Early reports suggested the English had been successful and our battalion HQ was moved into Jonocourt Railway Station on that basis. It was like the Germans knew we'd made such a move as they immediately bombarded the remains of the town for the rest of the afternoon. Despite the danger, all the battalion staff moved through the barrage and into their new dugout. Heavy artillery and gas pounded the area without mercy.

That night the battalion commander called his officers to a conference. When our CO returned, he told us that the 2nd Division would attack the enemy line with two brigades over a front of five thousand yards. We would have two thousand rifles against an unknown number of defenders. Our first objective was the take the Beaurevoir Line. Next, we were to take the village of Beaurevoir itself and finally the village of Montbrehain.

As we readied ourselves to move forward the line was to spread out an extra fifteen hundred yards. A patrol was sent forward to look at the German trenches. As expected, they reported a multitude of machine guns and more wire than anyone had come across before. An attack plan was formulated and sent out to all and sundry, zero hour set for 5.00am. B Company would take the centre of the advance.

The plan was simple; the 18th would spearhead the advance and take its designated section of the enemy line. The 17th would follow and push on for another four thousand yards. Artillery support would target German positions on the hill facing us. No-on knew what lay beyond and most doubted we'd get there in any case. A squadron of tanks had been ordered up to support the advance but hadn't turned up yet.

Once the Beaurevoir Line was cleared the 18th would push on to support the 17th as they advanced. The British 46th Division would cover our right while the Australian 19th and 20th battalions were to cover our left.

The Germans were obviously aware of our build-up and peppered the area with gas shells to try and disrupt our preparations. Our commanders made the decision to go straight to the jump off point rather than risk the men to incoming shells. We all moved up together and reached the start tape on the la Cateau Road where the air was clear. We even managed to get a hot meal before the stunt. My new CO came along to check on us,

"You all set son?" he asked.

"Yes sir."

"Just do your job and you'll be fine. I think we're going to be very busy today," and he placed a reassuring hand on my shoulder before walking off to another group.

I felt strange. I hadn't been a non-combatant before and I felt vulnerable. Being in a Lewis Gun crew had its benefits, particularly with several pairs of eyes to deal with any threats. As a medic I would operate alone. Butterflies welled up in my stomach as I tried to come to terms with my situation. I looked at the faces of my fellow medics, and they looked as intense as the infantry men. It didn't seem to matter what your job was, the fear still worked its evil on your mind. I vomited up some bile which left a nasty taste in my mouth.

On October 3rd, right on the dot of 5.00am, five Australian artillery brigades sent over their hellfire storm. It only took a few seconds for all of us to realise that something had gone dreadfully wrong.

"Good Lord!" exclaimed the man next to me.

The barrage was short and was falling on top of us. The screams of wounded men soon rang out all over the line. As a medic I felt compelled to do something, but I cowered into a ball, such was the ferocity of the bombardment.

Things only got worse when the German artillery responded, sending more shells into our line. A murderous metal avalanche was collapsing on us from both sides, and we had nowhere to hide.

"Cripes, who buggered it up this time?" Someone shrieked.

It didn't matter, we just had to hang on, but it was clear that many had been killed before they could take a step forward.

At last, someone made a decision and the order was given,

"ADVANCE!!"

No-one had to be told twice. Everyone who could rose and began walking forward. I waited with the other medics while the infantry men moved off. We would follow soon enough, once the first wave was well underway.

In less than a minute the familiar staccato sound of maxim machine guns rippled through the noise of the barrage. Lee Enfield rifles replied as well as a few Webley revolvers. Lewis guns sputtered along with bombs and mortars. The sounds quickly melded into one effervescent din.

My new CO then called out,

"Righto men, let's get moving.

It seemed like a very casual order under the circumstances, but the stretcher bearers and medics responded, and we all stood and walked towards the hell cloud erupting ahead. We walked into the maelstrom not knowing what to expect, not knowing if we'd be knocked by the enemy's defensive curtain. The air was thick with dust and smoke, and the smell of cordite stung my nostrils. Shell holes pockmarked the way ahead and bullets whined through the air like swarms of wasps.

"Stretcher bearers! Medic!" came the cries.

I found my first casualty not far away from the start point as more bullets spattered into the ground nearby. The man had taken several hits to the chest and lay on his back, knocked flat by the impact. He was dead.

I moved on as another body appeared through the smoke, crumpled up in a contorted pile. I didn't need to check on him and moved on to the next prostrate figure. This was truly awful. I'd never seen anything like this before. No battle I'd been in had unfolded in such a macabre and hideous fashion.

Another body emerged from the gloom, face down. This time the man was moving. I rushed over and knelt beside him, ripped a field dressing from my pocket and rolled him onto his back.

"Mick! Oh Jesus! Are you alright?"

Mick didn't answer, his face said it all. I searched for the wound but saw nothing. I ripped open his tunic and saw a single bullet wound in his right side. There was no exit wound. Blood was pouring from the hole.

"It's OK Mick, nothing serious. Just lie still and we'll fix you up!"

I mopped up the blood, looking at the wound. There was no way of knowing how deep the bullet had penetrated, but the darkness of the blood suggested it was in deep, perhaps striking his liver.

"STRETCHER!" I screamed as I placed a pad on the hole. Mick winced in pain.

"Sorry mate. Hang on a second, ok? STRETCHER!"

Two men suddenly turned up as I tied up the bandage, Mick was very pale and barely conscious. The men loaded him on the stretcher and soon set off. From my training I could only surmise that Mick would be lucky to see out the next hour.

I gathered up my things and headed off again attending to as many casualties as I could. There were scores of them. As I worked my way forward, I came across the first signs of the enemy; a reboubt full of dead machine gunners. They'd put up quite a fight judging by the number of Australian bodies that flanked the gun pit.

Further along was another machine gun nest, still surrounded by barbed wire. A maxim barked out from the position attracting the wrath of a Lewis Gun crew. Both teams exchanged a fusillade of fire. The Germans were outgunned as more Lewis gun teams opened on their position, forcing them the drop for cover. More soldiers worked their way through the wire and lobbed in a few bombs. They exploded, dispatching the German crew and their gun. A tank arrived at last and moved past me. Another group of Germans, upon seeing the beastly machine, dropped their weapons and surrendered.

I jumped up again and moved forward some more, finding yet another stricken Australian. I gasped when I realised, he was a medic. He'd been shot through the forehead. I took a deep breath and regained my composure, taking anything I could from the man's medical supplies.

As I moved on, I saw a savage fire fight ahead. Our men had reached the enemy line and the fighting was furious. The wire was still intact, stalling the advance. Our blokes were in a tight spot and were being enfiladed by machine gun fire. Suddenly the tank appeared again, attracting the German gunners. The tank ploughed on relentlessly riding up and over the German wire. Infantry men followed it through the breach.

I continued my work, skipping from man to man and was soon running low on bandages and iodine. There was a lull in the fighting, and a stream of prisoners were soon being led back to our lines. I stared up at their shocked white faces as they passed by. One of them tossed me a roll of bandages, and then a few more followed.

"Dunker!" I said and they nodded as they were herded away, most of them just boys. Unlike myself, I imagine that they didn't have any choice in the matter of fighting for their country. One of them dropped a leaflet which I guessed had been dispatched by our airmen. It promised food and safety to anyone who surrendered. They mingled with our own walking wounded, some even helping each other. It was a most odd scene indeed.

I stashed the rolls of bandages and moved on to another felled soldier. This time it was Lieutenant Irvine. He'd been wounded only a few weeks ago at Mont St Quentin, but it wasn't serious. Now here he was again.

"Hello sir," I said.

"Hello son, how does it look?"

"Not bad sir, but you won't be fighting again for a while I don't think. Best you go back sir!" I explained.

"Right, you are then!"

With that I called for a stretcher and watched them trundle away with my former CO. Just as they disappeared the crackle of rifle fire and machine guns grew louder. The short lull in the fighting ended suddenly as the Germans counter attacked at the breach in their wire.

It soon grew into a huge fight as the Maxims started pouring merry hell into our line. I knew that B Company was just ahead and hoped they were faring well. I looked back and saw soldiers from the 17th Battalion moving up to leapfrog the trench line, but I feared the trenches hadn't been taken. Things were about to get messy. I warned them as they passed, and they thanked me and pressed on.

I moved up with them looking for more wounded and caught a glimpse of the wire through the smoke. The Germans had certainly plugged the gap and were fighting grimly. I saw an officer from our side moving forward alone. He was in the open and quite vulnerable, but his luck was in. He worked his way through the wire labyrinth and thrust himself into a German machine gun nest. Those that weren't immediately killed quickly surrendered. His men took advantage of the opportunity and seized a foothold in the German line. On the right it appeared that A Company had taken their section of the trench while other sections appeared to be faltering. The co-ordination we'd hoped for was lost and the attack had dissolved into a series of small but heavy engagements.

Parts of the German trench line were barely a foot deep where our attacking troops were cleverly funnelled. It seemed like there were around fifty enemy machine guns firing down on Australians from behind the main trench line. Lewis gunners gave as good as they got but couldn't quiet the enemy.

As I scanned the area, I could see that at some points the trenches were up to three deep in places, judging by the coils of wire. The objective was a much tougher prospect than anyone imagined. The fire fight continued for what seemed like an eternity when, yet again, a tank arrived taking out some of the enemy strong points.

Fighting was fierce but the German line finally broke on the left allowing C Company to dig in while the 17th battalion boys jumped across the trenches and started working their way over the hill. The centre of our advance was still proving a problem. The wire was incredibly thick here, at least six coils of it at twenty foot intervals. The only way through was via a series of small saps which were all covered by machine gun posts.

The officer I spied earlier appeared again and decided to rush the enemy with a handful of men in support. Attacking in short bursts, the small band of men quickly set upon a Maxim crew. The Germans panicked and surrendered. That one brave move gave B Company the opening they'd been waiting for, and men streamed in and secured their section of the Beaurevoir Line. The men of the 17th Battalion behind the centre now had their opportunity and leapfrogged the position, firing on the enemy as they in turn retreated.

The number of dead and wounded was rising at an alarming rate. I simply couldn't keep up with the level of carnage. Stretcher bearers were few and far between now and those that were alive were run off their feet. I had to triage every case on the run in just a few seconds and was forced to leave several men to fend for themselves so I could deal with more serious cases. Basic training simply didn't prepare me for this, and I had to hold down the panic.

I saw bodies strung up on the wire while many of the wounded huddled in shell holes. German prisoners were recruited as stretcher bearers just to get the wounded out. There was total confusion all around. Some of our gains were now being heavily counter attacked while other units seemed to be forging ahead. Both sides were shooting sideways at times, so mixed up had the advance become.

I worked my way inside the wire to tend the wounded there and they were many. Machine gun fire continued to stream down from the hill and into our position. I noticed that my new CO and a few other medics were still working, which came as a small relief, but I soon realised that our ranks had thinned to only a handful of men. Orders were barked out and we followed them as best we could. Dead lay everywhere, most taken down by machine gun bullets. The barrage that was supposed to help us finally lifted and started targetting the hill beyond the trench line, but many had fallen victim to friendly fire.

I knelt by another wounded soldier, not taking much notice of who it was,

"G'day Stan!"

"Blue, oh my God...are you ok?" I blurted.

"Yeah, it's nothing," he replied with a bit of a slur.

I inspected the damage. His leg had been shattered and was bleeding badly but he seemed oblivious to his plight. Blood streamed from the gashes in his leg, and I just couldn't stem the flow. I applied a tourniquet and as much pressure as I could, but the blood kept draining away.

"Hold on Blue, just a little longer!"

I screamed for stretcher bearers, but none came...there were none. After a few more moments the bleeding seemed to ease.

"There, I got it Blue. You'll be OK," but as I looked up at his face, I saw his glassy eyes staring out at nothing. He was gone.

My heart sank,

"God Blue, I'm sorry."

I felt I was losing control and screamed out in anger. I marked Blue's position by shoving his rifle, bayonet first into the ground.

As I looked around again, I realised that the other medics were gone, probably dead. I couldn't be sure. I continued to work on the most urgent cases, scavenging anything I could get from the dead. We appeared to be making a bit more ground when the Germans hit us on the right. They were quickly pushed back but held the ridge which gave them a good field of fire on us.

The enemy started dropping mortar and gas shells to try and weed us out, but our men held on despite the escalating casualty count. To make things worse, German aircraft arrived and tried to strafe our line. They made a few passes before peeling off.

The fight continued to ebb and flow and continued like this for several hours. Some Australians were making ground while others were blocked. C Company was counter attacked and fighting hard. The 19th and 17th battalion boys hadn't made it far past the trenches when they too were forced to dig in. The 18th had been stopped dead and a runner flashed past carrying a note for HQ. Dead lay everywhere, some killed instantly but many bleeding to death because medics couldn't get to them. I tended to an A Company sergeant but was once again out of bandages.

"Don't worry fella. I'll be fine."

"I'll be back, promise!" and a scrambled off to fetch more supplies wherever I could get them.

Bullets sprayed in all directions, and I was forced to take cover in a deep shell hole, blown out of the trench by an exploding shell. I curled up in the space for as long as I dared until a new barrage was laid down on the German defenses. The runner must have got through. The machine gun fire eased, and I took the opportunity to climb out and continue to search for bandages.

Lewis gunners were frantically firing at a group of charging Germans who fell in the frenzy of bullets. I suddenly recognised Bert about thirty yards ahead desperately trying to hold his position. Dickie

had panniers ready but seemed to be struggling with his hand wound. With Mick gone they were finding it difficult and only had a few riflemen to back them up. I looked right and left but it seemed that very few men from my old platoon were left.

The Germans kept on coming, trying to take back their trench. Stick bombs rained down and exploded all around but miraculously did no harm. I watched as another German raised his arm, stick bomb in hand. He tossed it towards Bert and Dickie,

"WATCH OUT!" I cried but they couldn't hear me through the crescendo.

There was nothing I could do. The bomb hit the back edge of the trench and exploded. Smoke and dust filled the air between me and my mates. I strained to see what had become of them.

Bullets spattered the ground around me forcing me to duck again. I waited a few moments and looked up spotting a Red Cross bag next to a dead medic. I started moving towards it when I felt a terrific smack on the side of my face with a sharp cracking sound. It felt like someone had hit me on the side of the head with a lump of wood. The force knocked me flat on my back hard and I lay there dazed for a moment. A searing heat erupted from the point of impact, and I got up on my haunches but was overwhelmed by a dull groggy sensation. My eyesight went blotchy and a warm wetness trickled down my neck. I fell forward to the ground again, my thoughts becoming ever confused. Pain intensified around my mouth, and I tried to call out, but all I could do was gurgle. Blood had filled my mouth and I gagged and coughed, spitting out some teeth.

I was bleeding profusely and had little idea of what was happening to me. I tried to push myself up again, but my arms felt so weak and all the sound around me faded into silence. My arms could no longer hold the weight of my body. I collapsed face first into the ground while all my thoughts and senses evaporated into total blackness.

Chapter 15

The Aftermath

Voices....noises....sounds that came and went. Blurred images passing me by and pain thumping in my head. Confusion and then silence. No idea of time passing, no lucid thoughts. There was a feeling of being lifted and dropped, a vague realisation of movement along bumpy ground, blackness again. A sudden jolt roused me and I a caught a glimpse of men lying on the ground. It was night and it was cold, but I drifted off yet again. I dreamt, reliving the battle, seeing my friends blown up, running for the medical kit, then pain and blood.

I woke again, it was daytime now, but weakness gripped me. I tried to move but the pain racked my entire frame. My mouth crusted in blood, my breathing shallow. I faded away once more.

Voices again, an officer giving orders. I opened my eyes but couldn't see, something covered my face,

"Let's get to it men!"

I tried to talk but all that came out was a weak moan.

"You lot start digging. We've got a lot to do!" and I heard shovels hitting dirt.

Digging? Digging what? Trenches? I wondered.

I tried to move but could barely raise my head and the pain of trying ripped through my jaw and I let out another groan.

"STOP DIGGING!" someone shouted. He was close by. The shovels immediately ceased.

"What is it?" asked another.

"I thought I heard something."

"What?"

"I dunno, something!"

They were Australian voices. I knew I had to move and felt for a gap in whatever was covering me, but I was too weak and my hand flopped down.

But I felt, something...warmth. The sun toasting my fingers. I started wiggling them hoping someone would see.

"THERE! My God, this one's alive...CAPTAIN!!"

A blanket or something was suddenly ripped off me. Sunlight flashed white in my eyes. Hands were upon me in a few seconds and I was dragged away from what I now realised was a row of dead men. I tried to talk, my mouth aching with the effort but couldn't make more than a few muffled grunts and gave up.

"Jesus, look at his face! He got one right through the mouth!"

"Let me see," said another fellow, "Christ, that's a bloody mess."

Another man spoke,

"See if he can drink something."

With that I was propped up, I could barely hold my head up. Water was fed into my mouth, most of it washing straight out, but I reacted to the cool liquid and took a few sips. The taste of metallic, putrid blood forced me to cough, and I spat out a wad of congealed bloody phlegm. Fresh blood oozed from my face.

"Bandage that!" someone ordered, "Get him to a clearing station now!"

With that I felt myself being carried. Next thing I knew I was on a cart of some kind. I could smell horses and a fresh dump of manure. We started moving immediately, two men accompanying me, offering me more water.

"Not too much, he'll just be sick!"

I could tell one of them knew a bit about treating the wounded and felt some relief.

"What do you think happened to him?"

"He's from the 18th. They got smacked around badly from what I heard."

My thoughts immediately turned to Bert and Dickie. I tried to ask about them but again I could only gurgle and the fresh bandages were tight and held my jaw clenched. I remembered the bomb attack and the smoke but had no idea what happened. Was I lying next to them a few minutes ago?

The two men soon found something more interesting to discuss and I was lulled back to sleep by the gentle rocking of the cart, only occasionally shaken awake by the rough road.

Sometime later, I don't know how long, I was offloaded to a casualty clearing station. I waited in a bell tent, barely awake on an old bunk. My eyesight had returned and, even though things were still blurry, I could make out objects and people moving about outside.

My jaw panged with waves of pain, like a throbbing migraine and the bandages had soaked through with blood and other fluids and since dried like cement.

A man suddenly burst into the tent, a doctor I guessed. He was trailed by a young nurse, the first Australian woman I'd seen in a very long time.

"My word, you're a bit of a mess young fella. Let's take a look." He turned to the nurse, "Cut those bandages away will you dear?"

She delicately worked on the job. I winced in pain several times and she apologised profusely on every occasion. The doctor injected me with something and then helped the nurse complete the job. The rancid bandages dropped to the dirt floor. They then stuck a needle in my arm which was connected to a tube and a bottle of fluid.

"Now let's see what's happened. Do you remember anything?" he asked me.

I tried to talk and found that it was easier to whisper,

"Only flashes. Not sure."

"Understandable. You've lost a lot of blood, you're dehydrated and your wounds are filthy and look septic."

I didn't react to the news. I suspected as much given the taste in my mouth.

"Can you open your mouth for me?"

I tried to stretch my jaw which had been clamped shut for, I don't know how long. The jolt of electricity that seared through my flesh and bone caused me the squeal like a child.

"That's ok, try to do it slowly. Just a little bit will do."

I gave it another try and managed to ride through the pain, opening my mouth. I felt fresh blood washing down my throat as the doctor inspected the damage.

"You've lost several teeth and there's quite a bit of damage on both sides. Looks like a bullet went in your right cheek and through your teeth on the left side. You will need surgery and I suspect there are some fragments embedded in there. All that being said, you were lucky. An inch further back and it would have blown the side out of your neck."

A tear rolled down from my eye, brought on by the stinging in my jaw.

"Sorry son, I know it hurts. We'll clean you up as best we can. Then we'll have to send you on your way to hospital."

I looked at him as he filled in some paperwork. The nurse prepared to wash the wounds. He looked at my identity disc and read it out,

"6536 Dunkley S 18th BTN. What's the S stand for son?"

"Stan, Stanley," I replied.

The nurse leant over and started wiping away the gore with antiseptic. She was very gentle and smiled at me even though I must have looked and smelled terrible.

I felt dreadfully sore from the top of my head right down into my chest. The impact had sent a shock through my bones and jarred them badly. I was still struggling to stay awake and assumed that it was the result of the shock.

"How does it look?" asked the doctor.

The nurse replied, "Definitely infected sir!"

"I suspected as much. Clean it up as best you can," and he turned to me, "This won't be very pleasant I'm afraid, we must clean out your wounds. It's infected and full of dirt. We can't have you developing sepsis."

He wasn't wrong. As much as the nurse tried to be careful, it was terribly painful when she got down to the raw flesh. My jaw was swollen and tender to even the slightest touch. I spat up wads of congealed blood and had much trouble rinsing when asked to do so. Once the nurse was finished the doctor looked again,

"Sorry again, I have to get these fragments out!"

He plucked and poked away, my eyes watered with every pinch. It was worse than any dental experience I'd ever had, and he didn't offer anesthetic relief. Again, I could only assume it was pointless given the damage. I was wrapped in fresh bandages and readied for transport.

The doctor explained that my condition was critical due to blood loss and infection and that he couldn't remove the deeper fragments of teeth and metal. He draped a red tag around my neck which indicated my medical status.

"Thank you," I whispered as the doctor completed the paperwork.

"That's OK son and good luck." He smiled and I was helped up and carried by a pair of volunteers to a waiting area where several other wounded were sitting. A few of them chatted, while others slept or just kept to themselves. I was in no state to talk, so I laid back and soon fell asleep.

I was woken some time later and we were herded into a fleet of lorries and ambulances which ferried up across country to a railway station. The carriages looked like any other on the outside, except for the Red Cross marking but inside they'd been fitted with rows of double bunks, and a crew of nurses helped us all find somewhere to lie down.

After some time, we were underway, headed for Rouen where the 1st Australian General Hospital was based. The trip was slow and difficult and several of the more severely injured didn't cope well. I fell asleep on and off to the rocking of the train, pain a constant companion.

After many hours I started responding to the fluids that were being fed into my body and woke to find a nurse looking me over.

"Hello there. Are you feeling any better?"

I tried to talk, forgetting about my shattered face and winced in agony. I could still taste blood as it trickled down my throat.

"Oh, I'm sorry, don't speak, just nod."

I gave the nurse an indication that I was OK, despite the pain. She marked my chart and smiled before moving on to the next patient.

I looked around and saw that every bed was full of a few more men on the floor. I was desperate for news about the battle, but no-one here seemed able to discuss much. I wondered about my battalion, Dickie, Bert and Mick. I suddenly remembered Blue and felt pangs of guilt at not being able to help him.

Thirst overwhelmed me and I caught the nurse's attention as she passed by again. She eased a bottle to my mouth and I sipped carefully, ignoring the sting as it passed over my cuts, but I spilt more than I consumed. She was incredibly patient. And when I finished, I whispered to her,

"What happened with the battle?"

She looked at me, "You don't know?"

I shook my head slowly,

"We've pushed the Germans back!" she said.

My eyes widened as I absorbed the news,

"Beaurevoir?" I asked.

"I don't know the details, but we heard about a broke through. The Germans are retreating."

I was overjoyed to hear the news. It was indeed a relief. I took another sip of water,

"Not too much now, we don't want you to be sick. You should really try to rest."

Having been unconscious for so long, I didn't think it would be possible to sleep but I was soon lulled off again by the rocking of the train. I slept for what seemed like hours this time and it was restful sleep at last. I was jerked awake only when the train shuddered to a stop. It was now night and I couldn't see much. Orderlies soon filed on board and helped the most severe cases off the train. Ambulances whisked them away urgently.

Nurses checked our tags and offloaded the men depending on their level of need. I didn't have to wait long. Two orderlies came over and carried me onto the platform.

"Can you walk?" One asked.

I tried to put weight on my feet, but I was very wobbly.

"Never mind, we'll carry you," which they did with ease.

I crossed the platform and down a set of stairs and was quickly loaded into an ambulance with a few other men. The ride to the hospital was dreadful. The road was bumpy and my pain was amplified three fold with every pothole we hit.

Ten minutes later we pulled up at the hospital and the rear doors opened.

This time we were carried on stretchers whether we needed one or not. We burst through the hospital doors, and I was immediately aware of the strong smell of ether and other medicines. I was placed with a row of wounded men and waited, watching the goings on very closely. It was a hive of activity, people running in all directions, some giving orders, and doctors looking over the wounded and sorting them out. I was quite weak but was feeling much better overall. A terrible pang of hunger overwhelmed me suddenly and I thought that was a good sign.

The waiting was interminable, so I thought I'd try and get some more sleep, but the noises and smells made it impossible. Eventually a young doctor came over to me. He looked at my chart and started peeling back my bandages. They'd stuck to my flesh, and I flinched at the sharp ripping pain as they were torn away.

"I am sorry, but we must see what has happened to you," he explained with a French accent.

I nodded my approval and tried to ignore the pain. Some of the bandages were glued to the wounds by blood and the doctor had to take care not to cause more damage. A few minutes later the doctor looked at my wounds,

"Hmmmm, this is not too bad at all. You're a very lucky young man." he explained with a smile.

He barked out some orders, and I was carried off to a theatre and placed on an operating table. The doctor appeared again a while later,

"Your wounds are relatively minor but there is significant infection and fragments to deal with. We will clean them and try to repair the damage. It will be quite painful so we will put you under, ok?"

I nodded again.

"Do not worry, you will be fine." and he smiled again.

My world went black again and when I awoke, I was quite groggy, failing on several occasions to maintain consciousness as the effects of the anesthetic hung on. Eventually I realised that I was now in bed with clean white sheets. A new drip was feeding more fluid into my arm and fresh bandages covered my jaw. There was some pain but not nearly like before. A nurse noticed that I had awoken and came over,

"We meet again," she said smiling and I recognised her from the train, "How do you feel?"

I shrugged, not game to speak.

"It's ok; you can talk...what's your name?"

I hesitated but her reassuring smile gave me the confidence to try,

"Stanley, Stan!" I said through a clenched jaw.

"Nice to meet you Stan, I'm Catherine. Was there much pain just now?"

"No, not really," I replied.

"Good, the doctor did a great job. He'll be along shortly and tell you more."

"Thank you," I replied.

She tended to other patients as we all waited for the doctor. After some time he appeared, going from bed to bed and finally came to me,

"How do you feel....er, Stan?"

"I'm ok I think," but I didn't really know and he picked up on my uncertainly,

"You were shot though the face. The bullet went through clean on the right, grazed your tongue and went through your lower left cheek. It smashed up your teeth though and fractured your jawbone. Most of the damage is superficial. The left side of your cheek was a mess, but I repaired it. You'll be fine, minus a few teeth."

To me it sounded terrible and he realised what I was thinking,

"You might not have been so badly off except that you were out there for quite some time. That led to blood loss and exposure and ultimately your infection. Most of your problems were related to the time you spend unconscious," he explained.

I was still quite shocked.

"Oh, I'm not explaining this well, am I? It's the translation," he continued. "Let me say it like this, you'll be ok, really. It looked a lot worse than it really was!" and he smiled again.

I looked at him and took a deep breath, "Thank God!"

Catherine gave me a reassuring pat on the leg as I rubbed the back of my head, which was very sore to the touch,

"That would be your concussion," said the doctor.

"Concussion?" I whispered.

"Yes, everyone missed it, but you must have struck your head when you fell, and hard. The bullet didn't do much at all," he explained.

I couldn't believe it. That certainly explained the headache and the giddiness.

"Like I said before you're very lucky Private. Infection is still a risk so we will keep an eye on you for a few days."

"Anything else?" I asked.

"What do you mean?"

"Why did it take so long to find me?"

"They thought you were dead!" he blurted. "After the battle, they collected the bodies and you must have been unconscious, very weak and your face, well it must have looked hideous."

He noticed the shock on my face.

"They're not doctors out there. It has happened once or twice before, but don't worry about it now. You were found and you'll be ok."

"How long would I have lasted?"

He looked at me closely and deliberately, "No point thinking about what might have been. It didn't happen."

I let the thought go, "Thank you Doctor."

"My great pleasure" he replied and he moved on to the next patient.

I looked at Catherine and asked,

"What's the date?"

"The date?" she asked, "It's October 7th!"

I lay there stunned for a moment. October 7th? It couldn't be! I had missed my 18th birthday. In fact, I think I spent it lying amongst the dead.

Catherine again noticed my expression through the fresh bandages,

"What's the matter?"

"Hm? Oh nothing...but I am feeling hungry, "I explained.

"Of course, we'll organise something soon."

"Have you got any cake?"

"Cake? I don't think so, you'll be on stew for quite a while I think." and she gave me a quizzical look.

"No matter," I replied, "anything would be better than bully beef," and she giggled.

"Good to see you still have a sense of humour."

With that she left and followed the doctor on his rounds. Just then I spotted a man staring straight at me from across the room. His face was familiar, but I couldn't place it. He smiled,

"You don't remember me, do you?" he asked.

"I'm trying to place you..."

"It was about a year ago, you owe me a cup of tea!" the fellow claimed.

"Oh, my word....Sid!"

"Ah, you do remember me. Good to see you're still around."

"Well, it was a close thing, but I'll be OK. What about you?" I asked.

"Got me in the hip. Hurts like Hell, nothing serious but after a week in bed I'm pretty fed up." He explained

"Well, you might just get that wound patch after all!" I suggested.

I remembered the stories he told about his two incidents in Gallipoli.

"Yes, you might be right but somehow I'd have been happier without one."

"Me too!"

We both laughed but it hurt and I stifled my mirth very quickly. We chatted for hours, catching up on each other's news. I was shocked to hear that all of Sid's mates had been killed.

"You know they wanted to bet on what would happen to you. Looks like they were wrong," Sid explained.

"Well, if I knew what I was getting into I might have stayed in Sydney. I must have been mad!"

"Well, you can't carry that one on your own. Me and my mates all made the decision to come here between us...and now they're gone."

We paused at that point, both reflecting on the friends we'd lost,

"Anyway," he continued, "We're still in it and from what I've heard we've just about won the fight."

"I don't know much at all. Been in a daze for the last few days," I explained.

He went on to tell me that the German line broke at Beaurevoir. The town was taken and a day later Montbrehain fell. After that he wasn't sure, but we'd been successful.

We talked about all sorts of things...about home and family,

"I should introduce you to my sister, Edith, she's about your age, you'd like her," Sid suggested.

I'd like that very much," I replied.

"Oh, but don't call her Edith, she'll kill you. She goes by Rona."

"I'll try to remember that!"

After six days in the hospital, we were both getting a bit bored. We wrote letters home and passed the time getting back on our feet. I was feeling quite well and most of the aches and pains had subsided. I was able to walk the halls as my strength came back and even got to go outside when the weather was favourable. I regularly checked the rooms to see if any of my platoon mates were around and spotted a few blokes from the 18th, but there was no sign of Mick, Bert or Dickie.

Pretty soon Sid was up and about. His hip ached considerably but he kept quiet about it just in case the doctors tried to keep him in hospital any longer.

"They won't put us back in the fight with these wounds, will they?" I asked one day.

"Well certainly not me, but yours is only a scratch," and he laughed sarcastically.

I wasn't really that amused but it gave me a thought,

"I've probably got some leave due, what about you?"

"I imagine so, why what are you suggesting?" Sid replied with a glint in his eye.

"Well? I'd like to visit London given the chance!"

"Now that's a great idea Stan." And we both set about hatching up a plan.

That night I stole into the administration section of the hospital and got myself a pen and two sheets of paper with the hospital letterhead. I then wrote two letters, one to each of our battalion commanders suggesting we should be offered leave to recuperate. I signed them with my doctor's name and slipped them into envelopes, handing one to Sid.

"They'll shoot us if we get caught!" Sid suggested.

"So, we don't get caught!" I replied.

About four weeks after I was shot, I was given clearance to return to my battalion. My infection was clear and my wounds had healed quite well. Sid too was feeling much better but had a bit of a limp. Even so he was given clearance to leave.

After enquiring through the Hospital Administrator, we learned that both our battalions had moved back to an area near Amiens. We joined a few other fellows and walked to the railway station. We all boarded a train headed east and were soon rocking back through the French countryside.

The journey was slow as usual and the green was soon replaced by a pulverised wasteland. We arrived in Amiens late in the afternoon and sort information about the exact whereabouts of our units. We had to split up at this point and said our goodbyes,

"If I get leave, I'll find your battalion and we'll take it from there I suggested,"

"Sound like a good plan," and he winked as we shook hands and departed.

The 18th battalion was at Vignacourt, north-west of Amiens while Sid's 22nd battalion was at St Vast to the south-west.

"I'll see you soon then," I said as I set off.

"You can bet on it," he replied as he hobbled off and we soon lost sight of each other.

I walked for a while searching for by battalion's bivouac. I was feeling apprehensive because I still didn't know how we'd fared after the battle. It took me about two hours to find them, and I didn't waste any time reporting into headquarters. I found the battalion adjutant, Len Robson,

"Stan Dunkley reporting for duty, " I declared.

"Glory be," he said, we listed you as missing. I can see that's not the case. It's a good thing that we haven't sent off any letters yet. That would have been quite a shock for you family."

"Yes, indeed sir. Thank you, sir."

He looked me over and studied my bandages, which were hardly required now. I was ready to hand over my letter when he spoke again,

"Looks like you've been through quite a bit. What happened?"

I explained the entire story and was pleased to see that he was sympathetic.

"My word, that's quite an adventure. By the looks of it though, you probably shouldn't go back on the line. Let me see what I can do for you" I crunched the letter back into my pocket, "Come back and see me in the morning!"

"Thank you, sir."

I saluted and stepped outside and set off to find someone who could fill me in on the last few weeks. I was still technically attached to the Medical Corp, so I went there first. I hardly recognised anyone, most having been killed or wounded. Even the new CO didn't know who I was and I had to explain my story all over again. I then went to the quarter master and claimed back my gear which was, surprisingly, still in his possession. I couldn't believe my luck.

Once all the formalities were dealt with, I looked for B Company. I asked for some directions and found them a little way down the road. Before I could even start to look through the camp I heard a voice,

"We blow me down! You're alive!"

I recognised the voice immediately and can't describe the joy I felt,

"Dickie! It's good to see you!"

We shook hands vigorously,

"You too mate. I thought you were dead and gone, so did Bert!"

"Well, it was a close thing but I'm good as you can see. So, Bert, he's, OK?"

"Of course he is. Not a scratch on him!" Dickie said.

"I thought...they got you. I saw a bomb blow up behind you!"

"Yeah, well there were lots of bombs. Good thing those jokers can't throw!" and he laughed, "Come on, Bert'll be thrilled to see you."

We walked a little way and found some men relaxing, talking, playing cards, writing letters. As we approached many acknowledged my return, but most didn't. There were many new faces, which was most disturbing.

"Hey Bert, look what I found."

Bert was lying on his back with his slouch hat over his face having a nap.

"This better be worth waking me up Thorn or I'll...." he cut himself off as he looked up at me, "Bloody Hell! You slippery beggar! I knew they wouldn't get you. You're blessed remember!"

He jumped up and practically ran over wrapping me in the biggest bear hug I've ever had.

"Steady on Bert, I'm a wounded man."

"Wounded, you look...you look good." Bert gathered his excitement and revealed a bright red face, a little embarrassed that he'd let his guard down.

"It's good to see you too Bert. Looks like we all escaped."

There was a sudden silence,

"I know about Blue. I found him." I said quickly but their mood didn't change, "What is it?"

"He's gone mate," Bert replied.

I'd somehow expected this news, but it still came as a shock.

"God damn it all!" I said, "Poor Mick."

"Yeah, he was a good bloke," said Dickie.

"Well, you best fill me in on what's been happening. I haven't heard much news at all except that we pushed the Germans back.

"Well, you better get settled, we've got quite a story for you, "and we brewed up some tea and swapped stories.

They told me about how they'd fought off a major German counterattack and how they held the line until the 6th Brigade arrived to relieve them. B Company withdrew at 11.40pm with only thirty men, including just one office, Joe Maxwell who was recommended for a Victoria Cross. We'd taken and held our objective.

The entire 2nd Division had paid an incredible price for the victory, having faced machine guns, bombs, strafing aircraft, gas, shrapnel and explosive shells. After it was all over our divisions losses left us with barely enough men to form a single battalion. Five officers and one hundred and seventeen men had fallen during the engagement. In all the 5th Brigade suffered losses of around six hundred killed or wounded.

They went on to tell me that as the battalion retired; they faced another gas bombardment but kept going until 4.30am when they finally managed to sit down. Despite the roar of the battle they'd just left, most fell asleep and didn't wake until late afternoon.

They were then placed under the command of the 6th Brigade and sent back to the front to repel German counter attacks. They took over the line at 6am and held the position for the entire day. The next phase of the advance had succeeded in pushing the Germans back, liberating the town of Montbrehain. That evening the 30th American Division took over the line. The 18th then moved well back to Vignacourt and had been here ever since.

"So, when do we go forward again?"

"Dunno," said Dickie, "Never I hope!" and we all drank to that!

We chatted for hours and caught up on all the news, who made it, who was missing and we remembered our dead. Another day faded on the Western Front, and I was struck by how quiet it was. The rumble of guns that had been the norm for over a year seemed much more distant now.

Next morning I rose and had some breakfast. I struggled with solid food and still had some pain, but I was healing quickly. I then set off to see Len Robson. He handed me a pass and reminded me to be back in ten days. With that farewelled Bert and Dickie,

"Don't you blokes get into any strife while I'm gone" I ordered.

"Who us?" replied Dickie, "You're the one going on leave!"

I waved to them both, "See you in a couple of weeks," and then headed off with all my gear. I then reported to my CO and showed him my pass and set off again, back down the road; first stop would be the 22nd Battalion.

I'd been walking for an hour when a lorry approached, not unlike the others that had passed me by, but this one slowed down and finally stopped right next to me,

"Need a lift mate?" asked the driver.

I looked up and was about to say no when I saw Sid in the back,

"Hop in sunshine, you're wasting time!"

With that I threw my gear and myself into the back of the truck.

"We were just on our way to find you. If they didn't give you a pass we were going to pose as MPs and arrest you," Sid laughed.

"That might have worked!" I replied.

Sid wasn't alone and introduced me to a few other blokes from the 22nd, Chas Foster, Ernie Swan and Jim Hamilton," Stan here's with the 18th, a medic last I heard" explained Sid.

"A medic, very handy if we get into a dust up in London," said Chas.

We were all in a joyful mood and couldn't wait to get across the channel. We trundled our way back to Amiens getting to know each other better to kill time. We then caught the next train to Le Havre. It felt like I'd been going backwards and forwards for the last few days, but I didn't mind too much.

When we finally got to the coast it was midafternoon and once at the port were informed that we could only cross after dark. We found something to eat and rested, finally boarding around 9pm. Crossing at night reduced the odds of being struck by a torpedo. We zigzagged across the channel which added extra time to the trip, as did the choppy conditions. Once we docked in Dover the five of us caught a train into London, which took most of the night, so we slept until the train arrived. It was a huge thill to see the capital of the Motherland and civilisation again.

The day was only just getting started after our long journey and even though we were tired, our energy was elevated by our excitement. The hustle and bustle reminded me of life back in Sydney with men in business suits, women in stylish dresses and lots of men in uniform.

"Bloody Hell" said Jim, "It's like there ain't no war at all!"

"I dunno there are a lot of uniforms about. Look there!" and I pointed at two MPs chasing an Australian down an ally.

"AWL for sure," said Sid.

"Or he shortchanged them on a bride," suggested Chas which made us all laugh.

"So, what are we doing gents?" asked Sid.

I needed a new great coat desperately. It was getting cold and mine had been lost. We discussed it quickly and it was decided that we'd visit the Army Store first then find something to eat.

We wandered around looking at the shops and of course the English girls. There seemed to be quite a lot of them arm in arm with foreign soldiers.

"I've been warned about those girls," said Jim, "They get all cosy with you, spend all your money and then buzz off. Ain't right I tell ya!"

"Well, if they're willing then so am I," said Ernie. He was twenty three and looking for fun.

"Geez they'll wanna be desperate to give you a second glance," suggested Chas.

"Very funny!" said Ernie as we all laughed at his expense.

Asking directions, we found our way to the AIF War Chest Club in Horseferry Road. It was across the road from AIF Headquarters and the AIF Kit Store. There were Aussie soldiers everywhere and we felt more than comfortable booking rooms at the War Chest Club. It was a kind of hostel for Australians on leave and once I put my pack away, I went straight to the Army store. I discovered that it had two major roles. We could buy things that we needed like coats, puttees, boots and just about anything other kind of apparel. The second reason the kits store existed was more unsavory. They processed the personal effects of those killed and sent them back home.

I bought myself a great coat and immediately put it on. I also found a pair of boots that were almost new and put them on also. I paid the soldier behind the counter when a thought crossed my mind,

"Are you about to check something for me?" I asked.

"Depends mate...who is it?"

It was clear that he knew where I was coming from,

"I'm after information about Francis Curry, 18th Battalion."

"Mate, you're better off checking with HQ. They've got all the records."

"Righto thanks." And I hurried out of the store and walked to the AIF
Headquarters building. Two ornate stone pillars held up a banner identifying
the Australian administrative office. I stepped through the gate only to be met
by an armed guard. I showed him my papers and was allowed to proceed. He
pointed me towards the admin block, which was a bland, brick building.

I walked past a tobacco store which was certainly doing a roaring trade before
heading up the steps into the building. Heavy wooden doors gave way to a
large foyer. A clerk was standing behind an inquiry counter, and I waited
while the fellow scribbled down some notes. He eventually finished and
looked up,

"Yes?" he asked in a dismissive tone.

"Yes, good morning. I'm hoping you can tell me what might have happened to
a friend of mine...Francis Curry from the 18th Battalion?"

"Wait here!" demanded the clerk and he rose from his chair and vanished
through a rear door. I stood at the counter for twenty minutes and was
surprised that not one person entered or left the building in all that time.
Finally, the clerk reappeared.

"Francis John Curry, 6529 of Waterloo?" blurted the clerk.

"Yes, that's him, is he ok?" I asked excitedly.

The clerk paused as he scanned the paperwork,

"Returned to Australia!" he finally said.

"Oh...thank God! That's such good news. Thank you!"

I felt a great weight lift knowing that Frank was OK. I wasn't sure if he'd make
it when I saw him go down on August 8th, but he was young and fit and that
might have helped him pull through. Still, returning to Australia suggested his
wound was significant.

I immediately popped back to the store and purchased a postcard, writing a short note to Bert and Dickie explaining the news about Frank. I handed it to the storeman and left, satisfied. Sid noticed the smile on my face,

"You're very chipper; did they give you a pay rise?"

"No, they made him a general," said Chris.

I waited for the laughter to die down and explained about Frank. They immediately understood.

"And that calls for a drink!" yelped Chris and with that we headed for the nearest pub. The one we found was full to the brim with Australians on leave. It was rowdy and full of cigarette smoke. Beer flowed freely despite it being late morning and people were singing the latest songs around the pianola.

Jim took a sip of his beer, "Jesus, how do they drink this stuff?"

I must confess it was noticeably warm.

"It's a bit rugged at first but you get used to it," explained a private who'd overheard the complaint,

"You blokes just arrive?"

"Yes indeed," replied Sid.

"Well, you're in the right place. Just watch out for the MPs, they don't mind rounding us up at closing time," he warned.

Sid, Ernie, Jim, Chas and I found a table and sat down. We had a few drinks and sang a few songs, forgetting the war for a while. We stayed at the pub until closing time and staggered out with a mob on other Australians. I wasn't drunk but I was certainly dizzy while Ernie and Jim could hardly walk. It was up to me, Chas and Sid to get them back to our lodgings which were close by.

Military Police arrived on cue and the more experienced revellers quickly disappeared leaving the five of us stranded on the street.

"Had a nice time gentlemen?" one of them asked but no-one could answer before the second one spoke,

"I reckon we've got a drunk and disorderly problem here sergeant!"

"Now wait a minute," said Chas with a bit of a slur, "We're just minding our own business!"

There was no sense trying to run, at least two of us were in no state to escape. I looked at Sid and he just shrugged as if he were resigned to a night in a cell. I'd been through something like this once before and didn't fancy going through it again, not when I'd paid for a perfectly good bed. The first MP didn't mince words,

"How much have you go on you?" but before we could even think about taking up a collection three men came out of the shadows and crashed the MP's to the ground,

"Run like hell you blokes, we'll deal with these two."

We didn't have to be asked twice and took full advantage of the opportunity that had been offered. We high tailed it as the three men held the MPs to the cobblestones, making sure their heads were covered so as not to identify their assailants. We slipped away, fully expecting to hear the thunder of boots and the shrill of whistles but none came. I wondered what became of our rescuers but had a feeling they made a clean escape too.

Next morning we all woke with sore heads. The few days that followed were filled with sightseeing, shows, cafes and camaraderie. We even went to the London West End and saw Chu Chin Chow. It was a musical comedy, and we were surprised to learn that it was written by an Australian, Oscar Asche. The show had been running since August 1916 and had already been performed over a thousand times. It was a must see for most Aussies on leave and I enjoyed it very much.

The next day I decided to track down my new sister in law. I dug out a letter I'd kept of my brother's. Allan had given me Eva's address just in case I had a chance to call on her. Allan had been sent back to his battalion, leaving his new bride alone in London. I thought she might appreciate a visit from a relative, even though we'd never met. The taxi driver was typically chatty,

"So, what do you think of London squire?"

"Very nice."

"You off the meet a girl then?"

"Well, yes but it's not what you think. She's my sister in law!"

"Really, well a lot of young lasses have fallen for you Aussies, must be those accents, eh?"

"I don't really know about that."

The conversation was going nowhere but that didn't slow the driver down. He talked incessantly for the entire trip. We finally came to a stop in front of a little cottage,

"Here we are then sir," he announced.

"Thank you I said," as I fumbled for some cash and it handed over.

"God bless you sir!" he said with surprise. I'd obviously overpaid him, but it didn't matter.

I turned towards the cottage and saw a lovely young lady standing on the porch. She had shoulder length black hair, a pretty round face and snow white skin. She wore a white blouse, and her dark skirt hid her shoes. I guessed her age at around twenty or twenty one.

"Good morning, you must be Stan!" said Eva. Her English accent was soft, nothing like the cockney twang of the taxi driver.

"That's right, how did you know?"

"No mistaking you for anyone other than Allan's brother. The similarity is uncanny."

"Yes, we get that a lot," I explained. I held out a hand, "It's a pleasure to meet you, Eva."

She took my hand and I nodded rather than bowed in a semi-formal greeting.

"Please come in." I entered the dwelling and she showed me around. It was nothing like my home back in Granville. It had a short hallway which stretched past a pair of stained glass doors.

Beyond them was a sitting room. At the end of the hall was the dining room and near that the kitchen. Another hall led to two bedrooms and the bathroom. I thought the place delightful but too small for a large family. I looked at the photographs on the hall table.

"My parents," explained Eva. "They're both deceased now. I'm an only child, so this in my home now." Her sadness was obvious, but I didn't ask how they died.

"Will you be selling the house after the war?" I asked.

Eva looked up sharply, and I thought I'd offended her,

"I'm sorry. I assumed you'd be moving to Australia with Allan." I added.

"It's alright. I was a bit surprised by the question. You Australians really do get to the point quickly, don't you?"

"I suppose we do."

"Yes, I expect I'll sell. There's really nothing for me here now."

"Allan's a good man Eva. He'll make you happy, I'm sure."

"Oh, I have no doubts about Allan, but I shouldn't burden you with my troubles. It's not appropriate," she said.

"But you said it yourself; we Aussies get right to the point, so if there's something to be said, you should say it. Besides, you're family, who else can you talk to?"

"You're very kind Stan, but I hardly know you. Perhaps we can start with a cup of tea and talk after that." Eva suggested.

"Tea would be lovely," I replied but I couldn't help but wonder what was upsetting her so much.

Tea was prepared and we retired to the sitting room. I sipped from an ornately decorated cup and ate some delicious cake which Eva had made herself. I hadn't eaten anything so delightful in a long time. I'd just about finished it off when I realised, I'd forgotten myself. Living in the trenches for a year had caused my manners to erode somewhat. Eva was looking at me like I was completely mad,

"I'm so very sorry Eva, there's not much room for ceremony on the front line as you might imagine."

"That's quite alright Stan. You don't have to feel uncomfortable on my account." And she smiled.

I finished my cake which was indeed wonderful. I then embarrassed myself again when I slurped my tea.

"Have you heard from Alan?" Eva asked, again looking anxious.

"No, I'm afraid not but I'm sure he's ok. The mail is terribly slow as I'm sure you are aware."

"I know, but it's been so long and it makes me worry. It's a terrible thing to be waiting for news. I'm not even sure we'd hear if anything were to happen."

"Alan would have made sure that the AIF has you on record as his next of kin." The remark only seemed to make her worry more as she looked up at my fresh scars. "I can check when I get back to London if you like?" I added.

"Oh, would you? That would make me feel so much better." Eva seemed to brighten up a little at the suggestion.

"How did you both meet?"

"Oh, we met at the theatre in London when Alan was on leave from training. We saw each other several times after that. I don't know why but we just had eyes from each other from the very start," she explained.

"When he was wounded, he wrote me from hospital so I visited him as often as I could. We decided to marry there and then. The ceremony took place in the hospital chapel, and it took us two days to arrange a cake."

"And it was incredible. Alan sent me a piece in the mail. I don't know how it survived the journey."

Eva continued, "Before long he was sent back to his battalion, and I've heard little from him since. I know he tries to write but..." and she paused.

"Well, there's a lot going on over there Eva. We really haven't had much time to write letters lately. I'm certain there's nothing to worry about," but my words did little to allay her fears.

We chatted for hours. I told her as much as I could about Sydney and Australia. I talked about our family, not leaving out the issues. I didn't see any point in hiding anything. She listened intently and I was sure she heard it all from Alan anyway. We enjoyed a simple meal for dinner, vegetable soup but it was bliss compared to what I was used to. We continued to talk well into the evening, and I could tell why Alan was so attracted to her. She was indeed a delightful lady, and I was happy for them both. I didn't realise it, but I started to fall asleep while Eva spoke,

"I'm sorry Eva; it's been quite a long couple of days for me."

"That's quite alright and it is getting late so it might be a good time to retire," she suggested.

The hour was late and Eva suggested I'd have trouble getting a taxi and insisted I stay. Normally that would be frowned upon, but the war had changed thing socially in many ways and with me being family, it wasn't going to set tongues wagging. She prepared the master bedroom for me, and I fell asleep instantly in a large, soft bed.

Next morning I was awoken by sounds in the kitchen. I rose, washed up and dressed. Aside from the pink scars, it was almost impossible to tell that anything had happened to me.

Eva had prepared a wonderful breakfast, and I didn't dare ask how many days' rations she'd spent on the one meal.

"Wonderful, the best meal I've had in two years!" I announce much to Eva's delight, which made her blush.

We followed breakfast with a walk, and she showed me some of the more interesting parts of her little corner of the city. I enjoyed being in peaceful civilisation and the distinct lack of uniforms was also welcome. People looked me up and down as I passed, very few having seen an Australian soldier.

Before long a taxi cruised by and I waved it down as we were saying our farewells,

"Thank you for coming Stan. You have been so very helpful."

"My pleasure. I'm sure we'll see each other again very soon. I'll make sure to check in with HQ and send you word of Alan, rest assured."

Eva gave me a kiss on the cheek. This time it was my turn to blush. As I drove away, I looked back and waved. She seemed so sad and lonely, but I imagined she wasn't the only one after so many years of war.

When I got back to the city I went straight to HQ and came across the odd little clerk once again. He listened to my request, vanished for a while and returned. There was no recent news of Alan, which was good. It meant that he was probably very much alive and somewhere in France or Belgium with his battalion. I wrote a note and asked that the taxi driver take it straight back to Eva and paid him the fare to cover the trip there and back again. He disappeared with the message, and I hoped that Eva would be comforted by the news, or lack of.

I tracked down my new mates and got back to the business of enjoying our leave. We saw shows, drank too much, ate at cafes and sang. We had a wonderful time. Finally, the five of us had to face the reality of returning to the war. As we packed up a commotion could be heard on the street just outside.

We all hurried to see what was happening. People were literally spilling into the streets, and news began to filter through the crowd. It was Sid who caught wind of the message first. He turned to us and looked at us wide eyed,

"It's over...the bloody wars' over!"

We just stood there stunned. It took a moment for the words to sink in.

Chas finally broke the spell, "Strike me pink!" he said.

With that my mates all started whooping and hollering along with hundreds of others. I was in total shock,

"Come on Stan, give us a smile!" screamed Sid. I had a smile from ear to ear which stretched my scarred face, but I didn't care. I ripped off my hat and threw it in the air letting out the biggest hoorah I could.

All up and down Horseferry Road soldiers and civilians sang and cheered. Total strangers shook hands, hugged and kissed like it was New year. All thoughts of shipping back to France were gone as the five of us were absorbed into the exhilaration of victory.

Over the next several hours we watched as flags of the Allied nations were waved in the streets. Men doffed their hats to photographers who tried to capture as many moments as they could. Women danced and hugged soldiers they didn't know as the crowd swelled, choking the streets. Eventually there were thousands of people sharing the glory. Politicians gave speeches while pubs overflowed with revellers. Soon, newspapers hit the stands and people scrambled to read the headlines.

The Daily News, The Evening Standard, The Daily Express, The Chronicle and a host of others all released special editions. Germany Surrenders was clearly visible at the top of one paper but by the time Sid got to the news stand they were all gone.

It didn't matter as euphoria swept the streets like a plague. We worked our way through the crowd, shaking hands with some people while getting slaps on the back from others. The sound of people cheering and singing was rife and the celebrations continued well into the night. After several more hours things started to die down, and the Military Police started rounding up stray soldiers. The war might have been declared over, but we were still bound by duty. The MPs certainly didn't let their guard down and acted like the war had just started again.

Next day we woke after only a couple of hours sleep feeling like we'd all been worked over. We were back in our rooms at the hostel, and I noticed Sid slipping outside. When he returned, he held the remnants of a newspaper. We crowded around to read the front page. The headline read,

War Ends, Kaiser Flees!

We read about the signing of the armistice in a railway carriage in the French province of Picardy ending hostilities at the eleventh hour of the eleventh day.

"I still can't quite believe it," said Chas, "It's a bloody marvel!"

We celebrated for another two days. Chas and Jim paired off with some English girls, and I took the opportunity to visit Eva. The taxi driver couldn't stop talking about the events of the last few days, but I wasn't paying much attention. My thoughts were focussed on getting home and seeing my sisters and brothers again. People were everywhere and their moods were unmistakably high, although the number of ladies wearing black didn't escape my notice either.

Eva was thrilled to see me again and hugged me with excitement,

"Isn't it wonderful Stan? When do you think Allan will be here? Oh, I'd better start packing..." she could hardly contain herself.

"He'll be here first chance I imagine."

"I hope so Stan..." and we spend the day talking about the end of the war and how the mood of the people had changed so dramatically. Eva talked more about selling up and moving to Australia with Alan. Before we knew it the day was ending and I thought it time to return to my lodgings, however Eva urged me to stay and I was easily persuaded,

"I'm overdue back at Battalion but I doubt anyone will notice." I suggested.

We celebrated into the night and next morning had another lovely breakfast. Eva had written a letter for Alan and gave it to me,

"Please put this in the mail Stan. It might get to him faster if you take it with you." I agreed and happily took the letter. "The next time we meet we'll be on the other side of the world." Eva suggested.

"I'm sure you're right, and I look forward to it."

We hugged and I was soon on my way back into London. It was around mid-morning when I got to the hostel. I went into my room, but it was empty; no sign of my mates, the only thing there was my pack. *Sods*, I thought, wondering if they'd gone back without me. I grabbed my gear and wandered downstairs. I was about to head outside when two MPs came through the entrance, the same pair we'd run into on our first night if I recalled correctly.

"Show us your papers Private," they demanded.

I knew I was cornered but decided that running would be foolish. I handed over my leave papers and they looked them over.

"Looks like you're a little overdue." And they scowled at me expecting a response. I just shrugged my shoulders.

"Come on," and they grabbed me and led me outside. They marched me to HQ and when I entered the courtyard I was met with a huge cheer. Scores of Aussie soldiers were lines up; all charged with going absent without leave. They were cheering every soldier who was led through the entrance, and I couldn't help but smile. I spotted Sid and the boys who were smiling right back at me. I didn't worry about the MPs and steered myself toward my friends but was cut off,

"Not until you're processed Private!"

They took me into an office where I was charged and told I would forfeit two days' pay. I got the impression that it was just a formality given the circumstances and was sent outside again where I joined the others.

"Got you too, did they?" asked Jim.

"Yeah, but I gave them your name!"

Jim didn't know what to think but when the other started chuckling he realised it was a joke.

"Bastard!"

Before long we were across the channel again and on a train headed back to our units. This time all was quiet. No thunder in the distance, no observation balloons, no dogfights in the sky or smoke for that matter. It really was over!

We learned that our battalions were still near Amiens. Sid and I swapped addresses and agreed to write when we got home and try to meet up. I farewelled Jim, Chas and Ernie and was soon walking back along the road to join my battalion once again.

The traffic seemed much less frantic than before, and the air was still and quiet. The only thing that had changed was the weather, it was certainly much colder and very damp, but I didn't care.

Before long I saw our bivouac and stepped up the pace. I wanted to see Bert and Dickie and celebrate the end of the war.

Chapter 16

Peace

I walked through the fog and drizzle, back into the bivouac and reported to the command tent. Len Robson, the battalion adjutant scowled at me,

"You're overdue!"

"Yes sir, sorry sir." I said as humbly as possible.

"Lucky for you the war ended." He stared at me and then smiled, "They all listening to a lecture, you haven't missed much," and he waved me away.

Things were much more relaxed, but the army was still the army so the good cheer wouldn't last forever, and stricter discipline would soon return.

I walked through the camp and found the men crowded into a community hall. They were listening to a Colonel saying something about the three great powers. I didn't really understand what it was about and wasn't all that interested. I scanned the audience and eventually spotted Bert and Dickie. The looked terribly bored. I tried to get their attention, but they were too far off, so I had to wait for the lecture to end. It seemed to go on forever and several blokes were struggling to stay awake. About an hour later the colonel concluded and the audience broke up, some of the men being shaken back to their senses by their mates. A few others grumbled about having been tortured into submission after the service they'd given the Empire. Yes, things were certainly getting back to normal again. Finally, Bert and Dickie emerged, whining like everyone else.

"Would you rather be living in the mud boys?" I asked.

Bert looked up ready to clock the beggar who made the remark but quickly channelled his fury into a grin.

"I thought that scratch might have got infected and you died in London," came his retort as we shook hands.

"Did they toss you in the brig then?" asked Dickie.

"No...and the brig is for those Navy boys!"

Dickie looked confused.

"Come on Stan, we off to have a cuppa," said Bert and we headed for one of the battalions bell tents. I spent the next several hours telling tales of London and how we reacted to the end of the war. It was good to be back with my mates though, and the battalion.

"Any idea what we do now?" I asked.

"Nope," replied Bert.

"The boys were hoping to see Berlin but that's unlikely now," explained Dickie.

"Well, that's a shame. It would have been good to see their faces after all that's happened," I suggested.

"Yeah well, we're still here and we're still waiting. I don't think anyone knows what to do with us," Bert continued.

"I'm sure we'll find out soon." I concluded and I was right.

The next day orders were delivered telling us to advance to the Rhine River. A few days later we marched to Vignacourt Station and were herded onto trains. Delay after delay saw us spend several hours waiting. It wasn't until 1.30am that we finally got moving, headed for Busigny, about one hundred miles east. Some men cheered ironically while others grumbled about being woken. The trip was terrible with thirty five men in each truck. There were no seats and it was bitterly cold. After about ten hours there was another hitch. The train stopped at Bertry about ten miles from our destination and we tumbled out of the carriages and marched off to billets in a nearby town called Bohain.

The locals were very welcoming and adored Australians. Their hospitality more than made up for the horrid journey. Bohain had been a manufacturing centre during the war and was occupied by the Germans. The town was beyond the range of our artillery but had suffered some damage from air raids with some buildings destroyed. Most of the population had stayed for the duration of hostilities despite the danger.

We rested and enjoyed some entertainment before moving on again. Traffic in this sector was heavy, and the going was slow which prompted more dissent,

"I'm sure they're just going to walk us around until they find something for us to do!" someone said.

The battalion moved on to Mazingheim, then Prisches where we spend the remainder of November. Our battalion commander, Lt Col George Francis Murphy formed a committee which he called the Regimental Institute. At the close of the month, Len Robson recorded our battalion strength at forty five officers and seven hundred and three other ranks.

December 1st was a clear and sunny day at last. We were soon on the move again; this time route marched to Maroilles. We were accompanied by the battalion band and the Australian and Regimental flags were unfurled. We formed up on the side of the road and ordered to wait.

"Anyone feel like we're a herd of sheep?" Bert quipped. A few men chuckled only to be set straight by an officer.

"Pipe down and ready yourselves. You're about to be inspected by the King!"

"Struth! The King! I should have put on my Sunday best!" came the reply and another round of laughter burst out followed by the barking of officers.

After forty minutes the jokes had shrivelled, and we became increasingly restless. At 2.15pm a cavalcade of vehicles appeared down the road. They halted in a cluster at the head of the battalion column. We watched, wide eyed anticipating the arrival of King George V.

A door flung open on one of the lead vehicles and a little man scurried out and quickly stepped to the rear. He opened the door and saluted as King George stepped from the vehicle. Other men wearing an array of highly decorated uniforms alighted from other cars.

I looked at the King as he readied himself for the inspection and caught a glimpse of his short brown hair, parted in the middle and swept to the sides before it vanished under his navy cap. His face appeared friendly but was deeply wrinkled behind a grey handle-bar moustache and a short beard. His uniform was navy blue with a light blue sash that draped diagonally across his chest. His epaulettes were gold and dusted his shoulders while an array of medals covered his left breast. I was surprised by his stature, he wasn't a tall man by any means and his withered features suggested years of worry.

His appearance was enough to silence the ranks, and he chatted briefly with other uniformed dignitaries and was introduced to our commander, Lt. Col. George Murphy. He in turn introduced the King to the other officers. We were ordered to attention and looked straight ahead as the King began his inspection of the ranks. He didn't speak to anyone and walked the line briskly. I felt nerves ripple through my stomach as he swept past barely glancing in my direction. After the inspection the King stopped and turned to the assembly. With that an order was give and the men of the 18th Battalion gave the King three cheers,

"Hoorah, Hoorah, Hoorah!"

The King saluted then returned to his vehicle and drove off. We then marched to another town and settled into new billets.

Late that day a murmur swept through the camp. Len Robson, the adjutant was leaving. His tenure with the battalion had been terminated and he was ordered to report to London. The repatriation process had begun. Next day the battalion commanders met in the mess hall for farewell Len. He'd been with the battalion from the very beginning. We were told that when he left, George Murphy shed a tear. He had much respect for the adjutant and no doubt a close bond had developed. I was certain this pattern would be repeated many times over.

Still, it was going to take many months to transfer the thousands of soldiers back to their respective homes. For the Australians and New Zealanders, the longest of journeys awaited, to the opposite point on Earth from where we stood now.

The process was simple; those who had served the longest would go home first. I suddenly realised that for me and all the survivors of the 19th reinforcements that it would be a very long wait.

For the next two weeks the Regimental Committee and the newly formed sports committee tried their best to keep the seven hundred men of the 18th battalion busy. Educational classes were held; we played a great deal of sport including rugby, soccer, Australia Rules and Hockey. By December 17 the battalion was moved again. This time we headed north to Avesnelles. We only stayed one night and marched again to Clairfayt, Sivry, Barvencon and finally, after four days on foot we arrived at Walcourt in Belgium. This would be our home away from home for a while. It was truly beautiful, virtually untouched by the war, except that the Germans had stolen most of the furniture. It had a glorious Cathedral and a chateau. At first the locals eyed us with suspicion, and we didn't understand why they seemed so cold towards us. It was soon revealed that the Belgians thought we were Austrians who had been allies of Germany during the war. It took some explaining to sort out the confusion but eventually the people warmed to us and made us feel at home.

Once we were settled into our new billets, yet again, Lt Col Murphy went on leave to London. On Christmas Eve 1918 we joined the rest of the 5th Brigade to be reviewed by His Royal Highness, the Prince of Wales. We lined up in full dress uniforms and waited patiently and very soon the prince conducted his inspection. He issued medals to several men before meeting other notable medal winners including Lieutenant Joe Maxwell. Joe had been awarded the Victoria Cross for conspicuous gallantry during the attack on the Beaurevoir Line, the day that I was shot in the face. He was the most highly decorated soldier in the battalion having also received the Military Cross and Distinguished Conduct Medal.

Christmas Day 1918 was cold. We went to church and later enjoyed a generous Christmas dinner. Most agreed it was the best meal they'd had since leaving Australia. The commanders read messages from the British High Command including one from General Birdwood who congratulated the AIF on its success. He wished us all a safe journey home.

A few days later a collection was taken, the first money dedicated to the establishment of a memorial for the 2nd Division to be erected on Mont St Quentin. Everyone gave as much as they could. The year ended with a soccer match between B and C Companies. I enjoyed playing and our team was successful, winning 2-0.

New Year celebrations were low key, and classrooms were organised with the men encouraged to enroll. The AIF Education Scheme was an idea that came from Lieutenant General Sir John Monash. He had been appointed Director of Repatriation and insisted that the Australians be made ready for life back home. After years of fighting, many lacked up to date skills and knowledge. Courses were created for bookkeeping, first aid, mechanics, French, even veterinary classes. They were held at the 2nd Division University de Traile. In the weeks that followed we studied, played and became as much a part of the community as any of the local villagers. Sadly though, the war hadn't ended the suffering of many as influenza spread through Europe and was taken home by returning soldiers. Some who had survived machine guns and artillery shells were struck down by illness in the cruellest of ironies.

The AIF had also arranged for newspapers to be transported to the men. They might have been two months old, but no-one cared...they were from Australia and we absorbed every detail. One day we took in a tour of Brussels and the Battlefield of Waterloo, where Napoleon had been defeated. I was impressed by the city and found it very much unlike London. Bert too thought it amazing and quite ancient compared to anything back home. The buildings all looked like churches and had towering rooves, no doubt designed to stop snow piling too high. The cobblestone streets were slippery with ice while statues peered down from almost every vantage point. We wandered around taking in the sights while inquisitive Belgians stared at our strange slouch hats and larrikin ways.

On one of my days off I decided to find the 3rd Battalion and see my brother Alan,

"You're a site for sore eyes old chum," said Alan as we shook hands.

"You are too. I see you've come through it all OK."

"Can't say the same for you," he replied looking at the scars on my face.

"It's nothing."

"Let me look at you Stan. My word you've grown up. You were fifteen when I saw you last and every bit a boy. I can't believe it," he paused and then said, "Oh, I got a letter from Eva. She says you visited!"

"She's a lovely lady Alan; you've done very well there."

"Yeah, she'll do, eh?" and we both smiled.

We spent the better part of the day catching up on all the news and our adventures. It was great to be together after so long.

"Harold's OK, so Dad tells me," Alan said.

"Yes, I know, Dad wrote to me. I imagine he's married by now?" I quipped.

"He is, last year, didn't your hear?"

I looked up in surprise, "No, but he knows how I feel. Perhaps he was trying to avoid upsetting me."

"You need to forgive him Stan. He's been through a lot bringing us up by himself."

"I know, but you're older. You didn't have to deal with the thrashings like the rest of us."

"Oh, I got my share, don't you worry," Alan added.

"Well, his letter seemed genuine enough. Perhaps a new marriage will be good for all of us," I suggested.

"We'll soon see. Lots of fences to mend I expect," added Alan and I knew he was right. "Oh, I saw Arthur a few weeks ago. He's come through it too!"

Arthur was our cousin and his survival meant that all of us had come through the war, a rare thing for any family. We soon said our goodbyes, but I knew that we'd see each other again in Sydney. In the weeks that followed the men of the 18th battalion continued with study and play by day with lectures and shows at night. We heard about the Russian front, the search for radium, the new map of Europe and so it went on. The battalion held an election and formed its own government known as the Walcourt Parliament. Seats were based on various parts of New South Wales like Bourke, Mudgee or North Sydney. We even formed parties like the Liberal Diggers. Campaign flyers were handwritten with some candidates attempting artwork to better sell their messages.

Despite my local government background, I couldn't run for the Walcourt Parliament because I was too young. I found the irony most amusing.

The Walcourt Argus newspaper was published by the men and reported on the idea of soldier settlements for those returning home. There was even an astrology section, although the writer seemed to spend more time defending it as a science rather than making any bold predictions based on the stars. He was also very careful to keep his identity a secret, referring to himself as Stargazer. The last line of the paper said, *please do not destroy this paper before your cobber has read it, the paper supply is very limited.*

Soon, the first draft of soldiers from the 18th Battalion was sent home. Sixty eight men and two officers were farewelled with ceremonial toasts and a rousing celebration. They'd signed up at the very beginning; many having fought at Gallipoli and right through the Western Front battles and deserved to be going home before anyone else. Those of us that remained went about our business waiting for our turn to go home. We even managed to arrange a race meeting which was most enjoyable and some had even organised what was known as the *blue light room* where men were able to entertain their lady friends. It average about thirty appointments a week!

By the end of January, the battalion was down to forty one officers and five hundred and eighty nine other ranks. In early February it snowed and became too cold and slushy to play outdoor sport. After more than a month at Walcourt we received orders to move again. The entire town turned out to say goodbye, and we were very sorry to leave. We'd been treated like members of the family, and some strong ties had been created. We ended our stay in a typical larrikin fashion with a snowball fight before boarding a train and waving goodbye.

Next stop was Montigny le Tilleul about nine miles north and close to the rest of the Australians at Charleroi. We were thrilled to have access to bathe at the Le Grande Taille Charbonage. The bathroom was very large and could accommodate fifty men at a time. It had white glazed wall and floor tiles, and each man had his own compartment in which to bathe and hang his clothes. Best of all there was an abundance of hot water which could be regulated to suit each bather. I'd never seen such a thing before. The dressing room was also heated through steam pipes.

"I could get very used to this," suggested Bert.

"Me too," replied Dickie and I had to agree.

At the end of February, the battalion ranks had thinned by another one hundred men. March came and went with a hundred more sent home, then in early April I was approached by the battalion adjutant, Lieutenant Chillemon with orders,

"So, your papers say you were a clerk back in Sydney, is that right?"

"That's right sir," I said.

"Good! We need you to report to the Australian Base Reception Camp in France and help with the repatriation process!" he explained.

"Me sir?"

"Why not? You're qualified and single...no reason you should go home yet is there?"

It was a rhetorical question, so I didn't answer and simply saluted,

"On my way sir!"

"Very good. There's a lorry waiting to take you to the train. Be on it in five minutes!" he ordered.

He returned my salute, turned and left me standing. I ran off the gather my kit.

"What's the rush Stan?' asked Dickie.

"New assignment. I'm off to Havre!"

"Whoa, wait a minute," gasped Bert, "What about us?"

I paused and looked at my mates. In my haste I didn't give them a second glance and felt stupid and selfish.

"It's just me, helping out with repatriation." I told them.

"So, this is it then!" replied Bert.

"I suppose it is." I suddenly realised that I may not see my friends again and a melancholy feeling came over me.

Bert and Dickie stood and shook my hand. Dickie was suddenly very teary, and I too was on the verge. Bert pretended not to notice simply saying,

"It's been an honour!"

"Yes, it has," I replied. "It's a pity you blokes aren't from Sydney. Makes it hard to keep in touch."

"Yeah well, it only dredges up things we'd rather not remember, eh?" suggested Dickie. I know he didn't mean it. Even so we exchanged addresses.

"I expect I'll see your orders come through. Shouldn't be long now," I suggested.

"One can only hope," said Bert.

I saluted them both and it was a very good salute, worthy of a general.

"Have a safe trip home," I ordered.

"Thanks for watching our backs," said Dickie and Bert nodded in agreement.

"Thanks for watching mine!" I replied and I smiled; there was nothing more to be said. I turned and started walking away. I didn't look back because I knew it would break me, but I could feel Bert and Dickie watching. I just raised an arm and waved knowing they'd understand.

Within a few minutes I was on the Lorry and gone. A short trip to the station and before long I was in Le Harve. I was shown to a desk stacked with files and personnel records ready for processing and there I took station for however long I was required. Three hundred and thirty one thousand, eight hundred and fourteen Australian men joined up to fight in the war. Of those almost sixty two thousand were killed. That left well over two hundred thousand who needed to be sent home from Europe and the Middle East. Thousands were already on their way. It was a painstaking process.

An officer showed me what to do and I soon grew accustomed to the routine. For the next three months I processed files, helping to send our men home. I recognised a few names but didn't see Bert or Dickies' names cross my desk.

Then, on July 6th, 1919, I was called to the CO's office.

"Your orders came through Stan, you're going home!"

I just stood there for a moment. I'd been so busy I never really considered getting such news. It took a few moments to really sink in, but I was soon overwhelmed by happiness, a smile erupting on my face that I couldn't control. I took the papers and waited out my last few days in Le Harvre.

I boarded the ship nine hundred and twenty two days after walking out of my home in Granville. I learned that the HMAT Boorara was a converted merchant ship. Tall masts took up the forward and aft sections of the deck while the strangely tall funnel protruded amidships. Her hull was of a lower profile than most passenger type vessels while the bow sharpened and rose slightly, looking like a chisel. It turned out that the Boorara was a German ship that had been captured early in the war.

It was explained that in 1914, when war was declared the ship was in Port Phillip Bay in Melbourne and was known as the Pfalz. It had made a run for open sea after her captain learned about the declaration of war but was halted by the Royal Australian Garrison Artillery after they fired shots across her bow from Fort Nepean. She was captured and used as a transport between Australia and England for the duration of the war. The irony wasn't lost on me; I was going home on a German ship!

I found my quarters and settled in for the long journey home. As the ship inched away from the dock, I watched a small group of well-wishers waving and calling to men on the deck. Most were women who had befriended Australian soldiers. More tears flowed but not from me.

For the next two months we worked our way south back to Australia, via the Western European coast, then across to Africa. We stopped at Durbin, dropping off South African troops who were welcomed home as heroes. After a few days rest and having taken on coal and rations, we were underway again. We crossed the Indian Ocean finally sighting the West Australian coast. It was a sight for sore eyes and the excitement amongst all of us was at fever pitch.

I shared in the thrill of the celebrations and couldn't wait to get back to Sydney. When we docked in Melbourne, the crowd was huge. We were welcomed like I never could have imagined. It was bittersweet when I learned that the ship would not continue to Sydney and that the News South Wales and Queensland contingents would have to travel by train for the remainder of the journey.

We were finally bundled on board and spent two full days trundling along at a snail's pace. Even without the threat of attack or sabotage, the Australian train was slower than anything we'd used in France or Belgium. It added frustration to our journey, so close to the end but as we started through the southern suburbs of Sydney excitement grew again. We were ordered to get into full dress uniform and acknowledged people who took the trouble to wave as the train passed by, some with Australian flags. The crowds grew as we made our way into Central Station. When we alighted, we could hardly move for the number of people trying to find their much loved sons, brothers, grandsons, uncles and nephews.

We then marched into the city for a formal welcome home. Some had found their families and while the occasion was formal, the rules were overlooked. I didn't expect to see anyone even though I sent a telegram advising of my journey home. We were led by a band through the streets of Sydney and were surprised to see just how many people turned out to welcome us. They were five deep on every street. Flags flew and people cheered. When we arrived at Sydney Town Hall, I felt humbled by the enormity of the occasion. We stood to attention and listened to speeches from politicians and the mayor. It truly felt odd standing before my employer under such circumstances with so many familiar faces in the official party.

The whole affair took much longer than we hoped it would but finally wound up with three rousing cheers after which hundreds of slouch hats were flung into the air, followed by a crush of bodies as people tried to find their loved ones.

I began to work my way out of the crowd, hoping to catch a taxi. As I fought through the scrum I heard a voice,

"Stan...STAN!"

I looked around but didn't see anyone but then I heard it again. This time I homed in on the voice and there was my friend, Harry Robson with Alex Ironside. They waved and smiled and we struggled towards each other, finally meeting somewhere in the sea of people.

"My word it's good to see you blokes!" I yelled.

"You too Stan, welcome home!" said Harry.

"I see you came through it all too Alex?" I spoke.

"Rumours of my demise remain highly exaggerated," he replied and we all laughed.

"So how are things at home Harry? How's Dad?"

"Why don't you ask him yourself?" and he nodded for me to look to my left.

Just then, emerging from the throng was my father, Ernest Dunkley. With him were Harold, Alan, Eva, Jessie, Ruth and Eric. The sight of them made my heart melt. I dropped my pack and walked towards the clan. Words escaped me and tears welled up and rolled freely down my face. I was all choked up when I reached them and collapsed into my fathers' arms. He folded them around me and hugged me with more love than I ever gave him credit for. He too burst into tears and we held each other tight. It took a few moments for us both to gather ourselves. Dad released me from his embrace and looked me up and down,

"It's good to see you Stan, so good!"

I was overwhelmed and barely stuttered a reply,

"It's good to see you too Dad," a smile erupting on my face.

There wasn't a dry eye amongst us. Ruth ran up and hugged me followed by Eric and Jessie,

"Don't go away again Stan," Eric demanded!

"We've all missed you Stan," added Jessie.

I looked at my brothers and sisters,

"My word, look how you've all grown."

Harold came up and shook my hand, "Welcome back," he said with a certain look on his face. He knew what I'd been through and how I was feeling and I nodded my acknowledgement.

Finally, Alan and Eva came up. I shook Alan's hand, "Good to see you again Stan."

"You too Alan," I turned to his wife, "Hello Eva," and she gave me to most crushing hug.

"I'm glad you're home safe," she added.

"Come on Stan, Agnes has organised a welcome home dinner," said Dad, "and your room is ready and waiting."

I looked at Dad again, "I'm sorry Dad. I...."

"It's alright son. It's all over now," and we hugged once more, "For what it's worth, I'm sorry too," he added.

I felt a huge weight fall away. The pressures of the last few years had taken their toll, and the love of my family made it feel like I'd broken out of a hundred sets of chains.

Tears continued to flow as the crowd slowly thinned. I'd never felt so happy. I left home a bitter, angry teenage boy, blaming my father for all the problems in my life. It took the horrors of a war on the opposite side of the world to make me realise what was most important in life.

I forgave my father for not being there after the death of our mother, but more importantly he forgave me for running off to war.

Ernest smiled, looking me in the eye, "Come on Stan, time to go home."

Chapter 17

A word from the Author

I knew my grandfather very well and admired him greatly, or at least I thought I did but after spending a lot of time researching his AIF service during the Great War, my admiration for him grew even more.

As a child I loved to visit him and stay at my Grandparent's place opposite Maitland Gaol. Stan was a delightful man and very rarely raised his voice or lost his temper. He spoke often about anything I cared to ask of him, but my understanding of the war wasn't too keen back then and I didn't feel it right to pry. I regret that now.

I loved making model aeroplanes when I was young and one day took a model of a German WW1 Roland to show him. His face lit up as he recalled trying to shoot them down from the trenches. I asked if he ever got one and he replied that he was a terrible shot. We now know that's not true. A letter he wrote from the front to his friend Harry Robson indicated that he was a member of a Lewis Gun crew. To make the grade for a posting like that you had to pass a marksmanship test and only the best scores were offered for those elite roles.

We always believed Stan was a medic; he said as much but nothing in his record seems to back that up. Perhaps he just wanted us to know of him as someone who saved lives rather than taking them. It certainly enabled him to avoid telling stories about war, killing and death. His record does show he was attached to the Australia Base Reception Camp, so he likely did assist with repatriation after the war.

He remained a Private during his entire time with the AIF, possibly due to his age, although it wasn't uncommon for officers to be quite young as the war progressed.

Stan received two medals for his service with the First AIF: The British War Medal and the Victory Medal. When he returned to Australia he went back to his old job at Sydney City Council. He continued to pursue a career in local government, although we're aware that there was a period when he was in Victoria. This is where I believe he met his wife Rona (Edith Rona May Kohn). She was indeed the sister of Sydney Kohn, who I mentioned in the book. I don't know if Stan and Sid ever really met on the Western Front, but it is possible. I did meet Uncle Sid on several occasions and found him to be a lovely man too. I was always excited when he came to visit Nanna and Pop.

Stan may well have ventured to Victoria to assist with one of Australia's post war capital projects. Many World War I veterans worked on the Great Ocean Road. It's by no means a stretch to assume he was there.

Stan's local government career saw him leave Sydney, taking positions in Carrington, Campbelltown, Berrigan, Leeton, Blackheath (where my father was born) and Cootamundra. While there the Second World War broke out and Stan, once again put his hand up to serve. He was thirty eight and at the wrong end of the age scale to serve overseas, however he was recruited as Adjutant for the Citizens Military Forces, Australia's version of Dad's Army. They trained at home and were made ready to defend the country should the Japanese ever invade.

In 1949 Stan took up the post of Town Clerk at Maitland Municipal Council in the Hunter Valley. He was there for the two big floods of 1949 and 1955. He used to do radio reports on 2HR and told me they even offered him a job because they liked his voice. He did indeed have a deep resonating voice which I loved to listen to.

His wartime experience held him in good stead to deal with the crisis faced during those huge flood events. Even today the 1955 flood is often spoken about by the people who experienced it, including my parents. My father, Graham Dunkley, told me how he would wade along the railway tracks to get into town so he could deliver fresh clothes. Stan lived in the town hall at the height of the flood while the water lapped the stairs below.

In 1956 he wrote a commissioned report into the flood for the NSW Government. That report became one of the driving forces behind the creation of the Civil Defense, known today as the State Emergency Service.

Stan finished his career in Maitland in 1962 and was awarded an MBE (Member of the Order of the British Empire) at a ceremony held at Government House in Sydney for services to the community. He retired on his birthday in 1965.

Stan spent much of his time in retirement working at East Maitland Bowling Club. He'd walk there most days and meet with friends. He looked after the books as their treasurer for many years until the operation grew to the point where someone had to be employed for the task.

We tried to convince him to write his autobiography as one time; he handed over two typed pages which I now treasure. It wasn't that he couldn't be bothered, he simply didn't like to big note himself.

Many years after the Great War, Stan with his wife, travelled back to France. He'd always wanted to see Paris, something he hadn't had a chance to do when he served. He also tracked down the French doctor who looked after him when he was wounded. The man was still alive and well. Pop just wanted to tell him thank you. That sounds just like something he would do.

Stanley James Dunkley died in 1983 at Wallsend Hospital, aged 82. He smoked cigarettes, a habit he probably picked up when he joined the AIF in 1917. Rumour has it that he was sneaking a cigarette in the hospital toilet and had a heart attack. While that may seem a terrible end for a man with such a distinguished military and civilian career, we don't feel at all grieved by it. He was a proud and accomplished man and would have found it amusing to have gone out like that. He always told me that he wasn't afraid of death and often said to me "It won't be long before I'm up there," while pointing to the sky. I'm sure he enjoyed how I protested every time he did it.

To be honest I simply cannot imagine some of the horrors he witnessed and faced. I can't quite believe that he was able to raise a weapon in anger against another human being. The man I knew was mild mannered. He was a true gentleman and a great influence on my life. I loved him dearly and miss him every day.

He was a huge fan of ABC Radio and always listened to the news at 7.45am and Blue Hills at lunch time. These were the only times that he asked us to be quiet. I like to think he'd be very proud of where my career in radio took me, 22 years with the ABC and 30+ years in the media industry.

I'm certainly proud of his legacy and am equally proud to know that upon his passing his name was added to the official veteran's memorial at Rookwood. Wall 81; Row 8.

Whenever I visit my hometown of Maitland, I drive past the street they named after him in Rutherford. I know he protested against that, which doesn't surprise me at all.

I always make sure I glance over towards Maitland Park. There you'll find a little grove of trees that have been dedicated to Stan and Rona Dunkley for their years of service to the City of Maitland.

Fittingly they grow just a stone's throw from Maitland War Memorial.

By Andrew Dunkley

Other publications by this author

Parallax

5 Irons Don't Float

The Terranian Enigma

The Hitler Paradox

Web: andrewdunkley.com

Email: alliseeismud@gmail.com

A special thanks to everyone who assisted with th publication of All I See Is Mud. I coulnd't have done it without you.

My brother Steve for the cover art.

The Australian War Memorial.

Relitives of those who served.

Historians who gave me advice.

Authors who wrote refernce books that filled in a lot of blanks.

Thank you all!

LEST WE FORGET

All I See Is Mud

Andrew Dunley

Copyright © 2018.